ALONE & AFRAID

ALONE & AFRAID

LEVI JOHNSON MOUNTAIN MAN SCOUT

BOOK THIRTY-ONE

ASH LINGAM

WOLFPACK
PUBLISHING
EST 2013

There will come a time when you believe everything is finished. That will be the beginning.

— LOUIS L'AMOUR

ALONE & AFRAID

THE BOY

MONEY PENNY WALKED OUT THE DOOR OF THE CABIN, arching his hands over his head into a stretch. Today, he was the first to wake up. The nine-year-old walked to the edge of the porch and peed off the side. Steam rose from the yellow-stained, melted snow. He buttoned up and pulled his coat tight to keep the morning chill off, but knew that the temperatures would rise with the sun. Still, there was considerable snowfall on the ground. He squinted his eyes to block the light. White flakes floated lazily to the ground. That was when he heard the wild turkeys gobble somewhere on the other side of the brick-and-rail fence.

Without thinking, young Penny grabbed his twelve-gauge double-barrel shotgun from where it was leaning against the wall. He had learned his lesson when the Blackfoot Indian came out of nowhere and took a shot at Kit Carson, but nobody was armed. The warrior attacked unprovoked. The boy was young, but he wasn't stupid—he learned his lessons quickly. The click of two steel hammers broke the morning silence. With his gun in his hands, he held his breath and listened intently.

"Gobble, gobble, gobble, gobble." Now, it seemed there were several. If he got a couple of plump turkeys, they would have a feast tonight. He knew he only had two shells.

Money shot a glance over his shoulder, but the cabin window was still dark. He looked over at Rusty's house, and he saw a thin stream of smoke rise from the metal cookstove pipe. Of course, Angus was already up and busy preparing breakfast.

If I can bag a couple of turkeys before the first coffee of the day, I'll impress Levi.

When he glanced at the eastern horizon, he saw the first hints of daylight as a prism of colors shot across the sky and the carpet of stars rolled back toward the western heavens, quickly disappearing. Mountain blue-birds, three-toed woodpeckers, white-crowned sparrows, and American pipits tweeted and hammered among the trees.

Money followed the path to the outhouses, using them for cover so the turkeys wouldn't see him before he had a shot, as he carefully watched where he stepped. Halfway there, he stopped and listened. They continued to gobble. It sounded like they were between the stand of trees beyond the firewall, which they cleared of wood, and the compound fence. The only other sound was his moccasins squeaking as he tread in the snow. Gaining confidence, he stepped up the pace as he clutched his rifle with white-fingered fists, and his breath came short and fast.

Behind him, he heard someone cough and spit. He knew from his daily habits that it was Angus. He chanced a look back and saw the porches were bare. When he looked up, he saw a thin, lazy line of smoke rising from the main chimney, meaning that they hadn't stoked the main fire yet, so Rusty was still asleep.

Money brought his attention back to his prey. When he came to the brick-and-rail fence, he saw they weren't there. He had been convinced he heard them on the other side of the outhouses. He scampered over the wooden fence like a squirrel and down the other side. Again, he heard turkeys. Then he caught sight of several feathers as they puffed into the air and were then blown away by the wind. Now he knew exactly where the gobblers were. He smiled in anticipation.

With more confidence than ever, Money dropped into a crouch as he shouldered his rifle and scurried across the clear stretch of land. They made it as a fire-break, which also kept their many enemies at bay, with nowhere to hide in a firefight. Suddenly, the young boy felt exposed and naked. The first hint of paranoia began to gnaw at his stomach. He found himself alone at the edge of the Bear Tooth Mountain Forest.

He stopped right before he entered the dense bushes and close-standing trees that towered overhead, blocking out much of the light from above. Money glanced to his side and saw the fiery disk sitting squat on the horizon. It felt warm on his face. Just as quickly as his confidence started to evaporate, it grew again. It was full daylight by then.

You've got this, so don't get shaky now. They're just a step away.

When he turned back to the thick brush, he suddenly saw a man with a stick in his hand, but his reflexes were too slow. The piece of wood came roaring at his head. He felt the dull thud right before his head began to spin, and he fell to the ground.

A buckskin-clad man grabbed the boy by the scruff of his neck to keep him from falling into the snow. Little drops of blood sprinkled the ground.

"Don't kill him, or he won't be worth a penny. I have somebody up at Fort Boise waiting for us to head back east with a bunch of slaves. Some are runaways, and others are Indians, but none of them will fetch the price this young boy will. Why, look at those blue eyes. Yeah, I reckon he's the cream of the crop."

"Whatcha wanna do now, Hawkeye?"

"Throw the youngin' over your shoulder and let's get out of here before the others wake up. Be careful and head for the horses and the gang, Ven. But remember, he won't be worth a plug nickel if he's damaged goods."

When Money began to come around, he said in a hoarse voice, "What are you two doin' with me. Let me go, right now!"

Suddenly, a flash of white light shot through his brain, and Ven knocked him out like a light. This time, he didn't move.

"What did I just tell ya? Stick a sock in his mouth so he can't talk when he comes around, and tie his hands. At least he speaks English. Some of these settlers, this far west, are from foreign lands and don't speak a lick."

"You want me to tie his feet too, Hawkeye?"

"And then, how's he gonna ride the horse? We'd better move fast. This will be the last slave we'll catch, or the five of us won't be enough to guard them all. Two prisoners for each man are more than enough. The nine men will be heading for California."

"Why, California? I thought they would end them back east?"

"There are rumors that there's gonna be an uprising, and the Californios need bodies to ward off the Mexican assault. I hear there's gonna be a war. That's why Mr. Farnsworth Claymore is buyin' men to send west. I know California ain't really a slave state, but they knew they're gonna be in a pinch. I heard there are three prison wagons full of soon-to-be soldiers. They can't organize a draft because the land still belongs to Mexico. This is gonna be a revolution. It has already begun in Texas, with the dispute over the border, the Rio Grande, and the Nueces River, but California and New Mexico will also be involved. The government wants to declare independent states, but Mexico says it's their land. I reckon there'll be US soldiers all over the place by the end of the month, and Mexican soldiers will follow them."

"Gosh, I didn't know there was so much behind what we're doin'. And why in the world would they want children, too? You know, this young boy and the girl back at camp."

"Come on, snap to it. I don't have all day to answer questions. And clean your tracks like I taught you before we head back to the gang. Hopefully, they won't find out in time to take chase."

Hawkeye carefully brushed over the spots of blood with a pine tree branch until there was nothing visible, then he and Ven started on the tracks.

"If they want soldiers, why does this Whipple fella want young kids? Why, the boy and girl can't be much over nine or ten."

"Some questions are better not asked—especially

when they involve politics and politicians. They're payin' us three times the profit, so don't look a gift horse in the mouth. As soon as we turn over the bodies and get paid, we'll be on our way, just in case stealing the children comes back on us. The girl we stole from the Nez Percé Indians won't be a problem, but that boy might. There were three cabins of mountain men living there, and they might take offense."

"Why, I reckon they'll never know what happened. Children disappear all the time in the wilderness. They might think a wild animal carried him off. You worry too much, Hawkeye. You should relax like me. I ain't worried a bit. It's the Blackfeet Indians that concern me. You told me so yourself. You're the best mountain man in the Rockies and across the Great Plains. All we've gotta do is watch out for a band of dangerous Indians. Still, I don't see 'em attacking five heavily armed men.

"Unless we stole one of their braves. But I think that mostly Crow Indians live in this part of the mountain. When we reach Yellowstone Valley, things might change."

Just as quickly as they appeared, they disappeared. As the wind pushed the last of the snow drifts across the ground, it completely covered their light tracks. The buckskin-clad White man appeared to know what he was doing. The sound of muffled boots disappeared into the distance, as the woodpeckers continued to hammer on the lodgepole pines, and birds flittered from limb to limb.

———

HINGES SQUEAKED as the heavy timber door of the main cabin opened. Rusty Steel stepped into the cold as a shiver ran up his back. He liked the first brisk slap in the face of early morning. He took a deep breath and slowly exhaled, then sipped his coffee, feeling the hot liquid warm his body. Steam momentarily clouded his vision. First thing, as always, he scoured the compound for fresh tracks. The paths between the cabins and the outhouses were worn down, but Steel saw no signs of intrusions other than a light sprinkling of prints from crow's feet.

The compound leader sat on his chair at the head of the table, pulling out his pipe and tobacco pouch. In seconds, the sweet smell of tobacco mixed in the air with that of freshly perked coffee. Smoke floated around his head. Both were clear signs of the presence of White men. In minutes, more doors squeaked open and slammed shut as the compound members headed for the first coffee of the day and breakfast. Angus had been up for over an hour and nearly had the most important meal of the day ready to put on the table.

Marshal Joseph Walker helped himself to coffee from a gallon kettle. It was so hot that brown bubbles popped from the spout. He took his first sip as his eyes traced the outside of the compound. Since Virgil had let the Blackfoot warrior into their home and he had turned on them, they were on guard. The peace and quiet that they enjoyed when Crow Chief Hachta was still alive was no more. Now, the enemy took many more liberties. The stronghold was only a half-day's ride up the mountain from the north entrance. The Crow warriors didn't frighten them like they did only a year earlier.

Several of the more aggressive tribes were growing bolder by the day. Especially the Shoshone and Blackfeet, although the Nez Percé and Bannock were less friendly in the last months since Rusty's blood brother died. The current Crow Chief Wanata was disliked far and wide for his arrogance and trickery. The difference between him and the old chief was night and day. But he still had power from the clout of his band of warriors. That was his only redeeming factor—that, and the fact that there was no one to take his place.

When the old chief died, the dilemma the tribe faced was the lack of a suitable replacement leader. So, since Wanata was already the camp war chief, along with Levi Johnson's wife, Crow warrior Dahteste, he was given the honor, for lack of a better substitute. There had never been a woman leader of the Crow stronghold, and Dahteste, who could have been the only other choice, was happy living with her husband in the compound. She wanted nothing to do with the headaches that came with being chief. Still, she remained the war chief for the camp. She knew that in times of need, she would do her duty to her people.

The tribe managed to hold together, but not by anything their new chief had done. It was their adopted Tonkawa medicine man, Potak, who spiritually led the tribe. Like most American Indians at the time, they were superstitious and believed that the famous shaman was a man to be both respected *and* feared. Some even believed that he could read their minds and talk with the animals.

This was what saved Wanata because the medicine man was the chief's anchor. Without him, he knew his tribe would drift away, and chaos would prevail. As it was, the Crow tribe knew their leader wasn't feared as their previous chief was. In the wilderness, that was the only way to protect yourself from unwarranted aggression in advance. Now, with each passing day, the enemy became more and more bold.

Due to this unrest in recent months, compound members were even more careful. They had a taste of how emboldened some warriors had grown when a Blackfoot brave challenged Kit Carson at their front door. Luckily, the assailant had died in the act. Now they were wondering if the times of persistent Indian attacks had returned. When Angus, Mountain Dennis, Portland Pete, and Syracuse Sam first lived in the compound, hostile Indian attacks were the order of the day. All the tribes were up in arms because of the White men settling on the mountain.

Then Rusty Steel arrived from Montana, where he had lived with the Flathead Indians. Over the years, he and Chief Hachta had saved each other's lives on occasion. Thus, they became blood brothers, enabling his friends to live in relative peace. Of course, living on Bear Tooth Mountain was always risky business and a daily challenge. Besides the hostile Indians, there were grizzly bears, wild cats, and rattlesnakes, as well as winters with plummeting temperatures and forest fires. All things that this group of mountain men and women experienced living lost in the wilderness.

The campaign to push them out came to a stop with the help of Rusty and his blood brother, Chief Hachta. Back then, the leader of the Crow tribe protected them with a much stronger band of warriors. Many were too young for the job, and others were nearly old men. Many of the braves of fighting age had left for other

Crow camps. The unpopularity of Wanata was noted on all fronts.

MONEY STRUGGLED to breathe through his nose with the smelly, dirty sock in his mouth. A bandana wrapped around his head held it in place. His blue eyes showed his terror as tears ran across his freckles and down his face. Sometimes, he shuddered like a leaf, and at others, he looked lost and withdrawn.

This wasn't the first time Money Penny was stolen to be sold to the highest bidder. His mother had also suffered the same fate. After believing he had finally found the family he was always meant to have, it was suddenly torn out of his chest and hurt like it was his heart. After losing his mother and father, not a year had passed, and it was happening all over again. It looked like he was returning to slavery.

What Indian tribe is gonna buy me? Money asked himself. *I hope it ain't the Blackfeet like that fella Kit Carson shot and killed.*

"How much do you think the slaver will pay for the boy?" Ven asked. "He's gonna like his blue eyes and yellow hair. I wonder what they want with a youngin'. When we fill orders for Black folks or Indians, they always want healthy women and strong men."

"What do you care what they want the young fella for?" Hawkeye replied. "The same goes for the young girl we've got. All I'm interested in is what I was told. The young boys and girls fetched a pretty penny. Remember, the less we know about such goings on, the better. When a man is willin' to pay that much money for a healthy body, somebody rich is behind it all, and rich people always cause trouble for poor folks like us."

"You don't have to be so grouchy. I was just curious, is all, Hawkeye. I didn't mean nothin' by it."

"What you are is nosy. Remember, you're in charge of the two youngins, so make sure they don't get away. If they do, it'll be your hide. Me and the boys will take care of the rest of the young bucks, both red and black. All in all, this trip was good, even if we did have to ride way the hell off the beaten track. In the end, a few more weeks were worth the money. Those rumors we heard back in Fort Boise panned out. If it weren't for the gossip, we'd have never met Mr. Claymore."

"Findin' this White boy was a stroke of luck. I reckon if the young Indian girl were white, she'd be worth twice as much."

"She doesn't look to be Indian to me. Maybe she was kidnapped from White folks and made to live in some tribe or other. With all those settlers travelin' the Oregon Trail, women and children disappear every week. The Indians know if they get 'em young, they can mold 'em to how they like. I reckon we'll get top dollar for those two."

"I wonder what language she speaks," Ven Grim pondered.

"Why, don't you ask her and find out?" Hawkeye replied. "When I spoke to her, I ain't even sure she heard me. You know how some women go into shock as soon as we nab 'em. I reckon that goes tenfold for a little girl."

"Maybe, that's why she looks like she's starin' at nothin'. Or maybe she doesn't understand what we said."

"I know that boy speaks English because he mouthed off right before I hit him the second time. I must admit, boss, you're plenty smart. I was wonderin' why you had me gather all of them turkey feathers. He took the bait, hook, line, and sinker."

"That's an old Indian trick I learned over the years. They don't call me a mountain man for nothin'. Why, I doubt there is a frontiersman alive that can track as well as me or is as good with a gun. I can shoot the wings off a fly at a hundred yards."

"I could wear buckskins, too, but I find them too damned sticky when it's hot. Plus, I don't feel I need to look the part of somethin' I ain't. I like a cotton shirt in the summer and a wool one in the winter. At least you wear shoes, which is more than I can say for the young yellow-haired boy. We'll have to get him some boots as soon as we reach Fort Boise, before the buyer sees that he's nearly wild. He might be put off if he thinks he's more animal than a little human."

"He didn't give me any trouble."

"When you're sellin' your goods, first impressions are of paramount importance. If the buyer thinks the youngster is Indian-wild, he might not be so keen on the idea. We can swing by the town haberdashery before we meet up with Claymore. I figure by the time we get there, we'll be a week late. If we show up later than that, he might cut and run. These aren't the only slaves he'll be transporting back east. He brought three prison transport wagons with him. I reckon by the time he and his men pull out, they'll be packed in there like sardines in a tin can. I reckon when war breaks out, there will be a passel of men fighting."

Hawkeye smiled as he counted the money in his

head. They were on the home stretch, and in two weeks, they would be home free. The possibility of being unsuccessful never even crossed his mind. He knew how skilled he was, and determination was his middle name.

In the blink of an eye, they were back with their gang members, along with nine kidnapped bodies. One of them was a little girl. Her skin seemed dark, but it was only dirty and sunburned that made her look like an Indian—that and her Indian clothing. Underneath was fair white skin. The Bannock who had sold her to them hadn't mentioned whether she was already stolen or if one of her parents was white. All he said was that he kidnapped her from the Nez Percé.

The White man spat on the edge of his bandana while grabbing the girl by the hair, and he rubbed the dirt off. Ven exclaimed, "Why, lookee here, she's a White girl after all. Maybe we'd best let her wash up before we sell her. Maybe we should even buy her a new dress, so she looks good beside the little boy. We can sell 'em as a set."

"Whatcha thinkin' there, Ven? I know you. You leave that girl alone. As I said, there are no damaged goods. We only get top dollar if they're in good shape. All you've gotta do is keep an eye on 'em and keep your hands off. Remember what I said, now. If I see as much as a hair on that little girl's head that is touched, I'll beat you with my pistol until I knock some sense into that hard head of yours. Do you understand me, Mr. Grim?"

———

AN HOUR LATER, when they pulled out, two men led the string of mules, with one in the middle and the other two riding drag. Between them were their captives. Ven carried a baseball bat and used it on anyone who got out of line. They traveled hard and fast, so there was no room for unruliness or laggers. Out front, Hawkeye rode point.

His sharp eye caught anything out of place well before they were discovered. It was almost like he had a third sense. They raced through the whole day, only stopping at springs and streams to water the horses and refill their canteens. Then they would mount back up and ride some more.

When the moon rose at the end of the world, they continued into the night by the silvery light. The slavers were used to such hard travel, but it was taking its toll on the prisoners. Some of them refused to eat, and Ven forced food down their throats. They might get them there tired, but get them there they would.

DISAPPEARED

WHEN LEVI WALKED ONTO THE PORCH AND FOLLOWED THE worn path to the main cabin, he noticed a strange smell in the air. He stopped for a moment and sniffed, then shook his head and headed for a hot cup of coffee. At first, he couldn't place the smell and shrugged it off, but it remained to gnaw in the back of his brain. Since the incident with the Blackfoot Indian and Kit Carson, they were all on guard. If a hostile brave can walk right into their compound and even eat at their table and then turn around and try to kill one of them, things weren't on even keel.

Levi Beaver Johnson was lean and tall, with a sunburned face from living in the wilderness. It had only been days since the weather had changed, and the first hint of spring was in the air, but the sun was out and warm on the skin. He held his Sharps prototype in his right hand as he squinted into the glaring light. He looked down from Rusty's porch and at the rutted trail out of the south gate, which went curving out of sight below him. Two heavy Colt Walkers in cross-draw holsters hung from his waist. Despite the size of the four-and-a-half-pound revolvers, they appeared small on the six-foot-seven giant of a man. In his fists, they looked like toys.

There were rocky outcrops formed into mysterious shapes and shadows, creating dark places for a man to hide despite the glaring sun all around them. Everything around the compound within rifle range was mowed down to maintain a clear field of fire. The wilderness on that part of the mountain held a dark, desolate beauty, with pink bands and black rock covered in dwarf and cushion-shaped shrubs, bushes, and pine trees—a byproduct of the constant winds. There was also grouse whortleberry at these elevations, along with pockets of talus fiends. The three-point-six-billion-year-old mountain was located in the northeast of the Yellowstone caldera.

Above them was Bear Tooth Peak at ten thousand nine hundred forty-seven feet, which gave its name due to its appearance: like a bear's tooth. It was not only home to the White people living in the compound, but also to elk, deer, grizzly bears, wolves, mountain lions, pronghorn, and small mammals like birds and reptiles. Its expansive plateaus, high peaks, and pristine lakes made it suitable for a range of species, including man.

Something was eating at his brain, but he didn't know what it was or even why. Beaver shrugged it off and poured a tin cup full of coffee, then uncorked the jug to add a dash of corn liquor to take the chill out of the crisp mountain air.

Angus McFarlin opened the window and poked his head out and said, "Breakfast, I'm almost ready, folks. I hope you're hungry because I made flapjacks with maple syrup." He used pounded flour, mixed with water and cooked over a fire to make the most rudimentary pancakes. Despite everyone hearing the announcement, he rang the dinner bell anyway. They didn't know if he liked the sound that much, or if it was the fact that it bothered the Dickens out of the other members of the compound.

"I hope you made an extra-large stack for me, Angus. I'm starved," Levi said as he rubbed his belly.

"And, when ain't you starved, Beaver? But not to worry. I made plenty for us all. I even made some baby pancakes especially for Money. Where is that boy anyway?"

"He's probably with his ma," Marshal Joseph Walker replied, setting his half-empty coffee cup on the table as he sniffed the air. Everyone in the compound woke up as hungry as a pack of wolves.

When Bar-Chee stepped out of their cabin, she did so alone. Everyone turned to look her way. As soon as his Crow wife saw Joseph's questioning eyes, they all saw her face turn from sleepy to pure, raw panic.

"Where's Money? He wasn't in his cot when I woke up. I thought he was with you, Joseph." Her voice began to crack, and she wavered on her feet. It only took an instant before Joseph was at her side, then he disappeared inside as he did a second check, but there were few places to hide in their modest cabin.

"What's goin' on?" Virgil Lovejoy asked. "I reckon I must have overslept. He had his ever-present Bible in his hand. "Why, you look frightened to death, woman."

"My little Money's gone."

Nobody had to say a word. They all began searching the buildings and the compound for the nine-year-old boy. Levi burst into a run for the stables to see if he had taken his horse. He knew it wasn't like the boy to run off unannounced, but then again, he was adventurous and was always looking for a way to impress his mentor, Beaver. But when he got to the animals, he saw that his horse was still there, along with his saddle. It didn't look like he had even been in the barn because his horse wasn't fed yet.

Joseph ran out of his cabin, nearly in a panic. "His twelve-gauge shotgun is gone. Check for footprints, Levi. He doesn't seem to be here in the compound."

As soon as his wife, Bar-Chee, heard what he said, she fainted. Joseph managed to grab her just before she hit the ground and bumped her head. They could all hear Betty gasp.

"Take care of your wife, Joseph. You can't out-track me anyway. Captain, let's get our horses saddled up just in case. I thought I smelled something odd when I first woke up, but I still don't know what it was."

They began gathering their belongings to search for the boy. Still, they didn't know if he *was* lost or even worse. They didn't even want to think about all the possibilities that could happen in the wilderness. They were endless. All they could do was move quickly as they got down to business. When tracking someone, the last thing you could afford was to let emotions get in the way.

If you let them affect you, it would be impossible to think straight and conduct a calm, thorough search. Still, they had hopes that it was something innocent, but Levi wasn't so sure. The smell he had noticed was still stuck in his mind and began to bother him more and more.

They were just walking the horses to the hitching rail in front of the main cabin, where everyone had gathered. It was their fort in times of danger and their shelter in times of dangerous weather. It was a fortress compared to the other dwellings. Two teepees stood between the cabins.

"Where in the world did that boy wander off to?" Joseph huffed as he hugged his dizzy wife. Tears flooded down her cheeks. Money was the child she was never given, but finally had the opportunity to adopt, and now he had apparently vanished. She didn't believe it was something innocent in a million years. Bar-Chee knew how dangerous life alone in the wild of Bear Tooth Mountain could be. She had lived there her entire life.

When Rusty came running through the snow, they all turned their heads with puzzlement etched on their faces. By the time he got to them, he was out of breath from his sprint, finally doubling over with his hands on his knees as he gobbled for air.

"There are no tracks at the north or south entrances. I didn't see a trace of the boy. He must have left the compound over the brick-and-rail fence."

"Did someone check the outhouses?" Levi asked. "He may have fallen asleep while doing his business. It wouldn't be the first time."

"Of course, I did. Whatcha think I am, a fool?" Rusty growled. Of course, he wasn't angry at Levi but more at the world.

The aging frontiersman had taken quite a shine to Money Penny and knew how cruel the country was around their homes. It wasn't the place for a young boy alone, and with every second, minute, hour, and day that passed, the possibility of finding him diminished.

This was the first time such a thing had happened, but it wouldn't be the last. Not with the way the Indian's attitudes were changing.

Levi turned for the path to the outhouses. In minutes, he had his nose to the ground like a bloodhound. When he made a beeline for the fence, all eyes followed him as they held their collective breaths. He stopped for a moment, then put his hand on the top of the fence and leaped over to the other side. He studied the jostled snow and instantly knew this was where young Penny had exited the compound.

Johnson jumped back over the fence. "I can see where somebody tried to cover their tracks. Mind you, whoever it was is good at tracking and hiding. I only noticed where the fence posts meet the snow. Otherwise, I doubt I'd have seen it."

Levi moved all around the area with his nose inches from the ground. He stopped and picked up a clump of snow, breaking it open and smelling it, too. Then he dropped it to the ground and continued searching. With his eyes at ground level, he stared across the surface. It was one thing to cover your tracks from somebody who wasn't an expert, but Beaver knew how to look at the same picture from a different perspective.

He closed one eye and glared across the snow-covered ground, and then he could see its levels and the unnatural lay. He knew that somebody had covered their tracks. Using his hand, he brushed away the light powder and saw Money's track as clear as daylight. That was when he saw tiny drops of blood. Then he saw two more prints under the powdery snow. The top layer was beginning to get mushy under the relentless sun. When he looked back across the firewall cut from the forest and to the porch, everyone was staring, with eyes full of hope. Levi shook his head, and Bar-Chee started to cry again.

Levi followed his own tracks and jumped the fence again. He found himself the bearer of bad news. It seemed like such tasks always befell him. This time, it was especially tough for him since it was his apprentice.

"It looks like two men have nabbed little Money. Whoever it is, he's a good tracker. I barely found his sign. If I've gotta follow his footprints, it'll take me days, but there's only one way for White men to go, and that's down toward Yellowstone Valley. At least they weren't Indians. I reckon we've got us a pair of White men who stole the boy."

"*Stole...*" Bar-Chee mouthed the word like it had four letters. "Somebody's taken our boy?" She blinked like a bird in disbelief.

"I figure it's one of two things," Rusty said. "They've either taken him to sell somewhere, or they'll be snooping around for gold as a ransom, but I doubt it'll be the latter. If they wanted to parlay, they wouldn't have made such a fuss to cover their tracks."

"Go and find him for us, Joseph," Bar-Chee pleaded. Her eyes were so sad they almost made the hard marshal shed a tear, but he fought it back.

"No, Levi's right. He and the captain are the best two to find little Money. I'd just slow them down. He and Will are gonna fetch him back for us. Don't you fret."

———

RUSTY STEEL STOOD THERE GRUMBLING. Recently, he would have been the one to go and find the young boy, but he had partially retired from his position as the leader of the compound due to his age and his new wife, Silvia. They had recently been married and had managed to keep the newness from wearing off. He and she both knew that his days of trudging through the wilderness, risking his life, were nearing an end.

Money Penny was Levi's apprentice, so it was his duty to bring the boy back. As nature would have it, Beaver took over Rusty's old position, although no one ever said as much. It had become a given. Beaver was the finest mountain man within five hundred miles and maybe even more.

Levi stepped onto the porch and put his hand on Bar-Chee and Joseph's shoulders, affectionately. "I promise you I won't come back without him, no matter where he's disappeared to. He's one of us now, and the captain and I will protect him with our lives. Don't worry, my apprentice and your son have a lot more to learn here on the mountain before he's ready to go off on his own and live his life. Why, he's really no more than a boy."

Bar-Chee was crying so hard she couldn't talk. The marshal didn't trust his emotions by then, so all he could do was nod. Betty's face was streaming with tears. The captain's red-haired wife was worried about both Money and her husband, Will. Lately, things had been more difficult and dangerous, and with Money's kidnapping, it felt like things were going out of control.

Without another word, Levi and the captain climbed into their saddles, touched the brims of their hats, and wheeled their horses for the south gate.

"Let's ride over there by the tree line before we head

down the trail to Yellowstone Valley, Captain. I wanna see something that maybe ain't even there."

When they reached the point that Levi believed would provide the best opportunity for such an abduction, he dropped off his horse again and took a closer look. He brushed away a faint indentation in the snow with his fingers. He clucked his tongue and pushed his hand below the snow. When he drew it back, he had Money's shotgun in his fist. Two turkey feathers were lodged in the trigger guard.

"That's what I smelled: turkey." Beaver pulled the feathers free and held them to his nose. "They must have used the old Indian ruse to lure the innocent boy to them. No wonder there's so little sign of the two. Yep, this one knows every trick in the book. I wonder who he is. I ain't heard of any frontiersmen around these parts of this caliber of late. Keep sharp, Will. It looks like this fella might be as good as us."

Without another word, they started down the steep trail to Yellowstone Valley. They both had Fort Boise in their minds. They knew each other so well that they didn't have to voice their thoughts. There was only one place to take a White boy to sell, and that would be the fort. If it were Indians who had abducted the boy, they would have no concrete direction because the tribes stole children to repopulate their camps.

White men only stole people to sell to the highest bidder. That meant that whoever they were, they would be heading for Fort Boise, if only to stop and resupply, and then head onward either back east or to the west and into Oregon. Beyond that, they had no idea, but they felt sure that if they went by way of settlement on the Snake River, they would be able to find out who they were and where they had gone after a day in town. At least then they would have some direction to go in.

They also knew that they would have to keep a low profile in case the slavers were keeping an eye out for somebody coming to rescue the boy. If they found out, they might cut their losses and kill Money and get away scot-free.

TRACKING MONEY

THE RIDE DOWN THE MOUNTAIN WAS EVENTLESS. LEVI AND the captain knew the small, seldom-used trails like the back of their hands. Only the most astute warriors were aware of these hidden paths traveled by so few. In a matter of days, they reached a summit that allowed them to see the valley stretching far below, and it was all covered in a blanket of snow.

The icicles on the trees had disappeared, and after a few more weeks of sunshine, it would turn the white panorama into a lush valley of green. As they descended, the temperatures became milder. Horses' hooves sloshed down the trail, mixing snow and mud. Steam puffed from the animals' nostrils.

"We had an uneventful ride down the mountain for a change." Will smiled as he used the flat of his hand to stare into the distance. Yellowstone Valley was over seven miles across, both long and wide, and trails criss-crossed its entirety. "It's been months since we rode the valley floor. Keep an eye out for bears. They'll be coming out of hibernation soon, and they'll be hungry."

"I doubt our run of good luck will last much longer. We're in Blackfoot country from here on out, so we've gotta keep sharp or we could lose our scalps. Down here, if we run into them rascals, there'll be more than one, and they won't be crazy. I figure that warrior Brave that took on Kit Carson was plum loco."

"You don't have to remind me," the captain huffed. "He was mad with his desire for revenge. We've had a winter full of surprises, haven't we? Once we get across the valley and farther west, when we turn north, we'll only be a few days away. I could use a sit-down restaurant meal for a change. That and a proper haircut and shave." He rubbed his stubbled face and frowned.

"I'm hardly even hungry with all the worryin' about little Money. He's my first apprentice, you know. I should have kept a better eye on him. I feel responsible for what happens to the boy. Especially with him being so young."

"Why, he's tall for his age, so I don't see him as being that little. His personality is as big as a barn. There wasn't anything you could do about it, anyway, Beaver. You saw that he took off on his own to go hunting when he should have known better, going without an adult, so stop beating yourself up about it. You're just wasting time."

"Maybe I was tryin' to make him grow up too fast. I know I push the little fella hard. I thought he liked it. Every time I pressed him, he seemed to be willing and wanted more. But then again, maybe I misread him. I suppose I want him to turn out like me. I reckon that's a might egotistical of me, ain't it, Captain."

"From what I see, he loves it. You know, everybody

grows up fast in this country. If they don't, they don't last. Stop beating yourself up over this and focus on the target. Worrying about something never changed its outcome. Think positive. We're gonna find him and make whoever kidnapped him pay the price. There's no way we're going to go easy on this one. We've never let anyone down yet, have we? Surely, Money's not going to be the first. So, stop being so negative. You've always been the positive one of us, two."

"There's always a first time. I figure that truth is a byproduct of a fella's character. Honest folks reveal their truths with their every breath, and dishonest people will distort the same just as easily."

"And what is that supposed to mean?" Will asked, puzzled.

"That he who lies to himself is the biggest fool. Maybe we're both guilty of that at some time or another."

"You don't know what you're talking about. I make it a point not to worry. Only fools and horses waste their time on nonsense. If anything, I'm a practical man."

"That's just one of a hundred things you don't know everything about, Captain," Levi grinned. "Recognizing your own feelings ain't always a pleasant thing. But I reckon you're right about the worryin', yet, sometimes a man can't get his mind to do what he knows is best."

"Right now, you'd better focus on what you're doing, or like we said, we might lose our scalps."

As they carefully made their way, they came upon a cold campfire that held the remains of a dog on a stick. This was where an Indian war party had camped. Levi kneeled and felt the stones around the fire—they were still warm. He nodded to Will. Several teepees stood in the distance, surrounded by numerous Indian ponies. Their black silhouetted figures wandered grazing around the camp. Both men backed away before they could be seen. When the mountain men didn't want to be discovered, only the experts could detect them, and they had to be looking for them because they would never bump into them by accident.

———

AFTER CAREFULLY RIDING for two hours across the valley floor, Levi dropped off his gelding and kneeled beside fresh tracks. He counted the hoofprints of six riders plus six spare horses, and they were all shod. He stood, staring into the distance, wondering what White men were doing in the valley.

"I reckon the six of them must be White hunters, either that or they're lost," Beaver said. "Still, they make a big target, leaving all those tracks in plain sight. A blind man could follow this bunch. Quiet now, I doubt they're too far ahead of us."

"These men won't be those who snatched Money. They'll be here for something else."

Captain Forrester pulled at his shirt. It stuck to his body with sweat. The overhead sun pushed more heat into the valley, melting the snow, but Beaver hardly noticed. He seemed impervious to the weather, whether it was hot or cold. Levi's shirt stretched tight around the shoulders of the heavy-boned mountain man. He sat a full head above the captain on his big gelding. Shafts of light fell through the trees like rain.

Suddenly, everything was deathly quiet. One thing

they both knew for sure was that things were *too* still. Even the bugs stopped chattering, and the birds scattered. Their eyes flicked from one shadow to another, looking for signs of an ambush. Levi felt it was just a matter of time.

Suddenly, the day abruptly erupted into flashes of gunfire followed by a cacophony of bullets. Chunks of lead peppered the leaves on the trees as arrows sailed through the sky at lightning speed, falling from above. It was a miracle that the first volley hadn't hit them. Projectiles protruded from the ground like porcupines. When they looked, they couldn't see anything but the haze from the power flashes.

Levi quickly peeled back the hammers on his heavy Colt Walkers—in his massive hands, they almost looked small. They boomed when he pulled both triggers blindly into the brush. Will used his finger and thumb to empty all six chambers. Both men dove for the cover of a fallen tree while they fended off the hostile attack. Gray smoke hovered over the scene, with an overpowering, pungent smell of burned charcoal and sulfur. Using his arm's stump to hold the revolver, the captain quickly reloaded. You'd hardly notice he was missing an arm.

They popped up from behind the tree trunk and sent another eighteen bullets into the forage and brush. They heard grunts and two Blackfoot braves pitched forward, out of the bushes and across the path. The rest of the war party turned and ran while Levi and the captain reloaded, just in case, but all that was left was the buzzing of blowflies and the gurgling of a man with a shot-up lung. From experience, they knew he only had seconds to live.

"Let's get out of here, quick," Captain Forrester said.

"Now's not the time to linger. Every Indian and bandit within a mile in every direction must have heard all those rounds go off. Maybe more with the echo off the mountains."

They had been skirting the edge of the valley as they headed for the western side of Yellowstone before they turned north. The day drew toward its apex as the sun grew brighter, leaving their eyes defenseless to the bright glare.

"For one time, you're right." Levi managed to make a tired smile. "From here on out, we'd better travel day and night and only stop long enough to rest the horses. I hope they're up to the pressure of riding hard after such a long winter. Then again, there's no choice in the matter."

When they stopped to water the horses, the creek gurgled at their feet. Trigger, Levi's fourteen-hundred-pound gelding, bobbed his head as beads of water ran off his chin. Both horses twitched their ears at pesky flies as crows cawed at the intrusion into their space. A snake slithered through the grass.

With two dead warriors, they knew that their Blackfeet friends wouldn't go far. They would wait to retrieve their bodies for a proper burial and send them along to the Indian spirit world. So, the mountain men knew that the more distance they could put between them and the downed hostiles, the safer they would be.

Now, they wondered what else was awaiting them out there. Indians ran around the valley like termites in a rotting building. They both knew that these wouldn't be the last of their troubles. It was challenging to ride from Bear Tooth Mountain all the way to Fort Boise without running into an enemy or two, if not more.

That night, the wind whispered in the grass as owls hooted in the darkness and coyotes sang to the moon. They lay awake, unable to sleep, gazing up at countless stars light-years away. Despite the captain's bravado, they both worried about Money Penny. Still, not a word was spoken—they had said everything there was to say. After hours, they finally fell asleep under the great bowl of a sky in sober silence. They were so tired they didn't even snore.

———

LEVI WOKE UP FIRST. It must have been about three in the morning, but the moon stood nearly full, still high in the sky, casting silvery light across the countryside. They unhobbled their horses and set out again, carefully. Besides the sudden ambush by the young Blackfeet warriors, they hadn't seen another living soul, yet neither of them expected that to last.

A couple of hours after they started, and the sun had yet to rise, they saw flickering lights through the trees and smelled burning wood. Beaver sniffed the air like a jackal, searching out its prey's scent. All he did was nod, and the captain dropped off his horse and vanished. Levi grabbed his mount near the bit ring and held him still, giving Will time to get into position. After five minutes had passed, he grabbed the lead and calmly wheeled toward the campsite. Anyone camping in these woods would be taking a dangerous or foolish risk. Hopefully, it was the latter.

As the sun sat squatting on the earth's rim, he saw a thin line of gray smoke as it climbed high into the sky. Beaver slid off his horse and pulled a handful of grass, letting it fall, indicating the direction of the wind. He confirmed they were downwind to the campers.

When Beaver got close enough to see their faces, he saw six men, three dog-tents, and a flickering fire. Eight horses were tied to ground stakes as they grazed, whisking their tails, sliding their jaws, and blowing air. One animal raised its head and snorted, then nickered, but the campers didn't notice. Levi palmed a stale, molasses-laced biscuit into his horse's mouth and then the other half to the captain's Appaloosa to keep them quiet.

He saw thin-lipped, sun-darkened men in range cloths and dark leather chaps. Guns leaned up against nearby trees, and they all had Colt revolvers stuck into their wide belts. At first glance, Levi didn't know what they were if they weren't range hands, but why would they be there? Unless they were trying to follow the Oregon Trail and got lost.

They didn't look like trappers, as they had no traps. They weren't miners either because there wasn't a shovel among them. He wondered if the supposed buckaroos were coming from California or back east and were heading west. Whatever the case, they had a full day off the main trail, whichever way they traveled.

Beaver tied the horses a distance away and closed in on foot. Just in case he pulled his heavy revolvers while he covered the last few steps.

"Howdy, boys," Levi said in a friendly voice despite the guns hanging at his sides. He stepped up to the circle of light cast by the fire. "You fellas look lost."

"How dare you sneak up on us like that?" a young man with a pimple-covered face said and spat. When

Levi walked in, it startled him to his feet. "Who do you think you are, sayin' we're lost? You'd better watch that mouth of yours before I wash it out with soap."

"Atta boy, Earl. We don't take any sass from strangers, especially if they walk around dressed like Indians." A skinny man, not seventeen, replied, but his voice wasn't full of steel like his friend's. "Nobody barges into our camp announced. You liked to scare the wits out of us."

"You better be careful who you mouth off to out here," Levi replied, but the smile on his face had vanished. "Most folks in these parts don't have forgiving souls. You're lucky I'm a God-fearin' man. If you're lost, I can point you in the right direction. You fellas don't look like mountain men *or* scouts."

"What we are or ain't is none of your business," Earl snarled. "Move on out of our camp before we whip your tail. You don't know who you're messing with, hillbilly. Why don't you go back into the woods where you belong? Why, you almost look like a heathen. Now scat, before I get riled up. I can guarantee you, that's somethin' you don't wanna see."

Levi instantly rewarded Earl with a series of lightning-swift punches from his massive fists, knocking the mouthy cowboy to the ground. When he tried to get up, he fell over again. He lay there staring at the sky as his head spun around. Beaver had nearly knocked his lights out.

"Keep those hands right where they are," the captain said crisply, as he walked out of the dark with his pistol in his fist. "Your friend already got his tail kicked. I'd hate to shoot you, too, but I will if you make me. The other five of you mind your manners, and this will all be over real soon."

Levi didn't say a word, but he conspicuously hung his thumbs on his pistols' hammers just to give them notice. They weren't dealing with fools.

"If you know what's good for you, you'll stay down," Will said dryly from the edge of light. He leveled his gun at the strangers. The click sounded loud in the sudden silence. "If not, my friend will never stop, especially since he's so riled up. Levi doesn't take well to insults from ignorant men. You're lucky *we* found you. Were it somebody else, you'd have probably been shot just for being here. Where did you get that mouth of yours, Earl? You don't mind if I use your first name, do ya?"

Earl finally pushed himself to his hands and knees while swearing under his breath. Will walked right up to the fire and gave him a swift kick in the ribs to shut him up. He heard a distinct snap when his boot hit Earl's side, and he yelped in pain.

"I told you, you should stay down. The problem is you don't know who *you're* dealing with. Now, listen to what I tell you, or you're really going to get hurt."

The man Levi beat up opened and closed his mouth like he couldn't decide whether to talk or shut up. He blinked his eyes until they uncrossed.

"While we're here, we need you to answer a few questions," Levi said. It was clear that it wasn't a request but an order. "First of all, where are you comin' from?"

The second cowboy replied nervously, "Fort Boise."

"And you're headed to?"

"The territories and up to the settlement, Denver. We heard they paid top dollar for good buckaroos like us Californianos."

"You look like youngsters to me," the captain replied. "And you came all the way here for that? Why, I thought California was full of ranches."

"It is, but there's talk of war with the California Republic and Mexico, and we didn't want to get drawn into the conflict. We're cattlemen, not soldiers."

"I can understand that," Captain Forrester said dryly. "Did you see some men with a small boy about nine years old?"

"I remember seein' quite a few youngins runnin' around inside the Fort Boise walls and even more outside. Some of them were White, and others were dark-skinned. To be honest, we spent most of our time in McKay's Saloon gettin' drunk and don't mingle much with families. We're all bachelors, ya know."

Earl moaned as he sat up, holding his head. Again, he mouthed some words, but nothing came out. He fished his tongue around his mouth and spat out a tooth. It rolled across the ground, disappearing into the snow, leaving a thin thread of blood.

"You six ain't of much use, are ya? When you leave tomorrow morning, turn north for a full day. That will take you back to Fort Boise, then you ride west, not south. Before you know it, you'll be on the right trail again. You were headed toward more trouble than you've ever laid your eyes on. There are five tribes out there that say that land is theirs and don't want White men trespassing on it."

Without another word, the mountain men mounted up and wheeled their horses and continued north. These men were only dangerous to themselves and had no pertinent information.

"If you know how, follow our trail, and you won't get

lost," the captain called out over his shoulder. Horses' hooves slowly disappeared as the dark swallowed them up. They left the buckaroos heading west, among complaints but no more insults.

————

THEY TRAVELED deep into the night until it was almost dawn, and only then did they rest again. They found a close stand of trees with plenty of shade and threw their bedrolls out for a few winks. Their cold camp was impossible to see from afar, and one of them was always on lookout. Now that hostilities had shown their ugly heads, the Indians knew they were there and probably knew about the Californian buckaroos, too.

"I'll take the first turn," Captain Forrester said. "It would be just like those Blackfeet warriors to run these cowboys to ground and scalp them all. They have no idea of where they're playing."

"They sure were a strappy bunch for such young fellas. Hopefully, they don't get into serious trouble before they make it to Willamette Valley at the end of the Oregon Trail. This country eats White men like them."

It felt like Levi had just closed his eyes when he felt Will shaking his shoulder to wake him up. He saw the sun's rays filtering through the trees. Without a word, Levi grabbed his prototype rifle that Mr. Christian Sharps had supplied Rusty Steel and his men to test his weapons before putting them on the market, and the mountain men were all thrilled at the offer. Levi's shooting skills were even better with the new weapons. He had even surpassed his mentor, Rusty Steel, with his marksmanship. Something that his mentor begrudgingly admitted.

Will slept as if he were at attention. Everything he did had a military air about it. He lay with his eyes closed and his fingers wrapped around the grip of his saber—woe as to the stranger that awoke him.

TRAPPER JACK

BEAVER THOUGHT HE WAS HEARING THINGS WHEN THE first hint of a bell rang sharp and clear through the air. He cocked his head like a dog as he focused on the sound and took a deep breath to smell the air. He looked at the captain, but he was still sound asleep. His hand went for his rifle. He laid it across his lap. The smell came before sight. The odor was like burning green leaves. Then he heard somebody whistling a song he had recently heard from a traveler, their friend, Kit Carson. "It was The Hunters of Kentucky." Traces of white smoke floated through the bushes and leaves.

Will heard the whistling, which abruptly drew him from his dream as he sat up and pushed himself to his feet. Hip-cocked, he pushed his hat back on his head, pulling the drawstring tight against his chin. He waited, listening as the stranger got nearer. His .44-caliber Colt was cocked, but now it was pointed at the ground, dangling from his arm. They both watched as the stranger came into sight.

"He's wearin' a brace of pistols, so I reckon he knows

how to use 'em. Maybe he's trying to prove somethin'."
Levi whispered, uncocking his revolver and slipping it
back into his cross-draw holster. "Only a fool or a
friendly pilgrim would stroll into our camp and not
expect to get shot. But you'd better keep that gun in
your hand just in case, since he *is* armed. I'll do the
talkin'. We can decide how to proceed as we go. There's
no sense in startin' a fight we don't need."

"Everybody carries a gun in this wilderness. A man
would be mad to come out here unarmed, if only for the
dangerous animals," he murmured in his best friend's
ear. Will's eyes narrowed as his arm tensed, ready to
level his pistol. His empty sleeve festooned in the
breeze.

Both recognized he was a frontiersman because he
was dressed like them. The only difference was that he
walked like he didn't have a care in the world. He acted
like Levi and Will weren't watching, but they both knew
it was a show, and he was checking out their every
move. The buckskin-clad man pulled a stubborn mule
that was loaded with traps, hides, and knick-knacks. He
took a last puff on the bitter-smelling herb, dropped it
to the ground, and ground it out with the heel of his
boot.

A shiny brass bell hung from a thick string around
his mule's neck. They walked almost lazily, seeming to
have no direction or rush. When he pulled to a stop, his
eyes were as calm and still as a millpond. Then a
friendly smile stretched across his face, making it
wrinkle like an old prune. Only then did they realize his
age. Still, he seemed as spry as a teen and as healthy as a
racehorse.

The stranger must have been between Rusty and

Angus's ages and looked like he spent a good part of that in the wilderness. His visible muscles rippled under the tight hide across his back and chest, showing his muscles despite his age. Mooring lines ran up and down his neck. His gray beard hung to his chest, and his hair to his shoulders. The only traces of his Mexican mother's genes were his black eyes and heavy eyebrows. His white skin: sunburned.

"Whatcha trappin', Pilgrim?" Levi asked. "It's pretty slim pickings out here these days. Most of the beavers disappeared in 1840. A while back, we just arrived in time to catch the last rendezvous. We liked it so much we stayed, and that was six years ago. And you? What's your story, mister?"

"The name is Trapper Jack Reels. Believe it or not, I was at that same rendezvous in 1840. It's a small world, ain't it? Why, we sure did have a fine time back then, didn't we? I attended ten of the fifteen in all. It gave us somethin' to look forward to during those harsh winters. It's a shame how the world's changed. Then again, most folks call that progress and say it's good."

The white smoke of the foul-smelling hand-built cigarette still clung to his head. He made a face as if he had a bitter taste in his mouth and spat into the snow, leaving a green stain. He nonchalantly continued until he stopped right in front of Levi and Will.

"This is Captain Forrester, and I'm Levi Johnson. We live up in the mountains, ten days or so from here, with our friends. Been in the Rockies for long, have ya?"

"Mostly up in the Oregon Country, north and east of here. When the beavers were trapped out, I switched to hunting buffalo, but as you can see from the traps, I still chase muskrats, otters, minks, and even rabbits.

Anything that has a usable skin and is edible. I reckon it's more habit now than anything else because it doesn't pay squat. I've heard of the country around Yellowstone Valley, but I usually stayed away due to the hostility, although I have ventured there a time or two. They're a passel of tribes in the valley, and one is meaner than the other. I suppose that's what keeps 'em constantly riled up, bitin' at each other's backs and fightin' among themselves."

"The problem is, they don't like White folks encroaching on their land," Beaver said as he carefully eyed Jack Reels. "Until now, we're in the far reaches, so few settlers find their way up where we live, but the odd unlucky party or family finds their way to the valley and doesn't get what they expected. Most of 'em die."

A large Bowie knife stuck out of the small of the stranger's back, and the handle of a skinning knife from his boot. His frilly-trimmed buckskins were tattered and worn. Along the stitching, every few tassels were missing. He wore a pair of proper English riding boots, rather than high-heeled, pointed American range wear or even moccasins. They were solid, comfortable, and a safe barrier for rattlesnakes, which tended to bite men in the ankles or thighs, and the Rockies were full of vipers.

"That's true enough. A little farther east and south toward Texas, settlements are springing up like weeds. And at the same time, the army is pushing the Indians off their land and onto reservations. Two or three weeks ago, I was in Fort Boise. I had to stop there for provisions. Over time, some of those pitched tents and covered wagons outside the walls will decide to stay and build homes, which will only make the local hostiles angrier.

"As it is, there must be three hundred pilgrims living outside the walls for security. They know if they get attacked, they can hide behind the walls, saving them from assaults. Solid buildings mean that the White folks don't intend to leave, and the government back east makes it all legal. In exchange, they give the tribes small tracks of land hundreds of miles from their homes. It seems like a rotten deal to me. I'd say it's designed for a good part of 'em to die along the way, and many of the others starve. By the time they reach their destinations, half of them have died, and it'll all be designed to steal the Indians' land."

"Don't we all know it," Levi huffed.

"Indian Agency agents' positions are handed out mostly to men who hate the Indians. Many often profit by short rationing the reservation Indians selling their government beef and grain to local homesteads or even back to the army, who provided the meat in the first place." Jack pulled on his long beard, but his smile reached his eyes. "We're just pawns in the game, my friends, and have no say in Indian matters."

"That's been goin' on for a while now," Captain Forster replied. "Some years back, we were supposed to push the Comanche back near Fort Scott, but we were the ones who got pushed back. Levi here was my scout. Our weapons couldn't stand up against a bunch of warriors who could shoot twelve arrows per minute. Multiply that by a hundred, and you have a massacre on your hands with a thousand two hundred projectiles every sixty seconds. White men haven't invented anything that shoots that fast. Levi and I lost my entire expedition, save four soldiers, to Comanche war parties. Mind you, as soon as someone invents a reliable repeater rifle, that'll be the end of the show. The army has been losing this battle for nigh on ten years, and once the tables turn, it'll be vicious."

"I agree," Jack said. "It'll be a slaughter of revenge, and I know the politicians back in Washington won't lift a finger to stop it. They want to settle this whole country as soon as possible from the Atlantic to the Pacific coast, and top to bottom, and they'll let no one step in their way."

"I believe it's all part of their plan," Captain Forrester said. "Normal Americans have no idea of what is said behind closed doors in the White House, no matter what the newspapers say. I figure the government has them in their pockets, too."

"If you've been to so many rendezvous, maybe you've heard of my mentor, Rusty Steel? I reckon he's just about your age. That's who took us on as mountain man apprentices. That was our lucky break." Beaver couldn't help but grin. He was becoming more comfortable with the easygoing stranger by the minute.

"I've briefly met Rusty, but through his friend, McFarlin. Angus and I go way back. I do believe I heard tell that they share a cabin these days. Believe it or not, there aren't many secrets in the Rocky Mountains and the Great Plains—especially when it concerns White men. You know, Angus and I are the same age. I met up with him for two winters in the Crow stronghold on Bear Tooth Mountain, back some twelve or thirteen years ago. I think he was on his second Indian wife, Blossom. I forgot the name of the one before that. Angus sure could dance up a storm, and the Indian women love a fella fancy on his feet. Is that old rascal still alive?"

"Alive and kicking and as ornery as ever. He has another wife now, named Pine Needle. That makes three since he's been here in the wilderness. Excuse me, but I'm having a hard time believing he and you are the same age. Why, you look five to ten years younger. How can that be?" Puzzlement etched Beaver's face.

"Maybe it's because I've never been married." Trapper laughed. "Daunting women can put a passel of years on a man and shorten his life. Then again, I come from a good bloodline. My pa is ninety years old and he's still with us, or at least he was the last I heard."

Levi proffered his hand, and Jack grabbed it with the same enthusiasm as the younger, Johnson. For a moment, it almost became a contest, and their faces began turning red, until they both burst out laughing and released their grips.

"Birds of a feather. Pleased to meet ya, Mr. Johnson." Jack stuck out his scared mitt. Will conspicuously slipped his Colt Patterson revolver into his cross-draw holster. Another revolver hung from his hip, and his saber on the opposite side. They shook hands, but it was more formal than it was with Beaver. "Any friend of Angus's is a friend of mine." Still, the captain's voice was guarded.

There were reservations, both in his voice and his eyes. The captain never trusted anyone until they proved themselves worthy of his friendship or even his time, but Beaver made friends at the drop of a hat.

"Did you see anybody along the trail on the way here?" Levi asked. "You know, hostiles or bandits or the like?"

"Nope, I don't believe there's a soul for miles." He lifted his head and sniffed the air. "There ain't nothin' upwind that I can smell, and my nose is about as good as a hound's."

As Levi watched, the stranger dismounted and hobbled both his horse and mule. He felt like he was watching an older version of himself. Of course, he wasn't nearly as big, but he seemed to have that same feel and nature that Beaver had during his whole life. He felt he was destined to live in the wilderness, all the way back in Southern Indiana, on the Ohio River, where his parents had a cabin deep in the woods. Back then, he was only a teenager, but he was already certain of his destiny. As a boy, he longed for undiscovered mountains and valleys where no White man had ever set foot.

———

WHEN HE WAS YOUNG, Levi was such an excellent trapper that he invented a few of his own traps, which made him locally famous. Most of the Hoosiers even called him *Trapper Boy*, but it was Beaver that stuck. He was known to be the best shot on the Great Ohio River. That feeling was what prompted him to travel west as soon as he was old enough to endure such hardships, but he had trained his whole life, so it was effortless. He had always been the epitome of a frontiersman. With his size at six feet seven and two hundred pounds, he had always looked large for his age. He could hardly remember when people took him for a child.

"In that case, I figure we can risk a small fire for coffee and a half dozen frying pan biscuits. Whatcha say, Trapper Jack? How about you step down and we break bread together?"

Jack had glaring black eyes that looked like two chunks of coal. The wooden grips on his revolvers were worn and scratched, but at the same time, you could tell they were oiled regularly and well cared for. Signs of use shone on the metal. His holster fit like a glove and seemed like an extension of his body. Notches were visibly etched on the handles, something that gave Beaver pause.

Maybe we're not so much alike after all. I don't count the men I've killed, but that doesn't mean he's an evil man. Maybe he's more like another version of the captain, Levi thought.

The captain didn't have any notches in his wooden grips or rifle stocks, but Levi doubted little if he hadn't kept exact count. That was just how the captain was, and he cared little about what people thought of him. Everyone, except for his handful of friends and those he had protected with his life, just like his wife, Betty. She was no stranger to the wilderness either. As the niece of the famous Davey Crockett, she grew up deep in the Tennessee forests, and she and her family lived off the land.

"Which way are you fellas goin'?" Jack Reeds asked. "I've just pulled up all my traps and was headin' back to Fort Boise to resupply. I think I'm going to mosey along the Oregon Trail until I reach Willamette Valley, unless something more interesting pops up. I'm so fiddle-footed that pretty much any little breeze will change my direction."

"Do you always travel like that—free as a bird with little planning?" Captain Forrester asked. His curiosity had gotten the best of him. "When I decide to go somewhere, I'm full speed ahead until I get to my intended destination and refuse to be deterred."

"It takes an earthquake and a tornado to change the captain's direction." Levi laughed.

"Well, there was a time when I used to make plans, but I soon found that livin' in the wilderness, you can never plan too much because something always pops up that changes your future, be they good or bad, like it or not. Sure, sometimes I set up one of my teepees I have stashed away and spend a month or two in one place, but I'm usually runnin' away from bad weather. I just came up from Texas a few weeks back. It's fine weather in the winter, but be careful not to get caught in the summer, or you'll melt. Did you know that every place has a perfect season? All you've gotta do is find it."

Even though the small fire was hardly noticeable, the aroma of freshly perked coffee filled their senses and bounced along on puffs of air. Of course, after the White men introduced the Native Americans to coffee, they loved it too, but it was generally too expensive so they substituted it with chicory. Still, everyone in the wilderness, and especially the forests, knew that the aroma of hot java meant that White men were near.

Still, Jack seemed to know what he was doing, so there shouldn't be anyone on their point, and they knew nobody was on their drag because they had just passed. Sometimes you knew you shouldn't do something, but circumstances dictated that you did it anyway, and to a mountain traveler, it was almost imperative. All of them were grumpy until they had that first hot cup of the day.

The old trapper looked at his dull and tarnished pocket watch. He pushed the stem, and the top popped open. It seemed as ancient as he was. The captain nearly chuckled. Why would a man without a plan or much notion of time carry a timepiece? Then he thought it must be sentimental, because otherwise it didn't seem to fit.

Or maybe he was trying to read too much into the stranger. If he *were* friends with Angus, he must be a stand-up man. McFarlin had never tolerated poor behavior. Still, Captain Forrester was ever suspicious of anything he didn't know inside and out. That was part of what kept him and Levi alive over the last years.

"Did you know that Aboriginal people from these parts hunted the Great Western Plains for thousands of years? The original inhabitants witnessed the recession of the glaciers when the earth began to warm. American Indians hunted these same mountains and plains when it was densely forested, and now it's a sea of grass. Through all these changes, the people continued to live successfully as nomadic hunters on these vast stretches of land for the last 13,000 years.

"Now, the tides have turned, though. Is it possible for such ancient civilizations to disappear without a trace? That's what I believe we're seeing with our very eyes. Much like the beaver. Next will come the buffalo, and the Native Americans' demise will follow."

The talkative man had Levi and Will's undivided attention—especially the captain, who sucked up history like a sponge.

"The Indians of our time are colorful, mystical, although warlike. The antiquity of their rituals is estimated to be over ten thousand years old, too. They eventually developed an intricate organization of their many tribes. They're a hunting society built around the horse, even though the four-legged animal isn't native to our lands. When they came later, everything changed."

"It's hard to believe that there was a time not too long ago when horses didn't exist in North America," Levi replied. "It almost seems impossible now."

"Three hundred years ago, they weren't on the American continent. The Spanish introduced them before the other European settlers arrived on our shores. When the Spanish were nearly wiped out and abandoned their homes, the horses ran free on the ranges. They adapted until a sturdy and weather-resistant animal developed into the horses we use every day."

———

AFTER ANOTHER DAY OF RIDING, as they neared sunset, they saw antelope bounding across the hillside and on a distant ridge, shadows stood long beside a pack of coyotes. When they looked beyond that, they could see the lights of Fort Boise and thought they heard the familiar hammering on steel, which could only be the blacksmith. Soon, they could make the fort guards out in the gateway. The flames' shadows dance along the long exterior wall.

At first, the sound came gradually. It was faint as it emerged from the darkness. Initially, it was indistinguishable, but now the guards could hear the unmistakable clop of a slow walk.

Silhouettes suddenly stepped out of the darkness and walked toward the burning torches.

"Who goes there?" a soldier asked as the two guards

leveled their percussion lock rifles at the shadows in the distance.

"Don't shoot, it's me, Captain Will Forrester, with Levi Johnson and a friend. Stand at ease, men. I know it's dark, but don't shoot."

Of course, not everyone knew who Captain Will Forrester was, but anyone who worked at Fort Boise did, and the same was the case with Levi Johnson. Even though he was retired, he still acted like an officer and a gentleman unless he was mad. When he and Levi first visited the fort with the famous mountain man, Rusty Steel, everyone found them to be strange friends. They couldn't have been more different in every way.

Charlie Fox, the McKay's bartender, looked up at the mountain men as soon as they pushed their way through the batwing doors and whooshed closed behind them. When he raised his eyebrows, Will answered, leaning his forearms on the bar, "How about some whiskey and three glasses. This here is our new friend, Trapper Jack Reels."

"Why, I already know Mr. Reels. He was here a few weeks back." Charlie set a bottle of whiskey on the bar, wetting the tip of his yellow pencil with his tongue, and marked the level on the label so he would know how much they drank when they were done. The saloon charged by the inch. He grabbed three glasses with his fingers and deposited them on the table.

"Here you go, gentlemen." Charlie grinned. "I didn't know you boys knew each other."

The captain rested his elbow on the bar and held his drink up. Their glasses clinked, then they tossed them back in one go, allowing the harsh spirits to burn their way down, cutting through all the trail dust.

Charlie poured a second round and said, "These are on me." He poured himself a stiff drink, too. Now they sipped on their whiskeys, and they pulled out pipes, and the captain one-handedly built a cigarette.

Levi could see the captain relax the hard line of his jaw, his face leathery. When he looked at his friend, he couldn't help but smile.

"What?" Will snapped.

"Bottoms up." Beaver returned a broad grin.

"I'll warn ya now, Beaver." Charlie chuckled. "Jack here can talk your ear off. Why, he would give your mentor, Rusty Steel, a run for his money, and he can talk all day long."

"We've already found that out," Will replied. It was hard to tell if he liked it or not.

Usually, the captain wasn't a chatty man, but Levi was the opposite side of the coin.

"One more, before we tend to our horses, Charlie." He sipped a little more whiskey. "I feel better already. All I need now is a shave." He rubbed his stubble and growled. "We'll see ya around, Jack. We'll probably be here for a day or two."

When they finished off their glasses, the mountain men turned for the door. Boot heels hammered the porch. The street was mushy with dirty snow and mud as they stepped into the street to climb astride their horses. If they walked, they would be up to their knees in mud. Until the snow finally melted, everyone walked around with brown, slosh-caked boots.

A sign over the stable doors said, *FORT BOISE LIVERY STABLES AND FARRIER.* Two lanterns hung from the wall, casting half-circles of yellow light. A man sat on a bale of straw, digging at his fingernails with a pocketknife while reading a dime novel. Fifteen minutes later, they headed for the only bathhouse in town, right beside the local bunkhouse.

Many of the town's occupants were travelers spending a night or two in a real bed under a wooden roof, enjoying the most basic creature comforts before embarking on the last stretch westward on the Oregon Trail. That, and a few town citizens who called the bunk house home because they lacked the funds to rent or even buy a place. Due to high demand and limited availability, a place was hard to come by, so they opted to bunk with the wanderers and whoever might spend the night.

Others opted to live in covered buckboard wagons and tents beside the dozen Indian teepees scattered between the fort and the Snake River. There was plenty of available hunting game and fish to provide food for them all without encroaching on the Indians' reserves. Still, most of the tribes hated the White men for what they had already done, not only for what they were about to do in the near future.

There were the Shoshone, Bannock, and Northern Paiute tribes, who were referred to as the Snake Indians by White immigrants due to their ignorance of the Plains Tribes. They populated the area and often had hostile encounters with the travelers, especially the Shoshone People. As tribes, they were friendly enough with each other to intermarry and frequented the wagon trains on the arid Snake River Plains. These Indians had been involved in conflicts with the White settlers during the mid-nineteenth century. These conflicts derived from competition over resources and territory as more settlers migrated west.

Shoshone chiefs, such as Pocatello, began raiding settlements as soon as they could be built. They also attacked the smaller and more variable wagon trains in response to the encroachment on the land, as well as taking the food right out of their mouths. Due to these instances, the United States Army attacked Shoshone camps wherever found. The beginning of the end was just about to arrive.

Their main enemy, apart from the White settlers and overlanders, was the Blackfeet Tribe. Initially, when the first trappers and mountain men arrived, they were friendly and traded furs and hides and lived in peace.

But when the settlers began to come in hordes and wagon trains miles long invaded their land, they became hostile, like many others before and after them. They knew that if they didn't fight, they would perish, and perhaps even *then*, they might not be able to resist.

SEMBLANCE OF CIVILIZATION

FORT BOISE HAD BEEN BUILT WITH HOSTILE INDIANS IN mind and was constructed on a sloping hill. It stood a way off the banks of the Snake River with a single entrance opening onto the small dock where rafts and barges sailed up and down the waterway. A small guard-house stood between the fort walls and the water, also armed with a single guard. A lantern glowed inside, spilling light out the wedge of an open door. A cigarette's cinder glowed orange in the dark.

A tall, square turret rose out of the corner of the fort walls with an additional lookout inside. It was topped off with the stars and stripes of the red, white, and blue. The chapel bell was just visible above the fifteen-foot-tall walls. Fishermen sat on the riverside with cane poles in their hands, hoping to catch a cutthroat trout, rainbow, sturgeon, or smallmouth bass. Baby bluegills and tadpoles darted about the shallows at the river's edge as a turtle awaited the warm sun, where it would lazily lie in the reeds. For now, its head was hidden in its shell.

They could hear the faraway creaking and the muffled rumble of wagons. Of course, the fort was a steady stop to rest and resupply on the Oregon Trail. Six years prior, there was a sprinkling of brave explorers, but now, every Tom, Dick, and Harry was blazing westbound. There were so many that the strings of wagons and animals went on for miles, sometimes as far as the eye could see. When they suddenly saw the six-horse team against the blue sky, it billowed dirt.

Wagon wheels churned up dust as hammering hooves raced toward the fort's gates. Levi raised his hand, but saw the driver make no attempt to stop. When he finally reached the entrance, the bullwhacker held the reins high through his fingers as he booted the brake lever, and it skidded sideways to a stop. The spokes were covered in mud.

That was when the three mountain men noticed the arrows protruding from the sides of the covered buckboard wagon as the feathers fluttered in the wind. It looked like a huge porcupine with four wheels. They had apparently been hit hard, but there were no wounded visible.

"What the hell?" Jack exclaimed.

As soon as the guards stepped aside, they rolled into the fort's compound, and the driver pulled up before the livery's corral. Before climbing down, he punched the empty shell casing out of his pistol, replacing it with new bullets. He shoved his revolver into his holster, swearing all the while.

Arrow-leaf balsamroot, fescue, blue bunch wheatgrass, and bitter brush covered the river's sides, along with huckleberry and sagebrush. Every tree between the fort and the river had been cut down to make a clear field of fire. This, along with the fifteen-foot wall made of heavy timber, locally quarried sandstone, abode bricks, and reinforced with stones, made it all but impossible to breach the entrance and raid within its walls. Time after time, there had been attempts, but to date, they had all failed.

The Fort Boise location was initially established as a fur-traders' outpost in 1813 by the Pacific Fur Company. The early settlers of the fort were soon killed by the local hostile Indians. Others escaped to reach the friendly Walla Walla Indians on the Columbia River, but in 1838, they built Fort Boise as a trading post along with Fort Hall, three hundred miles east. This created a safety zone for trappers and travelers alike along the Oregon Trail. Between the two forts was no-man's-land.

The same went for the trail between Fort Boise and the Willamette Valley. Only the occasional refuge was available, but these same places provided the provisions in the way of trading posts they needed to continue their journey along the Oregon Trail. These were the only safe havens on the highway across the Great Plains.

Inside Fort Boise, they found a wall with small store-fronts. There were saloons, a bathhouse, a boarding house, a barbershop, and a hardware store. Every man's needs were provided within the confined space of the sizable compound. Mixed in with Americans from the East Coast traveling across the country were a large share of immigrants from Europe.

One and all were chasing the pot of gold at the end of their imaginary rainbows. The government had assured them they would find green valleys, free land, and riches beyond their wildest dreams. In the European newspapers, they even claimed that you could pick up gold nuggets right off the ground. Many desperate people believed what they read and boarded the many ships that transported the millions of immigrants about to descend on the United States of America.

They weren't near the large centers of vice and crime, such as San Antonio, Denver, or San Francisco, among many others, but that didn't mean that everyone in the out-of-the-way settlement was honest. Many men, this far west, were running or hiding from their past or maybe even the law. Where better to disappear in blind sight than in the middle of the wilderness, surrounded by wild Indians? Not even the bravest lawman would chase an outlaw that far.

As they walked out of the tavern and entered the courtyard, the first signs of light began to show on the eastern horizon, and the moon dropped off at the other end of the world. The two guards hardly glanced at them after standing watch all night.

Once they tended to their animals, they were free to rest and do whatever they wanted.

"I know what I want," Will said and grinned. "A haircut and a shave."

"I'd rather drink whiskey after such a long, hard ride. You know, we hardly slept for the last ten days. First, we'll tend to the horses, then we'll get another drink, and you can go get your shave while I have something to eat. Then, after a good sleep, I'll have that bath. I'm plumb worn out, Captain."

"All you think about is food. No offense, but you could use a bath right now, too. You might not notice it, but you're getting ripe. Washing up in a stream isn't the same as bathing in a hot tub filled with clean water, using a scrub brush and a bar of soap. I guarantee you, you'll sleep better, too. I can't wait to get out of these clothes and into a tub."

"As soon as my stomach is full and my gullet's wet enough, I'll be up for that bath. Then we'll get back to work. There's no sense in runnin' off half-cocked anyway. It'll just spoil things in the end. Before that, I ain't doin' nothin'. A steam engine doesn't run without wood, and I don't run without food."

They stopped in front of the shop beside the saloon, and Levi and Will could smell the smoke from the forge and hear the loud clang of the smithy's hammer as he worked on a piece of red-hot, gleaming metal. The captain's boot heels clattered across the porch's wooden floor.

When they walked in again, the mountain men stopped, framed in the doorway, two silhouettes in the morning light. One had a missing arm. As soon as they walked into the restaurant, the women stared at the handsome men.

They stepped past the door and into McKay's Saloon. Charlie Fox smiled and shouted, "Come on in, boys. What'll ya have this time? I didn't figure you had enough with a couple of drinks. I bet you're hungry, ain't cha, Levi? There's some tasty black bear meat on today's menu. That and mashed potatoes, mush, and canned peaches. How will that do ya, Levi? Just sit down over there in the restaurant and Geltrude will be right with ya."

"Whatever you say, Charlie. We thank ya, kindly. Black bear, it is then. We'll have that same bottle at the table." Levi grinned, especially as he got his way.

The captain was full of plans and rules, but Beaver

let his heart lead him, and it rarely failed. Right then, he knew he needed fuel in his engine. The maintenance would come later. Will was obsessed with his stubble of a beard. When he wasn't clean-shaven, he felt dirty. If it were up to him, he would shave every day, especially if it was in a proper barber shop or some semblance thereof.

They raised their shot glasses of whiskey in a toast, nodded, then bottoms up, making their Adam's apples bob up and down. Gertrude mysteriously appeared out of nowhere and was suddenly standing beside their table with a notepad in one hand and a sharpened pencil in the other. She tapped her foot impatiently as she waited to take their order.

"I'm off to get that shave I was talking about. Then I'll come back and eat too." Will placed his hands on the table, pushed himself up, and looked into Beaver's eyes. "We're going to find that boy. You just watch." Then he turned for the exit and disappeared behind the swinging doors.

"I'll have two menus of the day, please. Do you have fresh milk?" Levi asked.

"Yep," Gertrude replied. She was a woman of few words. "One for you and one for your friend when he gets back. Should I keep it warm or what?"

"No, ma'am, they're both for me. Bring me a pitcher full of milk with my meal, and give me a double helping of everything else, ma'am." Levi smiled so wide you could see his wisdom teeth.

"That's a gallon of milk, young man."

"I know. I doubt it'll be enough either." Beaver chuckled. "I'm as hungry as that bear you're servin' for dinner."

"Did you run into any trouble on your way here, Levi?" Charlie Fox asked.

"It was one hell of a fifteen-day journey from Bear Tooth Mountain to here, and we traveled day and night. We only stopped for meals and the occasional wink of sleep," the captain said. "Marshal Walker would never have been able to keep up, but still, I know it left a bad taste in his mouth having to stay behind and wait. I'd much rather be solving a problem than sitting on my backside, waiting for someone else to complete the task."

"By the way, Trapper said that he'll see ya when he sees ya. As soon as you boys left for the stables, he hit the hardware store and vanished. That old fella is a strange one, all right. He can never seem to stay in one place."

When the waitress brought out a tray of donuts, Beaver's eyes spread as he grabbed two in each hand.

"But that's dessert," Gertrude scolded. "If you eat everything we've got, there won't be anything left for anyone else. Now act your age and mind your manners, Mr. Johnson. That's right, I remember your name."

"Who said I can't have dessert first, Geltrude? Go on then. I doubt I'll last long on four donuts, but it'll help tide me over. You don't wanna see me when I'm really hungry. It's an ugly sight. Thank ya kindly, ma'am."

"How is the marshal, anyway, and of course your misuses, fellas? I hope they're all well and fine. How'd you fare the winter? And what are old Rusty and Angus up to? They come down the mountain less every year. I haven't seen McFarlin for ages."

"Why, Marshal Walker isn't doing very well these days. Somebody stole his boy," the captain whispered.

"But mums the word, hey old buddy. We're looking to find him and bring him back home."

"You mean, little Money? Who in the world would do such a thing?" Charlie asked as the blood drained from his face and he popped his tongue.

"I'm afraid so," Beaver replied.

"Pshaw," Charlie said, then spat a stream of brown juice into a spittoon behind the bar, making it ring. "I ain't ever even heard of nothin' like that. Who would want to harm such a young boy? Who would go up the mountain to steal a lad?"

"Slavers. There were more tracks, too. There was a string of captives, but I reckon all of 'em are Indians, except little Money, but I ain't sure. It's not the first time slavers have been around the valley. They know that there ain't no law, so if they're a strong enough force, they can take who they want, men, women, and apparently children. I figure they nabbed him by pure luck. What do they want with a boy that age is beyond my imagination. He's too little to do heavy chores. I intend to get him back, though. He's my apprentice, you know."

Beaver was suddenly filled with conflicting feelings, unleashing a cataclysmic storm of thoughts. He had to force himself to calm down and finally got a hold of his emotions before they ran out of control. God only knew what he might do then. Despite his anger, Beaver's voice was even and impossible to read, just like his face.

"Have you seen any suspicious characters in town of late? You know, folks capable of such a thing."

Charlie's mind was buzzing with the story he had just heard. Like most towns, McKay's Restaurant and Saloon was the center of gossip for Fort Boise and a hundred miles around it. The town bartender knew everybody who lived there and watched the others come and go, having contact with all but a rare few who didn't drink or eat in sit-down restaurants. If you were crossing the Oregon Trail and you had the money, you were bound to run into Charlie Fox.

"Unusual characters in town during the last two days, you say? I saw a couple of wiry fellas—one with hawk-like eyes, and the other had a small, flat nose. They've been hanging around the saloon for the last day or so. One of 'em is dressed like you boys. I took him for a mountain man, straight away. The other one was dressed like everybody in town: normal."

The captain removed his cover, raked his fingers through his hair and down his beardless face, then pulled out the chair and sat down. "I needed a shave more than even the drink of whiskey after that ride." Will replaced his hat and passed his shirt sleeve across his forehead, pulling the brim low over his eyes. "I hate rubbing my hands across a stubbly face."

"Why don't you have those fingernails manicured, too, while you're at it? Captain—you're the fussiest man I've ever known. Then again, I haven't shaved since I was a kid. My wife, Dahteste, trims my hair and beard every few months. That does me fine. I ain't so fussy about the way I look."

The captain shot Levi a dirty look, but he didn't say anything. He was guilty as charged, and he knew it.

The local sheriff, Tom Hand, walked in the saloon door, dropping his hand to his hip, as he brushed his coat aside, showing the Colt revolver in his holster as he eyed everybody in the room. That was when he recognized his friends.

At first, the Fort Boise law stared at the two like they

were curious anatomical specimens from another world. When the realization hit him, his face broke into a grin of recognition, showing tobacco-stained teeth. "Why, it's been since last summer that I saw you two. How're ya doin', Levi...Captain?"

They drew the town law away from the others to have a private word without the customers hearing, huddling together while they told him the story of what happened to Money Penny.

As Levi explained what had happened, his face darkened as he spoke, and his voice rose, but he didn't notice. He was more upset about Money than he ever admitted. Will worried about him keeping focused on the target. In an instant, Beaver's eyes became dark and dangerous. The captain could hear the threatening tone in his voice.

"That's one thing that I can promise fellas like those who took that boy," the sheriff growled. "If they do their dirty deeds in my town and they don't surrender, they die. But you know how many people ride through here. Why, some weeks we have more than one wagon train, and some of them are a mile long. Right now, the place is full of that bunch of overlanders that just arrived not an hour ago. You just watch how chaotic things are gonna get in an hour or two. Everybody comes in wanting something at the same time and complains when service is slow."

When they weren't looking, Sheriff Hand looked Levi and Will over, sizing them up afresh after such a long and brutal winter. It was true that you couldn't judge a book by its cover, but then again, some things and people never changed. Johnson and Forrester appeared to be two such men. They were as solid as a boulder and as faithful as dogs. The sheriff's dark mustache curled down around each side of his mouth, contrasting with his clean-shaven cheeks.

Will nodded...then he sat silent for a moment as he tried to put the pieces together. They lounged until late into the night on the porch with cigarettes and cheroots glowing in the dark. They believed that the kidnappers had to have come close to town, if not inside the fort itself. That would mean that Money was close by. Then again, if they were smart, they would hide out on the outskirts and wait until they were ready to continue or sell their merchandise right there in Fort Boise.

Beaver struggled to mask his frustration and a near state of panic. Will patted his friend on the back to remind him where he was. He knew that he was too upset to think straight, and that was a perilous state of mind in their business.

Somebody sent a shrill whistle from across the saloon and then a little yelp. The captain's eyes snapped toward the stairs, blazing like branding irons. "What is it now?"

"It's nothing, Captain. Just one of the customers gettin' too rambunctious with one of the ladies."

An oblong pine table stretched across the restaurant in the middle of the room. On it, food was piled high, ready to be served. At the end of the room sat a squat potbellied stove. Heat radiated across the dimly lit room. Shiny brass spittoons were scattered across the sawdust-covered floor.

THE COMPOUND

RUSTY TOOK ANOTHER SIP OF COFFEE, TOSSED THE remains off the porch, jammed his pistol into his empty holster, and headed for the corral. The snow melted into a black stain. He slung his rifle over his shoulder. Angus watched from a distance, his eyes half closed in the glaring sun. He lit a hand-built, then sat unmoving as he watched his friend disappear. The soft clopping slowly vanished. McFarlin picked up his book from the table, dropped off the porch, and headed for the outhouses.

The morning was crisp. Vapor disappeared inches from Rusty Steel's mouth. The bear claw necklace clicked around his neck. He knew exactly where he was going. By noon, he would return with fresh meat for dinner. Some good food may help raise their morale, which was currently at an all-time low. The disappearance of Money had affected everyone.

Rusty wheeled his horse up a squirrelly trail until he reached a stream. He kicked his leg over his mare's neck and slid to the ground with his rifle in his hands. One shot would be all it took. He walked to the edge of the fast-running water, which pooled below, spilling into the small pond, muffling all sound. He peered over and had a glimpse around the watering hole to make sure he was the only human around.

He sat at the edge of the drop, using his hands to push his body as he slid down the trail, raising dirt and snow until he disappeared into the gully. He came to a stop in a blind of trees right beside the water. He knew that any white-tailed deer around would go there for their morning drink. He also knew that their prey could appear, too, so he kept his eyes open for mountain lions. Maybe even a grizzly bear. If you weren't careful, sometimes the hunter became the prey. He licked his finger and checked the breeze. He was still downwind.

Rusty crawled forward in the wet snow. He rolled over and parted the bushes to look across the opening in the trees where the small spring lay. He poked the barrel through the branches and drew back the safety trigger as he began his wait. He sat as motionless as a reptile bathing in the sun. After an hour, he saw motion out of the corner of his eyes, and he held his breath to see what it was. Finally, he slowly breathed out, preparing for the moment, and smiled. Without another thought, he aimed and pulled the trigger. The other three deer drinking beside it seconds before, bound for safety at lightning speed. One remained, dead on the ground.

Rusty reloaded his rifle but didn't take it out just yet. First, he waited to see if anyone else showed up. If there were an Indian within a mile, he would hear the shot. Bugs buzzed through the air as the sun bore down, melting even more snow. After half an hour, he knew if any were within a mile, they would be there by now. He stepped out of the bushes and the cool shade and into the sunny, warm day. It was a plump young deer, just like he wanted, so that the meat would be nice and tender. He would skin it too, but not there alone with no one to stand guard. It would be safer back in the compound even if the animal was stiff by then.

An hour later, the gutted and dressed white-tailed deer dangled, limp across his horse's rump. Blood stains from his kill ran down the horse's hips and thighs. Steel's arms were bloody up to his elbows. After having a careful look around, he squatted at the water's edge with his bare feet as he wiggled his toes while tadpoles darted around his feet. The cold water sent a pleasant chill up his back. Rusty used sand from the bottom of the pond to clean away the blood. Darkened, dry claret stained his fingernails.

He had made short work of a day's chore, bagged dinner, and returned in a few hours. At this time of year, the mountains were bounding with all sorts of game animals. His mind wandered to what he was going to hunt for tomorrow's dinner. Perhaps he could cheer up his friends through their stomachs, but not everyone was like Beaver.

"Here you go, Angus," Rusty said when he pulled up to the hitching post in front of his cabin, where McFarlin was standing in the doorway like he knew that he was going to arrive at any minute. "You can dress it down enough for supper and strip the rest and hang it to dry. I'll come and help you remove the hide as soon as I tend to my horse. I've gotta brush her down good to remove the blood.

"My-oh-my, we're gonna have a tasty dinner tonight.

I have just the thing to go with it, too." When he took a deep breath, he smelled the peach pies in the oven. "Take a guess what it's gonna be, Rusty."

———

WHILE STILL IN HIS DREAMS, Joseph Walker heard someone scuffling outside. The marshal blinked his eyes open in a panic, grabbed the revolver by the bed, and crawled across the wooden floor to the opposite wall. Sweat beaded on his brow and ran down his face. He wiggled on his belly, edging toward the door. He carefully pressed his face to the edge as he opened it a crack. Joseph slowly rose, hugging the wall. When he heard the familiar sound of the outhouse door slamming, he sighed and relaxed.

It's only Angus. Damn, I must be gettin' paranoid with all that's happened, he thought, shaking his head. He dropped his arm, his pistol still dangling by his side. He was lost for words.

Joseph turned back to their bed. He watched as his wife's eyes opened. It was apparent at first that she wondered if it was all a bad dream, a nightmare. He felt sorry for Bar-Chee as she bit her lower lip and stared past the fence and through the trees. It was as though he wasn't even there.

The Crow woman turned and looked at her husband, her eyes still bore the uncertainty of staring blind. He could see the questioning face, but he didn't have the answers. He knew her heart was breaking, but there was nothing he could do but wait. Of course, he knew that Levi and the captain could travel much faster without him, but it still got to him that he had to stay behind when his son was out there somewhere, hopeless. He knew he needed him then and there.

It was only his wife who held him back. He knew if he disappeared too, she would take her life. It was the Indian way after such tragedies. There would be no other way out. He knew she felt she could never go back and live in the Crow stronghold, especially with her brother as chief. Then he would be out, both his wife and son.

"He'll be back, darlin'," Joseph whispered. "Mark my words. Levi and the captain will return any time now."

She nodded as she turned again and stared across the compound through the open door. For her, seconds were like minutes, minutes like hours, and hours like entire days, and each day seemed eternal. Joseph was silent as he watched the broken-hearted mother. He fidgeted because he didn't know what to do, so he sat mute, in concern, trying not to shed a tear. He wasn't that kind of man, but this time he was struggling to maintain his composure.

Bar-Chee sat on her blanket with her head buried in the crook of her arm as her shoulders convulsed and she sobbed. After a few minutes, she stopped crying but didn't raise her head. She knew she should be brave like a warrior, but she was devastated. For her, all hope was nearly lost. Joseph stood staring at his wife, then he crossed the room and sat in a chair near the window. It wasn't long before he heard her crying again.

The territorial marshal sat listening to her muffled sobs as he stared through the glass, lost for words. He sat with a dazed expression on his face. The marshal never expected to get married in a million years, let alone have a son. All things had come to him in his later years in life as a great surprise. Now, he had everything he wanted, and it was torn from his grasp. It felt like his heart had been ripped out of his chest. If Levi and the captain didn't bring Money back, he knew he would lose Bar-Chee, too. He suddenly noticed their cabin was quiet. Then came a noise.

Virgil entered the main room. He let Joseph and Bar-Chee live with him since his old roommates had passed away. Mountain Dennis Breed had been there the longest. Then there was Syracuse Sam, Portland Pete, and Yosemite Bob. All had lived years on Bear Tooth Mountain, and now all four lay in their final resting place under the white crosses at the northern corner of the compound. Over the years, others had passed too. Over their graves stood markers. With his Bible clutched in his hand, Lovejoy looked closely and saw that her eyes were puffy from crying.

"I feel useless and foolish sitting here," Bar-Chee said. "Terrible things have happened, and I don't know how to deal with it all. I don't seem to understand how all this could have happened. It seems that all I can do is think of myself. I should be ashamed."

"You just rest now. I've been prayin' and know that Beaver will return soon. If you don't believe it, too, we're lost. Hope and faith are what you need right now. I know we worship different gods, but you can trust in your friends to pull you through. Even though we're different, I'll pray to Jesus for you anyway. I know it can't do any harm."

"I don't care what happens to me," Bar-Chee said, shaking her head. "I feel I don't have the strength to carry on. Not without my little boy, Money."

"Feelin' sorry for yourself ain't gonna change nothin', ma'am." Virgil scratched his close-cropped, wiry hair.

Joseph grabbed his wife's shoulders and turned her toward him. "I care what happens to us, no matter what. As long as we have each other, we'll get through this."

"Come on, let's go have something to eat. Angus hates it when we make him wait." Virgil led the way.

When they stepped into Rusty's cabin, Angus offered her a plate of food, but Bar-Chee shook her head and turned and sat cross-legged on the floor.

Angus grumbled and said, "Suit yourself." He set the plate of food and a steaming tin cup on the floor where she sat on a bearskin rug, beside the fireplace. He walked outside to finish making jerky from the deer Rusty shot.

Steel walked over and kneeled, sitting on his heels silently as he watched with concern. After a while, he said, "You can't go on like this, woman."

"What do you want me to do? I've already lost all the self-respect that I had. Do you want to take more?"

"I want you to stop all this foolishness. You've lived your whole life in the wilderness, and you know how dangerous things can be. Folks die or disappear here every month or so. You know as well as I do that if anyone can find Money, Beaver can. You know he won't leave any stone unturned. Levi ain't gonna let Money become another statistic."

Bar-Chee bit her lower lip again and looked at Rusty with moon-sized eyes. He could tell she was trying to believe, but it looked like she just didn't have it in her.

"All right, everybody, sit down. It's time for the most important meal of the day: breakfast. Come on now, get it while it's hot." Angus wiped his hands back and forth on his grease-stained apron and forced a grin despite the situation.

In minutes, soft-boiled eggs filled wooden bowls as steam rolled off the large pie pan of hot biscuits beside a jar of thick molasses and goat's milk butter. Slabs of venison lay on large cutting boards as blood pooled under the steaks. A cup of hot coffee sat on the table before every chair. Angus knew that the whole compound was affected by what had happened, and he was doing his best to try to turn the tide of sadness that had fallen upon them all, possibly bringing some little happiness to their stomachs. For Levi, that went tenfold, but unfortunately, he wasn't there to cheer them up with his immense appetite.

"I've never seen such a bunch of sorry faces. Virgil, I reckon that today's the day everybody could use a prayer. I've never seen us all so down in the dumps."

Once they were all seated, Virgil opened his Bible to a special passage that he liked to read. He mumbled as he spoke, making it hard to understand. He, too, was nearly in tears and was too choked up to speak clearly. Still, he murmured on. They could all tell it was heartfelt.

"Pull yourselves together, right now!" Rusty growled. "None of y'all are actin' like mountain men and women. You're all actin' like a bunch of daisies."

Angus's effort to lighten the mood failed miserably, and they all ate in silence. Without Levi at the table, for the first time ever, there were leftovers after the meal. For some reason, this just made them feel even worse. The delicious venison sat there getting cold.

When they returned to the cabin, Joseph grabbed Bar-Chee and pulled her toward him. His arms circled her shoulders. When he kissed her, holding her lips to his, he finally felt her body relax, and she made a final shudder. Then she kissed him back. Joseph brushed his lips across her cheek.

"He'll find him, you just watch. He's never let us down yet."

When her hair brushed his cheek, he knew she was nodding yes. Joseph felt his heart speed up, and he felt a little lighter. It was true. Beaver had never let them down.

That night she awoke, and her eyes crawled to the silhouette in the doorway. The sun was not yet above the trees when the marshal opened the door. He looked back and saw that his wife's features were softened in the shadows. He hadn't been able to sleep all night, worrying about both his son and wife. He was afraid he was about to lose them both. Sure, he knew that such tragedies were as everyday as the rising sun in the Rocky Mountains, but this one had hit home with them all, unlike anything ever before. They were like birds in tailspins, and they couldn't pull out of the dive.

PRISONERS

FRESH HORSES AWAITED THEM AT THE FOOT OF THE mountain, and as soon as they hit the valley floor, they all rode off, pushing their animals to their limits from the start. Hawkeye led the party to ensure they weren't riding into an ambush, keeping them well off the beaten trail. He had studied the route on the way to Yellowstone Valley and knew exactly which way to go. He knew the location of every camp along the way for each of the tribes. As usual, he had done his homework.

It would be more likely to remain undetected if they stayed off the main road, trails, and paths. At the end of the day, they continued to ride into the night under the light of the moon. The kids fell asleep in their saddles as the twilight twinkled above them. All that was heard was the soft clopping of horses' hooves in the dwindling cover of snow. Mud sucked at the animals' feet.

The young boy's head nodded off and on, as if he were half asleep. Money must have been dozing off when he was suddenly pulled off the horse with his hands bound, slamming him to the ground. Ven snickered when he hit with a thud. The boy pushed himself up as he sat and blinked the dust from his eyes. He rubbed his forehead where a lump the size of an egg formed.

They had stopped for a few hours to rest the horses. Anyone who couldn't keep up the pace would be tied across the back of their mount and pulled. Nobody was going to hold Hawkeye up. He knew from experience that time was of the essence.

The gang leader knew that guerrilla warfare and hit-and-run tactics were what worked best. You went after your prey when nobody was expecting an attack, then vanished into thin air without a trace. He was a master of these skills. It was dodgy business kidnapping people. Especially wild Indian men and women who would take your scalp the very first opportunity they got.

His trick for them was laudanum. The opium-laced chicory he gave them masked the bitter taste. He had been at this for some time now and knew the safest way to transport an Indian was drugged. Just enough so they functioned, but did not put them to sleep.

It also made the long, tiring rides painless for the intoxicated captives. Of course, Hawkeye didn't use the potent drug on the children because they could easily overdose, and he would lose easy money. He subdued them with his wickedest stare or sharp words. When he last spoke to the little girl, she wet herself, so he wasn't worried about the kids. He knew he had them scared, into submission.

Despite the laudanum, if any of them became stubborn, they would be beaten into submission and made to run beside the horses rather than ride until they surrendered to their destiny. Eventually, the women would be taken as maids or, in some cases, even wives. There was still a shortage of White women who weren't percentage girls from the saloons in the far west. In some cases, women were considered more valuable than gold.

Many a settler had taken Indian wives for lack of women of their race and color. Such was the case of many in the compound. For them, it worked out just fine, but Dahteste, Bar-Chee, and Pine Needle were never slaves and were given their say in how things were done. That made all the difference in the world. They had married their husbands willingly and loved them as wives should. Still, for some men, including Indians, out west, women were treated like possessions, especially those stolen or kidnapped. Some even continued to work as slaves for the rest of their lives.

"What did I tell you about roughing up those prisoners, fool? Especially the boy and the girl. I see how you've been looking at the child, and the hate in your eyes when you look at the boy, too. It ain't his fault that you're stupid and don't do as you're told. Now, don't take it out on the youngins. They're the icing on the top of the cake with this deal." Hawkeye looked back to make sure his men were close on their drag. He didn't want any of the drugged Indians to wander off along the trail.

He certainly didn't want any of them to get away now that they had them in their possession. A string of horses followed, but the boss kept the two children close to him. He trusted the other two about as far as he could throw them, but they were hired guns for the job, and up until then, they did as they were told.

Everybody but Ven, stayed in line, and he had to be

watched like a hawk. His unseemly habits often got the best of him, and he disobeyed orders, therefore, the boss knew he would have to keep a close eye on him and scold him when he went too far. Why he tended to beat children was anyone's guess, but Hawkeye wasn't about to let him damage his valuable goods.

Ven had been working for Hawkeye for a couple of years and was a good hand as long as you were prepared to ride him all the way. Besides being lazy, he was mean in an unusual way, and Hawkeye had seen his share of ornery men. As soon as they hit Fort Boise, he would pay the hired hands and cut them loose and lock up his captured men, women, and children until he could arrange their delivery.

He had it all worked out in his head, and he knew it was just a matter of time. He even had a stash house where they would go completely unnoticed, in a small shack and cabin, only a few hours' walk and a river cross from Fort Boise. The mountain man had done his homework and expected no surprises. He had worked the details out to the letter. The only thing that lingered, stuck in his mind, were cabins back on the Bear Tooth Mountains.

The more he thought about it, the more he realized how skillful these men must be if they could survive in such a place. That and the time and energy it took to build such a compound in the middle of nowhere. They might be more determined than he had initially believed.

Still, he made himself push concern out of his mind since they were so close to their objective. Hawkeye took a deep breath and smiled. Nothing would stop him now. Their next destination was California, with a stake to make a fresh start in what he had read to be the land of milk and honey.

"Break out those stale biscuits and hard tack. We can't chance campfires. We'll be heading north in the morning. Once we get farther along, without seeing anyone trailing us, we can let our guard down a bit. On the way to Yellowstone Valley, I saw a deep gully where we might heat up some beans. Until then, we've gotta keep a cold camp and do with what we've got. And no smoking tobacco until we turn north and can get farther off the main trail. Mind you, now, I won't tolerate any laggers, so keep up with me, or you won't get paid. I don't backtrack for stragglers either. If you fall behind and get lost, it's on you and you're on your own."

"I need a coffee if I'm gonna keep up this pace," Ven complained. "As it is, I'm pretty near runnin' on empty. If you want us to ride hard and fast, we've gotta be fed, just like the horses and our prisoners, too. We can't all run on air."

"All right. I'll make an exception just this once, but first thing when we wake up before sunrise. We'll use that stand of trees over there. We can't afford to take any unnecessary chances. If we slip up now, we could lose them all. I'm countin' on that money to give me a stake when I arrive in California. Without it, we ain't goin' and that ain't an option I'm willin' to entertain. At the end of the day, everybody wants to get paid, right?"

"You sure do run a hard shop, Boss. But I reckon you're right. Just make sure you let me know if any Indians are close, so I'm ready. Travelin' across Blackfoot country makes me edgy. I'd hate to lose my scalp now that we're almost done."

"Don't worry, you won't lose your scalp. I can smell

an Injun when they get within a few hundred yards. My nose is as good as some bloodhounds. I wonder if those folks in those cabins up on the mountain have decided to come after the boy. The girl I ain't worried about. Ain't nobody gonna come after her. If I were them, I would come for the boy, but then again, there ain't many men as stubborn as me."

Hawkeye laughed at his own joke, but nobody else even broke into a grin. All that was left were forced smiles all around. They were all as serious as death and wondered if he was leading them to their demise.

"Do you really think we've got to worry about a bunch of crazies who live lost in the Rocky Mountains? You'd have to be out of your mind to settle down way the hell up there. They ain't gonna risk their lives for this little whippersnapper. Now, if it were a beautiful woman we'd stolen, a man might just be so foolish as to take chase. I know I might."

"Don't fool yourself, Ven. I've lived on the Great Plains with Flathead people for three years. That's where I learned my Indian knowledge. It appears I have a knack for it and picked it up with little effort. Even the Indians I lived with said I was gifted. Blessed enough to have learned their language, too. I reckon I'm part Indian by now. And that tells me that anything can and does happen, whether it makes any sense or not."

"Who's gonna take first watch?" Ven asked. "I'm dead on my feet and need a few winks of sleep before I'm ready to climb astride a horse again. Wake me up in a few hours, Boss."

No sooner did Ven hit his bedroll than he started snoring up a storm. Hawkeye considered putting a rag in his mouth to shut him up, but he knew he needed his rest just like everybody else.

"Go ahead and sleep, everybody. I'll take the first turn at watch," the boss said. "You boys get yourselves a few minutes of sleep. I'll wake one of ya when I'm tired. Go ahead, you can rest easy with me on guard."

In minutes, all the men and even their prisoners were dead to the world, in a deep, exhaustion-induced sleep. But Hawkeye could run day and night for a week. Surviving and enduring the pain was something else he learned from the poor Flathead Tribe he spent all that time with. He learned much more than met the eye. Horses on ground stakes pulled at tufts of grass and slid their jaws while other horses already slept. They unconsciously twitched their ears and swished their tails at flies and bugs.

———

FIREFLIES FLASHED off and on in the darkness as an owl hooted, and its mate replied. The breeze made the leaves in the trees rustle. Little animals scurried about the brush. A blanket of stars stretched across the sky above the canopy of trees. Falling comets raced across the heavens until they burned out when they entered the earth's atmosphere. A steady breeze whispered through the grass.

A colony of bats silently flew overhead, creating a wavering, snake-like silhouette between the earth and the moon. Silvery shadows cast long across the countryside. There wasn't a soul around as far as Hawkeye could see or hear, but then again, sometimes the obvious was deceiving. You just never knew what could be lurking out there beyond the circle of light.

No sooner did Hawkeye turn around to do something than Ven got up and moved over toward the girl as he stared vulgarly.

"I told you to stay away from that girl. You're crazier than a dog humpin' a pig, you nincompoop," Hawkeye growled.

"Take it easy, boss. I wasn't gonna do nothin', I swear. There's no call for you gettin' all angry with me."

"I don't need to control my temper. I need you to listen to me to stop pissin' me off."

Despite the scolding, Ven's eyes went back to the little girl. Suddenly, the truth settled in, and Hawkeye blew his top. Fear kicked up a notch, and he got Ven's full attention. He knew better than to cross the boss.

Hawkeye tried to control his temper and managed to curl an amused smile, but it looked like an evil grin.

Ven forced a tight smile, just to make the boss happy, not feeling much like laughing. "All I did was look."

When Ven looked at her, Annie's blood rose with a jolt of panic. She swallowed grudgingly. Tears welled up in Money's eyes, born of frustration and confusion. He leaned forward, taking her slightly trembling bound hands in his, squeezing them in his own. He still had something in his eyes that she no longer possessed. It was called hope.

"Attaway!" Malcom yelled as he slapped his knee when he saw Ven take a chance and tried to sneak a feel. That was when he felt Hawkeye's backhanded fist. He tumbled over and went out like a light. Then Hawkeye turned for Ven.

Tears flushed her eyes, but there was defiance there, too. Annie reeled from the narrow escape, but still her heart sank. She saw the look in the evil man's eyes and knew it was only a matter of time. Who was going to save her? Sure, Money said he would try, but he was just a boy, almost as young as her. The pallor of terror crawled into her eyes. Now all she needed was a little hope.

Money knew he had a one-in-a-million shot, but still, he had to take a chance and try. The only option was too dark to imagine. He also felt that Levi would be somewhere out there. He would never let them steal him without a fight. He could only hope that his mentor could find them in time, because he knew, as they were nearing Fort Boise, the clock was ticking. If he didn't find them in time, they would be swallowed up by the Great Plains and tens of thousands of other overlanders and settlers. Then, no one would ever find them.

Money's heart was in a sprint, and his mind was jumbled and confused, but he knew he had to keep his head if he wanted to save his Annie before...he could hardly let his mind go there and imagine such a thing. He kept remembering the look in Ven's eyes. His anger flared, and again his mind spun despite his struggle for control. He had to figure out what a nine-year-old boy could do against grown men.

They had them resting in a stand of trees, barely visible from a little-trodden path. Money peeked out, and bright sunlight flashed in his eyes.

"Why did you have to punch me so hard, boss?" Ven pushed himself into a sitting position, but he still struggled to see straight and stay upright. "If you hit me any harder, you'd have killed me. You won't find another right-hand man as loyal as me. You shouldn't be treatin' me so harsh."

"The day you outsmart me will be the day monkeys fly out of my ass," Hawkeye spat. "If you don't do as you're told, I'll hit you again. Maybe next time I'll rupture your liver. Don't make me damage you for life, Ven. You might be my right-hand man, but everybody's replaceable, even you. There are some things I won't tolerate, and one of 'em is messin' with youngins. Now, if I were you, I'd lay off before it's too late."

Ven seemed to be in a free-fall descent into malice. His heart was full of poison, as was his mind. He knew what the gang leader had told him, but he did things before they formulated in his mind. He also knew his intentions were despicable, but he somehow rationalized it to himself. Still, he knew he was playing with fire. If he went too far, Hawkeye would see that he died.

Reece and Malcom didn't open their mouths the whole time. They even averted their eyes. They were there for the fifty dollars each Hawkeye promised if they gave them a hand. If they had known that someone like Ven was going with them, they would never have hired on, but if they still wanted to get paid now, it was too late.

Money knew he would have to wait until everyone was asleep before he told Annie what he planned to do. He hoped she would go along and was up to the challenge. Both their lives and futures depended on it. Without her participation, there was no plan, and he doubted that he could come up with another idea before they hit Fort Boise and were sold.

For the briefest of moments, everything froze like in a black-and-white picture. A sudden revelation hit

Money in the face like the hot kiss at the end of a hard fist. All his thoughts had instantly come together, and he was surprised when he felt he knew exactly what he had to do. The epiphany shocked even him.

———

IN THE MORNING, well before sunrise, the small clearing was illuminated by orange glowing coals and a flickering fire, creating a circle of yellow light. The smell of coffee filled the air as soon as Hawkeye was done cooking, pushing dirt with his boot over the coals and putting them out, as white steam rolled off the dying fire. Just like promised, Hawkeye made a quick breakfast to keep both the troops and prisoners fueled. He wanted to make better time on this last leg of the journey and come onto the fort from the north, and the other side of the river, rather than the south, drawing as little attention as possible.

The kidnappers undid the cinches, pulled down the saddles, and hobbled the horses' legs before setting them out to graze and drink from the small stream Hawkeye had located. Ven dropped to his hands and knees and ducked his head under the cold, quick-flowing water. Soon, they were preparing to have one of the first real sleeps at night. Hopefully, the break would last four or five hours.

"Buffalo boats will get us across the Snake River to the hideout. We'll have horses waiting on the other side. They'll be waitin' at the end of the portage trail." The water bull boats were made of raw buffalo skins and wood and were smaller and easier to hide.

EVERYONE WAS at their wit's end with the pace of travel until now. But as they neared their destination, they felt safer every step of the way. Soon, they would be hidden in a small cabin not far from the fort, and he would go into town to make contact.

Of course, Hawkeye knew there was always a chance that Ven would disobey him again and harm the little girl, if not the little boy as well, but he trusted the two hired guns even less. He would have to be quick, or maybe he should give Ven a beating before he left, for good measure.

She drew in a sudden, deep breath as his eyes widened. Annie sat there staring blankly into space like she had forgotten where she was. Money looked at Annie, his face not six inches from his as he pressed his lips into a tight smile, and his heart rate flew off the charts. Money dared to push a wispy strand of hair out of her eyes and gave her a hopeful smile.

Ven turned his head and pinched his nose with thumb and finger and blew twin strings of snot onto the dirt. He wiped his fingers on his cotton shirt as he drooled.

They tracked a spiral of smoke rising obliquely from somewhere just over the rise. Hawkeye looked at the two trees he used as markers. From there, all they had to do was follow the stream that ran into the Snake River. A raft would be waiting in a growth of reeds. It too was run down and weathered, but more by design than actual wear and tear.

Inside the cabin was warm and dry, and the roof didn't leak. A series of bunks lined the front and side walls. An oblong wooden table stood against the wall, and at the back window stood a cookstove. Heat radiated from the cast iron.

Most of the boats on this part of the river were flatboats, constructed of rough-cut timber. It was designed for shallow running to prevent it from getting hung up on sand barges, submerged tree trunks, and branches.

Inside the small, ramshackle cabin, nestled among a stand of trees and clusters of bushes, the wind moaned like a distant beast. Late into the night, Money eyed the strange man over the dying flames of the fireplace. He could tell that Ven was waiting for Hawkeye to leave.

"Y'all take a bunk and stay put while I figure this out. Anyone who gets out of line, you'll pay the price. You got that, Ven? If the Indian women act up, you can whack 'em one. If they men act up, before you let them escape, shoot 'em where they stand. I won't have a revolt on my hands. But I'll warn ya now. Those two children are tied up, so we know they won't give us any trouble. So, you make damned sure they're untouched when I get back, or I'm gonna lay my hands on you and it won't be a friendly punch in the mouth. I'll rip your head off and take a crap down your neck. Do you understand? I can't hear you, mister."

Both churlish-looking gunhands sucked their teeth and looked around with crazy eyes. They were waiting for their money and wanted to leave. Even though they knew that things were about to go sideways, they didn't want anything to do with it.

"You two look like a couple of vultures." Hawkeye chuckled. "Here's your double eagles so you can go. Don't show those ugly faces of yours in Fort Boise for a few days. I don't want you two to get into trouble and have the law ask questions. But you can't stay here. There's not enough room for all of us, so you can be on your way." The boss turned and walked off, as if they weren't even there, but they did as he said, and they vanished into the darkness. In seconds, there wasn't a trace.

"Yes, sir, I heard ya. You don't have to repeat yourself all the time," Ven said.

Money's face shone pale, like the moon's rays that fell through the window and spilled out in a square on the hard-packed dirt floor.

"I have an idea," Money whispered into Annie's ear. Despite the situation, her smell surprised him. She smelled like flowers or something sweet, like the candy store. He shook his head and remembered what he was doing. "If you can distract Ven for a few seconds, I can take care of him."

Her first reaction was to shake her head no, with wide eyes. She shot a glance at their captor, but he was still busy.

"It's our only chance. We've gotta try something. Once we disappear on the Oregon Trail, my mentor, Levi, will never find us. We've gotta help him buy a little time, and the only thing I can think of is for you to make eyes at that horrible man. You saw the way he looks at you. We've gotta use that to our advantage. If it doesn't work out, we might both die, anyway, but I'm ready to try. Anything is better than being sold as a slave."

"Maybe," Annie said, shrugging. Money could tell that she was uncomfortable with the idea, but that was the only one he had. They had to distract Ven because Hawkeye was far too smart.

Still, she could see the hope and excitement in

Money's eyes. He was obviously convinced, plus what choice did she have? Anything was better than being traded again and sent off to God knew where.

They listened until the last hoof-clop of Hawkeye's horse died in the distance. They knew he was headed for the boat he had talked about. He had swung wide of the fort and rode upstream until he found a shallow enough place to cross. The river beside Fort Boise was too deep and the currents too dangerous. Money took a chance and glanced over at Ven, and he was listening too.

Ven obviously had no intention of doing as his boss said. It was almost like something he couldn't resist. Money remembered his mother reading the Bible before all this began. It was something about tasting the forbidden fruits, and now he thought he knew what it meant.

MEDICINE MAN

"WHAT IS IT YOU SAID ABOUT LITTLE MONEY PENNY, again, Rusty?" Potac asked. His brow was so wrinkled it bunched above his eyebrows in concern. "What would White slavers want with young White children? It's common enough, between the tribes, to kidnap men to work as slaves and women to take care of braves and maybe even make wives. Sometimes they might take small children to raise as their own, too. But White folks kidnapping a White boy? That's something that I've never even heard of in the Indian gossip. Even when they are the children of a tribe, their outcome ultimately depends on how well the captives adapt to their new environment. I'd swear that's one I've never heard of."

"Somebody kidnapped him, and whoever it was is skilled and brash enough to come to the compound to take him right out from under our noses. It happened before we even got out of bed. Apparently, Money went off to shoot a turkey or two for supper without an elder tagging along. He didn't even tell anyone that he was going. I've told him a hundred times not to ever go past the brick-and-rail fence alone. Up here on the mountain, there's a dozen ways to die, not a half mile away from home."

"What was he thinking?" asked Potak. "The wilderness is no place for a young child alone. I believe the slavers were looking for strong men and good child-bearing women, and they accidentally ran across the boy. But I believe there would be a slim market for nine-year-olds. Why, I doubt Money could swing a pick, so he won't be much good in the mines. That's where many captured people end up. Free labor that the miners can work to death without having the law get involved. I don't know that slavery is legal here, in California or Oregon, but even if it is, for a bribe, the law would turn a blind eye. In the Indian's world, it is common enough."

"I believe it was all our fault. We're making him grow up too fast. Me, Levi, and the captain included. The only ones that seem perfectly satisfied with his skills at his age are Bar-Chee and you, Marshal Walker —all the women, too, except Dahteste. Even Virgil encourages him to enjoy being a boy and doesn't push him to be a man. Everybody else seems to say, hurry and grow up as fast as you can." Levi's frown deepened.

"Now, don't go beating yourselves up over this. Youngins in the Rockies are like no others. At least now that he's in trouble, maybe he'll have a fighting chance if he keeps his head. After spending a fall and winter in the Rocky Mountains, you're tested like no other. We've gotta think positively. Anyway, the slower he grows up here, the bigger the risk of something happening, just like this. If he had had a little more frontiersman education, he wouldn't have done something so dumb."

"There's nothing like fishing to take your mind off our problems," the marshal said out of the blue. "Do you have that fishing line, hook, and sinker you always carry? Lookee there, that pond is teaming with trout. Why don't we stop and fish some? I ain't been fishing since last summer. Above all, I need to take my mind off Money, if only for a spell. As it is, I can't even think straight."

Rusty shimmied up a catalpa tree nearly as fast as a squirrel. He grabbed two dozen catalpa worms as they ate the leaves and dropped them into a tin can. Then he skinned down, and by the time Joseph had found a solid length of pole, he was preparing the bait. He used the hook to carefully turn the caterpillar inside out so the smell would draw fish. There was little pond life that could resist such a morsel, especially with a powerful sense of smell. The native cutthroat trout developed an acute sense for finding food, and the pungent odor of the caterpillar was unmistakable, making it a delicacy.

When they looked into the crystal-clear pool of water, large trout stood on pale fins. Tadpoles darted between the horses' hooves as they drank jaw-to-jaw, bobbing their heads as water dropped off their chins. They shivered their coats to rid themselves of flies.

Fallen leaves lay like golden paper on the damp, snow-white trail. Sun rained through the trees, leaving moving spots of glitter on the water's surface. Fish surfaced here and there, nibbling at insects as they effortlessly glided through the pond. The waterfall thundered in the background, but the fish stayed in the still water away from the strong currents, where it was full of food flying just over the surface.

Rusty had a round, red cork floater. When Joseph tossed the bait in the water, the red ball sat motionless as they watched trout swim all around it. For the first few minutes, they didn't even get a nibble. The fishing line remained slack as the marshal's patience faltered.

"How do you like that?" Joseph spat. "My luck is so bad I can't even get a fish to bite when they're wall to wall from bank to bank." The only time the floater moved was when the trout inadvertently hit the fishing line with their tails, but there was no nibble.

"Here, give me that pole, Marshal." Rusty grinned. "And here I thought you were a master fisherman. Let me show you how it's done. They've gotta think that the bait's still alive."

Rusty grabbed the cane pole and began to slowly pull the bait through the water, making the occasional sudden movement, when he jerked the tip, as though it was fleeing from a predator. That was all it took, and suddenly he had a five-pounder on the hook. It doubled in size when he pulled it out of the water and lowered it to the ground, as it flapped desperately to get free. Joseph deftly removed the hook from the fish's throat and put more bait on the hook.

"He was a hungry bugger." Joseph grinned. "That caterpillar was halfway down his throat."

This time, when the red ball floater hit the water, it disappeared upon contact with the surface. It sank and never resurfaced. The Lahontan cutthroat trout, waiting a few feet down, shot off like a bolt of lightning with the flick of its massive tail.

Now the fishing pole was completely doubled and

was almost ready to break. Joseph *whooped*, and Rusty hollered. This whole time, the Tonkawa medicine man seemed to observe, as if he were studying a science project, completely detached.

"This one must weigh all of twenty pounds," Rusty yelled.

"There ain't no twenty-pound trout that ain't from saltwater. Only then will they go up to twenty pounds and even forty."

"Not if it's a Lahontan cutthroat trout. They can be anywhere from six inches to forty. If I'm right, we've got a fight on our hands."

But true to his words, despite the norm, this one did weigh all of twenty-two pounds. It was a whopper and probably as old as seven years, if not a tad more. Rusty grinned, showing a mouthful of teeth.

They tossed the hook in again, and the line rose from the water and tightened like a fiddle string, as water drops fell like tiny bombs. The fish crashed through the surface, splashing on its side, out of oxygen, giving up the fight.

Lank, greasy hair fell around the Tonkawa's large butterfly ears, but there was some ancient knowledge in his eyes that you couldn't get past. The old Indian was buckskin-clad with a light blanket wrapped around his shoulders. He rode a bone-tale mule. Everything from garlic to strange roots from South America hung from his Indian saddle along with several bags of cure-all concoctions.

The shaman wore his hair in many braids, which hung around his head and down to his waist. His perpetual pipe was always in his hand. He had a hooked nose and dark skin. Feathers hung from his ears, and black hairlocks from enemy warriors were sewn into his buckskin shirt. Under his blanket was his vest decorated with metal studs. A curly frizzle of hair sat on the top of his head.

———

THE TONKAWA PEOPLE had more enemies than any other tribe on the North American continent. All the Great Plains Indians considered them their enemies. Time and time again, the nations had joined in a common cause and tried to wipe their people out. Initially, there had been thousands strong in Texas and the north, but over the years, their tribal customs were finally discovered by all, and their tribe was banished from their remaining allies.

The meaning of their name, Tonkawa, was, *THEY ALL STAY TOGETHER*, and that they had, as they neared the bitter end. What had started as a tribe of two thousand strong had shrunk to a few hundred, and even that number was dwindling every day.

Yet, Potak, the Tonkawa medicine man, was given a free pass across all the Indian Nations in Yellowstone Valley and the surrounding mountains. His feats and skills were known across the Rocky Mountains and even the Great Plains. He was a renowned healer, and at times, an intermediary politician, mediating disputes between the tribe and Whites.

Potak was known to speak eight Native American languages, in addition to English and some French, from the time of the early trappers. Everybody trusted the shaman despite the reputation of his disliked people. To them, he was their spiritual leader, not just with one tribe, but with all of them, including the Blackfeet, given the circumstances. Nobody dared harm a man with a direct connection to the Indian spirit world, knowing that if disease struck, they could always turn to their multi-tribe medicine man.

The shaman studied the two frontiersmen carefully and observed how they were acting like nine-year-olds. It made the aging shaman smile. Rusty was his close friend and an exceptional human being. For him, Marshal Walker had yet to prove himself. The Indian gossip had told him what kind of man the territorial marshal used to be. Potak had yet to see if he had changed with his new life in the wilderness or not, but he knew when the time came, he would be tested. Everyone who lived in the wilderness was at some point. Unfortunately, Money's time had come much earlier than expected.

Their shadows grew longer every minute as the sun moved toward the horizon, but the two were having so much fun they hadn't noticed. Only Potak saw the signs and knew that soon darkness would fall upon them. He pulled his stubborn mule to a cluster of green grass and tied him to a tree. Then he pulled the bag of buffalo chips he had been collecting all day from the side of his saddle and began to prepare a smokeless fire. It even burned hotter than dry wood, and it was readily available due to the large herds in the area. Above all, it had little to no smell, unlike burning pine, especially if it was green.

"We should camp here by the stream. The noise of the waterfall will cover any sounds we make. We are running out of daylight. You can leave the fish on stringers overnight, staked to the water's edge, so they'll still be alive in the morning. Then it's only one day back to the compound."

"I fancy trout for breakfast too," Joseph said. It was true that the excitement of fishing gave them a break from stress, and it did both of them a world of good.

By then, the riverbank was filled with fish trying to flip-flop their way back into the water, but to no avail. In minutes, they had stringers passed through their gills and mouths, tied to ground stakes they used for the horses as they swam against the current but couldn't get away.

"I can make supper with a special recipe from my mother," Potak said, surprising them both.

The medicine man seemed so ancient and wise that nobody ever thought about him having a mother and father. At times, he seemed like the oldest man alive, although he was as spry as a racehorse and could walk or run farther than any of them. They gazed out across the rolling hills and mountains peppered with lodgepole and ponderosa pine. Dark clouds dotted the tree line and were heading their way, as lightning flashed from cloud to cloud.

———

THAT NIGHT, they camped in a mountain pass among a cluster of bushes, where they could make a fire without anyone seeing the flames. The little smoke left by the buffalo chips disappeared a few feet above their heads into the night. The only thing that smelled was the tobacco from the three men's pipes. They could see fire-flies in the distance—moving from place to place, flashing their tails, calling their mates. There were so many, they were impossible to count.

A waterfall thundered out of the near dusk and into a large pond, spilling off downhill into several quick-flowing creeks. The flow trickled over the stones and rocks. They sat beside the small, flickering fire, giving out just enough light to see their faces. Scattered sprinkles made the fire hiss, but it stopped nearly as soon as it started and turned into tiny flakes of snow.

Potak slapped the flies away with his hat as he stared toward the horizon like he could see something that the White men couldn't. Usually, he was a man of few words, but then, upon occasion, it was hard to shut him up. He raised the mule's leg with one hand, looping the hobble and slipping it under the other hoof.

Once he had taken care of his animal, he prepared two trout grilled on woven green sticks held together with bark from the weeping willow overhead. They roasted over the glowing orange coals. Fat spat and sputtered from the heating, sizzling fish. Once they were cooked, they each had a large portion of pink meat. That, and all the creamy sweetbreads they could eat for dessert, and they still had over a dozen fish to take back to the compound. Those they would salt so they would keep.

Little birds chirped in the wind as vultures rose from the ground with their bony wings, doing the seemingly impossible: flapping their massive bodies into the air.

The earth floated off in a long curve to the end of the world, where the sun was about to set. It seemed to grow as it approached the horizon, then it began to shrink, closing like a great fiery eye. In four minutes, it was gone. All that was left was a rainbow of colors in a dimming sky. As night took over the day, stars millions of miles away came out of hiding, although they were always there.

A stark silence came over them as the full moon rose over the first mountain they saw. It climbed into the sky, as though it was being reeled on a string. It cast a light across the vast valleys stretching for miles. On the opposite side of the world, the sun disappeared, and the moon grew so big it felt like it was towering right over their heads. They could see the clear outline of craters. Rusty looked, but didn't see the man in the moon like he suspected. Then again, Rusty was almost as superstitious as the local Indians, and that was going some.

The silver sphere stood frozen and glowing over the mountains. It was so high that they dimmed out part of the stars. The distant snow-covered peaks shone silvery in the moonlight. Up there, the temperatures were still below zero, but down where they were, the snow was slowly melting away.

———

THE FOLLOWING MORNING, they rose before daybreak and began climbing down the mountain. They rode clopping over rock and stone as they passed through rifts of cool shade. When the sun rose, black shapes of the riders lay like moving objects stenciled on the ground, but there wasn't another soul in sight. Still, both men knew that looks could be deceiving while in the Rocky Mountains.

Lodged in crevices high above were straw nests. Golden eagles used their towering perches to spy on prey below. They launched themselves into the air, tucking their six-foot wings into a dive toward their target at two hundred miles per hour, making it one of the fastest diving birds as they targeted rabbits, squirrels, other birds, and even reptiles.

Their horses stomped their hooves and stretched their necks as they nickered and sniffed the air. Rusty knew there was another nearby. The mountain men stopped and listened for the other horses to nicker, but all they heard was the wind whistling through the grass.

As soon as they reached the top of the ridge, they came face-to-face with a massive fourteen-pointer. Its enormous body was solid muscle, with a prominent hump on its back that helped support its neck and antlers. The large mass of muscles and ligaments helped the elk hold up its heavy head. The antlers alone could weigh up to forty pounds.

The gunshot sounded flat and muted in the heavy air, but the rifle kicked like a mule, traveling at one thousand eight hundred fourteen feet per second. Instantly, the male elk grunted. Rusty hit the target: his heart.

The big wapiti sank under its own weight with a pneumatic sigh. The elk was over a thousand pounds. The shot to the heart stopped it in its tracks as its front knees buckled and dropped to the ground. The elk wheezed through his teeth, trying to gobble air. Rusty reloaded his rifle and slipped the strap over his shoulder.

Three vultures hobbled out to pick at the dead with yellow beaks. Rusty ran them off with a pistol shot from his Colt Walker revolver. The 44-caliber six-shooter had a nine-inch barrel, making the boom deafening. Pink froth showed on its dead, colorless lips.

Whirlwinds stood like smoke in the distance as the white powder swirled around, racing across the ground. Cloud banks stood among the mountains, threatening to bring more snow, or if it warmed up even more, perhaps even rain.

Potak's mule bucked its head and sniffed the air. Its sense of smell was significantly better than that of a human. When it shook its head, the medicine man smiled.

"We should be at the compound by the end of the day," Potak said as a tiny smile curled at his lip's edges.

"We'll have to step up our pace if you want to reach the compound before nightfall, and with the Blackfeet about of late, it's best not to travel at night," Rusty said in a low, even voice. "They'll probably have ambushes set up out there somewhere."

THE SNAKE RIVER

MONEY AND ANNIE SAT SIDE BY SIDE, WAITING TO SEE what happened next. Neither of them could make any sense of what was going on. All they knew was that their abductors talked about a man in Fort Boise being interested in purchasing the two, along with six Indians, four men, and two women. They tried to push themselves deeper into the corner, hoping to hide in the shadows from the light that seeped from the large gap under the door.

There was no window in the room, but it was clearly near water, as they could hear the gurgling as it passed and the sloshing of the Snake River against the shore. Money stuck his ear to the wall and listened, but the voices he heard from the only other room were muffled and impossible to discern. Still, he knew that their abductors were still in the rickety-looking cabin. Little did they know that it stood on the opposite bank of the Snake River from Fort Boise.

"Whatcha think they're gonna do next, Annie?

We've got to figure out how to get away while we're still here near Fort Boise. That water outside must be the Snake River. Once we leave here, we'll be back in the wilderness somewhere along the Oregon Trail or maybe even north to who knows where. I won't lie to ya. It'll be dangerous to take a chance to make a break for it. We'll be easy pickings for the hostiles, especially Blackfeet, but the alternative ain't an option. Hopefully, everybody, but Ven and Hawkeye, has gone. If we can get away, we might be able to make it to Fort Boise on our own. Can you swim?"

Annie timidly nodded her head and said, "Sort of."

Money whispered so low that Annie could barely hear, even with his lips nearly touching her ear. He unconsciously smelled her skin, fresh and young. It sort of made him uneasy, and he didn't know why. He was still too young to understand the birds and the bees, as well as the facts of life. But he was aware of the presence of evil men, both Red and White.

"I reckon they're waitin' on the money from the buyer. That means we'll only have two to deal with and not all four. The others were gunhands, that much I know from the way they wore their holsters and revolvers. Hawkeye is some sort of mountain man outlaw, as far as I can see. What that foul-mouthed Ven is doing with such a skilled man, it's hard for me to understand. What we need to do is wait until he goes to the settlement to arrange the meeting. Hopefully, Hawkeye won't send Ven, and he will go himself. When money is involved, it's usually the boss who takes charge. Only then will we have a chance when we're alone with Ven. Hawkeye seems to be almost as good a frontiersman as my mentor, Levi, but his second is a clown, even though he's still dangerous. What we need to do is trick him once we're alone."

"You want to trick Ven?" Annie asked in shock. "He seems too dangerous to mess with for us. We're only kids, Money. I wanna go back to my Indian mama. My White mother died trying to save me. You don't know what it's like to lose two families in a row in so few months. I wish I had died with my White family. Then I wouldn't have to go through all of this. I just want it all to end and for everyone to leave me alone."

"I know exactly how it feels. I've lost my parents and a brother, too. Now I reckon I've lost my new family as well, just like you. Like those Indians you were livin' with. I believe home is where you call it, maybe where your heart is. Sometimes we have no choice in where we live or who we live with. Now, it looks like we're both in a mess, don't it? But not to worry. I'm a mountain man apprentice, and I'll never give up. I may still be young, but I know I was taught by the best. Luckily, I'm like a sponge and suck everything up. I don't know how, but I'm gonna figure out a way to free us. I've gotta. It's our only shot. Both our futures depend on it. Now, let me think. What would my Levi Johnson do if he were in my shoes?"

"What are you talking about, Money?" Annie asked, wild-eyed. She was so nervous that he could hear her teeth chatter, and her voice almost broke. "What's a mentor? All this is making you talk crazy. I hardly understand a word you say."

"You think I'm crazy, do ya? Don't you want to escape? A little bit of hope goes a long way, Annie—

Levi's my mentor: sort of like a teacher. I'm what you call a mountain man apprentice. Or at least I was until Hawkeye and Ven stole me just like they stole you, and right out from under everybody's noses. The gang leader is clever, all right, and sneaky too. He'll be too tricky to deal with, so our only chance is to trick the dumb one, Ven."

The only other way out of the room was through a shuttered window, too far away to reach, but it was also secured with a padlock. The shackles on their legs were only six feet long, giving them enough slack to pee in the tin bucket. Something that humiliated both Annie and Money, even though they turned away, careful not to look. That and get a drink of water from the goatskin pouch hanging from the wall in the opposite corner, barely in reach. They sat on a hard-packed dirt floor between heavy wooden walls. It didn't look like it, but the building was built to last.

The chains clinked every time they moved, making it easy for their captors to know precisely where they were and if they were up to something. They both did their best to avoid drawing attention by sitting as still as stones, and when they did move, they did so slowly so that the metal links didn't jingle.

———

BOOT HEELS HAMMERED THE FLOOR, and they knew that their abductors were walking toward their door. Annie closed her eyes and covered her head with her arms, expecting the worst. Hinges groaned, and a blinding light shone in from a large front window. They squinted their eyes to block out the sun. The only other person in the room besides the gang leader was Ven. At least, this confirmed that the gunmen had already left.

Money sighed a little breath of relief. Maybe he could work out a plan after all, if the cards continued to fall his way. He knew that without a bit of luck, he could never pull it off, but he was also aware that it was a matter of do or die. From where he stood, he saw that they had no other choice.

"What are you two up to in here?" Hawkeye grumbled as he eyed the children. "I heard you both whisperin'. Didn't I tell you, no talking? Or do you want me to turn Ven loose on ya? How about you, little girl?"

"We've gotta buy a new dress for Annie, iffin we wanna fetch top price," Ven said with greedy eyes. Saliva dripped from his lower lip and rolled down his chin. He wiped it off with the heel of his hand. He couldn't seem to break his stare away from the small girl.

"A pair of boots and britches for you, too, boy," Hawkeye said. "We can't deliver you to your new owner lookin' like a couple of heathens. He might think you're too Indian-wild and turn us down. Don't you worry none, he'll make a good master for you both. At least until he gets you to *his* buyer."

Both men laughed so hard they got a stitch. They knew they were a pace away from success. All that was left was for the boss to go to Fort Boise and inform the interested party that their goods were there. Once they arranged their meeting, they would cross the river with the slaves and turn them over to Mr. Farnsworth Claymore and his men.

"Mind you now, Mr. Claymore has a half dozen slavers out looking for more captives just like us,"

Hawkeye warned. "The word is he's taking three wagons of slaves to California. There's talk of war with Mexico, and they need bodies. At least you won't be alone, hey, children. This Farnsworth fella is said to be one of them Californianos."

As soon as they had their money in their hands, Hawkeye planned to ride westbound along the Oregon Trail immediately after he was paid. They would travel just off the trail. The fewer people they ran into, the better. There were another two sheds outside the main cabin, and they, too, appeared to be in dire disrepair, but what was inside was the complete opposite. One was a storage room, and the other was where he was holding the six Indian captives. Both had heavy timber doors and thick steel locks, and Hawkeye had the only keys. In the prisoner hold, there was an additional lock on the heavily shuttered window.

The adult prisoners' quarters were Spartan and had nothing that could be turned into a weapon, except for large buckets in each of the two corners. The room stank of urine and sweat, and soon it would get worse. But Hawkeye didn't intend to wait long before the bodies and money exchanged hands. If he could get it done first thing in the morning, all the better. In the storage room, he had all their supplies for the trek west to Willamette Valley. In the corral, they had an additional two floppy-eared pack mules. Bedrolls and supplies were already loaded and fastened onto the aparejos, ready for the journey. All he had to do now was make the exchange, and within the hour, they would be on their way.

They planned to leave as soon as they returned from the second and final trip to Fort Boise and be on their way. Hopefully, within an hour, they would be long gone and untraceable. Hawkeye even went so far as to plan to set the buildings on fire when they left, so there would be no visible trace of their presence, leaving no evidence. If someone had tracked them to the hideout, all they would find would be ashes.

The same went for the buffalo boat. He planned to sink it in deep water as soon as he reached this side of the riverbank. A hatchet would make short work of it. The intention was to leave everyone clueless about what side of the Snake River they were on, making it that much harder to follow. He was sure it would be thought that they were on the Fort Boise side or somewhere downstream, which would be the easiest escape. From then on, the slaves would no longer be in his charge, and he couldn't care less about what happened to them. All Hawkeye was interested in was getting paid and heading on his way west.

Hawkeye believed once the little boy was out of his hands, he could forget about the mountain men, too. He hadn't seen any signs of them being followed, but his gut feeling said something else. It stuck in his mind what he would do were it his kin. There would be no mountain high enough, no valley deep enough, no ocean vast enough to keep him away.

Hopefully, none of the mountain men were like him. Soon, it wouldn't matter anyway. Once the children were with Farnsworth, anybody chasing them would turn their attention to them. There was no sense in chasing someone who didn't have the children. Now, he knew, despite his gut feeling they were nearly home free.

By then, Mr. Claymore would be their new owner,

and they would be out of Hawkeye's hair. In twenty-four hours, it might all be over, and he and his nitwit friend would be a few hours along the westbound Oregon Trail. Why he continued to allow Venom to ride with him, he wasn't quite sure, himself. Sometimes he wondered why he didn't run him off. He was usually more trouble than he was worth.

In the back of his mind, he had always known if the hounds got too close, he could always leave Ven in his dust, between him and the law or whoever was chasing them. He also happened to be his friend, if that were possible, and the only person he trusted. These things were what tore at his judgment. If he had looked at it coldly and without emotion, he should have fired him over a year ago. He is far too much of a troublemaker.

If anyone following them caught Ven, he knew it would hold them up the time it took to hang him and probably camp for the night. When Hawkeye tried to think of another quality he had, he couldn't. Maybe it *was* time to cut Ven loose, too. Twice the money would go a long way toward his plans in California.

But did he want to do all the hard work on his own? Sure, Ven was as lazy a man as he'd ever met, but when pushed, he eventually got the job done. Hawkeye knew he was too intelligent to be a laborer, and his time would be better spent working on his next plan. Now he had to consider a new eventuality. Still, his mind wasn't made up. The only thing he was sure of was that he was headed for California. He had read in *The Boston Herald* that there was so much gold you could pick up nuggets as big as your thumb right off the ground.

"It must be humiliating to be bought and sold like so much beef." Ven sneered as he carefully watched the children's faces for a reaction. When Annie burst out crying, he started laughing again. It was obvious he enjoyed the children's suffering.

"Shut up, Venom. You're scarin' 'em needlessly. Remember, until we get paid, keep your hands off. I don't want 'em to spook when they go on the auction block, and I don't want that little girl to be damaged. You know good and well, if there's a mark on her, she might not sell for top price. I know what goes on in that twisted mind of yours, and I've had just about enough. You'd better shape up, or you're gonna get shipped out."

"You know I don't like to be called by my real name. I don't like *Venom*. My pa was so ornery that he gave me that damned name to curse me for life. Call me by my nickname, boss. I prefer Ven, if you don't mind. You know how that offends me. It ain't nice."

"And what do you know about being nice? I figure he probably had a good reason to call you Venom. Was that your name from birth, or did he call you that when you were growing up? Maybe you did something to deserve it." Hawkeye chuckled. He loved to taunt Ven, much like he did with others. It was mainly to give him a taste of his own medicine, but it never seemed to sink in.

"I can't remember that far back. All I know is that as soon as I was old enough, I set out on my own. Not that I believed my ma or pa would follow me. I reckon they thought it was just their good fortune that I was gone. I know it was mine."

"Look at me, Ven," Hawkeye demanded in a serious tone. "I said, look at me and stop starin' at that young girl, fool! If I come back and find as much as a hair ruffled on her head, I'm gonna take it out on your hide.

Don't make me kill you. You know I will if you push me. I ain't said a word to you about many things that you do, and I don't like, but this is one I can't let pass. Now go and sit in that far corner, and when I get back, I expect to see you still sittin' there."

"There you go again. Blaming me for things I ain't even done. You rest easy. Nobody's gonna move until you return, Boss. And I ain't gonna lay a finger on the youngin. Neither of 'em."

When Ven felt a blow, the wind rushed through his ears, and a red flash seared across his brain, and he blacked out. A couple of minutes later, he sat up, shook his head, and asked, "What'd you do that for?"

"That's just an advance on what you'll get if you ignore my orders." Hawkeye's eyes—white caged in ridged, red lines.

"Uh-huh, boss," Ven replied as his eyes uncrossed, and he could finally see straight again. He gritted his teeth and blinked away the tears. They were born of frustration, and it was building up to a climax inside. When it would finally come was anyone's guess.

Ven waited until the heat of embarrassment drained from his face. He knew he was no match for Hawkeye, so he shut his mouth and swallowed the embarrassment. Luckily, nobody but the children saw what happened. Maybe he would take it out on them while the boss was gone. He knew he would have to do it without leaving marks or blood so that he would be careful.

Just because the boss ordered him to do something, it didn't mean that he intended to do as he was told. He wondered why Hawkeye couldn't understand that he couldn't control himself, more than he could stop the sun from rising the following morning. Hawkeye didn't know his right-hand man as well as he thought he did.

There are more ways than one to skin a cat, Ven thought as he rubbed his head where a knot was forming.

FARNSWORTH CLAYMORE

HAWKEYE WALKED OUT OF THE CABIN, GRABBED HIS horse, turned, and raced around the back to a hidden trail not much bigger than a rabbit path. The water was so close he could hear it lapping on the shore. The river smelled foul due to the decayed waste from the fort and wagons surrounding it. As soon as he was out of sight of the cabin, he broke into a trot with his head down until the fort on the opposite banks was out of sight. Only then did he make a sharp turn for the river. He had planned everything out to the letter. If anything, Hawkeye Burns was meticulous.

Thunder muttered somewhere in the distance as more dark clouds wavered on the horizon. For an instant, everything lit up as bright as daylight, then just as quickly, night returned. Every few minutes, he would pull to a stop and wait for a spell, then continue. If he was careful, he knew that everything would work out as planned. Only the reckless suffered the price of discovery and capture.

He wasn't worried about being discovered with the

Indians because he knew there was no precise law against what he did, but the White children were another matter. If he were caught with them, the discipline would be severe. Maybe even to hang by the neck until dead. He wasn't so sure about the girl captured by the Indians because she was already tarnished. But the boy with the blond hair and blue eyes could cost him his freedom if his kidnapping was disclosed. Still, he was confident that everything would go as planned and he would get away scot-free.

Across the river on the opposite bank, a retinue of wolves trotted silently in a single file behind the pack's leader. The alpha male occasionally looked over his shoulder to ensure they followed. They cast long shadows under the silvery moonlight. A thunderclap and a frigid wind set the trees and bushes gnashing, but still, it didn't rain or snow. It was like the weather couldn't make up its mind to let spring come or for winter to return.

He dropped off his horse and tied it to a tree, then crept cautiously from cover to cover when a mournful sound cut the stillness. Hawkeye remained stone-still for a moment until a smile crept across his face and he whispered, "Night Birds." He smiled, pushing himself to his feet and carrying on. For a second or two, he was a barely visible blur, then he would disappear into the next shadow. The mountain man crept across the distance like an animal, slow and with his back arched. He used the shadows and hard places to see and go undetected.

Hidden under river reeds was his bull boat for ferrying back and forth across the river. In two minutes, it was uncovered, and he slipped the bowline from the post he had pounded into the dirt just far enough from the water to tether the craft. It kept it tight against the water's edge. He climbed aboard with his two hired Tonkawa Indians as Hawkeye turned it toward the middle of the river. The braves paddled on either side as he manned the rudder. When he was halfway there, they struggled with the heavy currents as they dodged floating branches that could sink the boat.

The few remaining Tonkawa Indians often hired themselves out for unusual jobs, and many even worked as scouts for the Texas Rangers. Since they were everyone's enemy, this made them the most trusted by the White intruders. An Easterner knew if he hired a man from this tribe, he wouldn't turn on him at night and take his scalp. They, too, worked based on their individual reputations. These two came with the highest recommendations and were warriors, too. Hawkeye couldn't forge the river alone and needed someone to make sure the bull boat didn't disappear before they were done.

When the bow of the boat ran aground in the mud on the other side of the river, Hawkeye sat as mute as a tailor's mannequin as he listened for an alarm to sound out. But it was just as he suspected, nobody was looking for him. He sighed a breath of relief and helped to pull the boat out of the water and covered it with branches he had stashed nearby, days prior. He looked around to see if anyone was watching, and when he saw no one, he stepped out of the shadows and onto the trail that ran right before the fort. The Tonkawa stayed behind to guard the boat with their lives.

The two Indians and Venom were his only loose ends. Of course, he had to trust someone because he couldn't execute such a job without assistance. Still, he knew that if anything went wrong, it would be the fault of one of the three or all of them. Still, this was his stake for California, and he knew if he didn't take a chance, he wouldn't have money to make a new start when he arrived on the West Coast of America.

In the distance, he could see the lights from the campfires from all around the fifteen-foot-tall walls. Dozens of teepees and at least fifty covered wagons camped side by side under the safety of the local guard, initially provided by the Hudson's Bay Company. Although it was a waystation for the travelers along the Oregon Trail, there were rumors of gold nearby, so a new kind of overlander began to arrive. Then again, like many such stories, it was probably more rumors. Just the same, every day, more people arrived as they headed west toward Willamette Valley.

There was so much hustle and bustle inside the walls that the guards didn't even give Hawkeye a second glance. There were enough mountain men in the settlement that it was easy for him to blend in. The United States government sent limited patrols of American soldiers to protect the settlers and run off the hostile Indians, as Washington pushed more and more people to venture west, claiming unsettled land that wasn't really theirs to give. Still, the push went on, and they even advertised in the European newspapers, telling them all about America, the land of milk and honey, and that free homesteads awaited them. Flames from the torches on the fort walls yawned in the night winds, making their shadows dance on the wagons.

As he walked by a teepee, an old Indian man wore an eye shield made of a crow's wing and a rosary of fruit seeds. Strange trinkets hung from bracelets on his wrists and neck. He sat and stared at every move that Hawkeye made. His face was wrinkled like an old sheepskin. The mountain man stopped and turned to look, but there was no hint of expression. He wondered if he knew who he was.

Over the years, Hawkeye had stayed quiet and wasn't a wanted man anyplace, including Mexico, but when you lived so long on the Great Plains, people were bound to hear of you, and some might even know what you were and what you did for a living. He turned and hurried for the closest ally, where he took a minute to wait and look for anything strange and out of place. Despite the hour, the courtyard was full of people, some busy and others enjoying the small dose of civilization in the middle of nowhere.

He stayed in the shadows as he made his way to a private quarters with an elegant porch and two windows that spilled squares of light on the ground. He made no more noise than an alighting bird as the veins on his temples pulsated like fuses. He continued to wait beneath the slow wheel of stars pulsating light-years away. The slaver studied the scene stoically beneath impassive eyes. Hawkeye looked both ways before speedily walking across the street.

He moved as fast as he could without appearing to run. Long strides took him to the doorway. When he reached the green door, he pushed his back up against the wall and had a look around again. Without looking, he made a fist and rapped three times on the door.

No sooner had he knocked than it quickly swung open, and he slipped into the lamplight, making him blink. The door closed behind him with a *clack*, and he could hear a key turn in the lock.

"You're late, Mr. Burns," Mr. Claymore said. "I was just about to leave, and then you would have missed out. Next time you work for me, make sure you're more punctual. Do you have the items that I ordered?"

"Yep. Six Indians: four strong men and two women. You don't have to worry about them. They're so drugged up on opium, they're as meek as lambs. I also remembered what you said to me before I left. That you were interested in children, if that order still stands, I have a couple of fine specimens for you, but they won't come cheap."

"Boys or girls?" Farnsworth replied, seemingly all business. At first, it was hard to tell if he was really interested or not.

"One of each and they're both White."

He quickly turned his head and locked eyes with Hawkeye and asked, "What?"

"The boy's got blond hair and blue eyes and all. The girl's been living with one of the tribes, but she's White, too."

The slaver's eyebrows rose as numbers flashed in his eyes. He replied, "White children, you say? I have some special clients in California who are interested in just such items. That's where we're going, by the way. I have three wagons of slaves to work for the revolt against Mexico. In a short time, California will be a state founded by the Californianos, like me, and Mexico will no longer be part of our political lives."

"Well, I've got 'em on the other side of the river. They're all healthy and clean, and none of 'em has any diseases. If you have one of your people meet me on the riverbank with the money, I'll hand over the cargo, including the boy and girl."

"We have a deal, then, even if it is sight unseen. I assume you wouldn't dare to cheat me, would you, Mr. Burns? Me and my associates wouldn't like that and would surely take offense, and I can assure you that we are not the kind of men with short memories."

"You've already asked around and know the answer to that. Although I must admit that this is an unappealing business, I'm a professional at it, just as I am with everything else, I do. It's my reputation that's at stake here. Mark my word. Everything will go as planned."

———

WHEN HAWKEYE RETURNED to the boat, he heard rustling in the reeds. That was when he saw two Nez Percé Indians making ready to launch his buffalo boat and paddle off. Two lightning-fast flashes of steel cut through the night. The sand on the riverbank's edge turned dark with blood. The Indians he hired to paddle him across suddenly stood appearing among the reeds with bows and arrows in their hands. They had already been in position to thwart the attempted theft. Their actions confirmed he could trust them.

Hawkeye pushed the dead men over with the toe of his leather boot. His neck was slit from ear to ear, just like his friend's. He was not only a first-class tracker, but he was also deadly with a knife. He nodded his approval as they helped him drag the bodies into the water, where the current would whisk them away.

His face glistened with oily preparation. He paused

to catch his breath. He wiped the sweat from his face with the back of his hand. This was the first warning of things going wrong, although not completely unexpected. He was aware that anything outside the fort that wasn't nailed down was fair game with the Indians. Even for those who lived around the fort, they kept their illegal acquisition of others' goods for the travelers, knowing that in a few days they would move on, and no one would be the wiser.

A strange boat, never seen before, with no crew, was too much of a temptation for anyone to resist, including White men. A portion of the fort's population was there with fleecing the travelers in mind. Whether it was gouging prices or out-and-out extortion, Fort Boise was no exception to what was going on in every one of the frontier forts. Where supplies were difficult to acquire, merchants took advantage and raised their margins as much as they dared.

Even the Indian agents were grifting the men, women, and children that lived on the reservations against their will. Often, the food sent for the Native Americans was offloaded and sold on the cheap to a co-conspirator. Without extensive courts and too few soldiers and lawmen, there were no limits as to how far they could go. Even as far as starving the people they had confined to reservations. As usual, Washington didn't care because it worked in their favor. Due to such actions, there would be fewer mouths to feed and less resistance.

Under the moonlight, beclamored with yapping coyotes, amid cries of owls, one of the wolves lingered like a marionette from the heavens, its saliva dripping from its tongue and lips. It finally turned and raced to catch up with the others. Even a lone wolf was afraid to be out in the wilderness at night, alone.

As soon as they reached the other side of the river, Hawkeye paid the Tonkawa warriors, and they vanished before his eyes. It was like they had never been there. Not even their strange scent lingered. Still, he knew they would be there the following morning at six sharp. That was when the exchange was to take place. He planned to load the slaves onto the bull boat and wait on the bank until almost six, when they would strike out, and only then would they ford the river to disembark their captives and trade them for gold coins.

The last part of the deal was the most dangerous, because all the elements would be in one place. The slaves, slavers, and the money, so if discovered, then, at the very least, they would be robbed or locked up in the fort jail. Of course, they would set the Indians free and keep the children under lock and key until they discovered from where they came. But this was something that Hawkeye knew wouldn't happen. Not with his cunning as a frontiersman and his planning skills.

The last leg of the journey would be the easiest. With his knowledge of Indian ways, they would vanish into thin air and become impossible to find among all the travelers heading west on the Oregon Trail.

VENOM GRIM

VEN SAT IN THE CORNER LIKE HAWKEYE TOLD HIM TO, BUT his mind was already wandering. He fantasized about what he might do if he were the owner of the two children. Nobody knew it but him, but sometimes he couldn't distinguish reality from the imaginary visions in his head. Luckily, he was good at hiding the fact that he was always the craziest person in the room.

Sometimes, he wasn't sure whether it was Hawkeye who had told him to do something or if it was one of the other people living in his mind. There were three of them, and he never knew which one would come out. He smiled at the fact that only he was aware that he was as crazy as a loon. It was something he had done with ease ever since he could remember.

Of course, his parents knew all about it and had also discovered his secrets. That was why he had killed them after locking them in a dry cellar for months on end. He remembered it as if it were only yesterday. When he did it, he didn't feel one way or the other about his actions, although he did find it amusing when their eyes asked,

WHY, at the very end. That was something that he couldn't even answer himself, so it was really a stupid question. In his heart, he did it because he *could* and felt no remorse for his actions. It was something else that stirred deeper feelings inside his very being.

At first, he had asked himself, *why would anyone in their right mind want to own a couple of children as slaves?* As soon as the thought got into the wicked one's mind, he could think of nothing else. That was what Ven called him. The third one hardly ever said a word until something went wrong, and then he reprimanded them both while trying to make things right. He was the good in Ven, trying to break out, but was dominated by the other two, who were both maleficent and cruel.

Today, the evil one suddenly took possession, and his stare shifted from the window to the two children in shackles and chains, a wicked grin etched on Ven's face, but it was somehow different. The children watched as his other identity overcame him. Both Money and Annie knew there was something different, but they couldn't put a finger on it.

Venom got up nervously and paced back and forth in front of the door, stopping to look out the window with each pass. It was as though he was worried Hawkeye was playing a trick on him and would sneak back to catch him in the act. When he turned to look at Money and Annie, his face appeared to change into a mask of violence and cruelty. Right then, they both knew what he was capable of, and it wasn't just death. His plans for the two were much viler and more twisted.

Money grabbed Annie's hand and squeezed it hard to keep her on track. If she backed out of his plan now, it would be too late, and who knew what this nefarious man before them might do. In their imaginations, although young, the possibilities seemed limitless. They had seen Indians do things that kept them awake at night, but they suspected Ven to be even more of a monster than even the hostile Blackfeet.

Money did his best to feign sleep as Annie turned her big eyes on their captor and blinked invitingly. Ven's mouth watered as saliva dripped down his chin, splattering on the floor. When she got his undivided attention, she batted her eyelashes as enticingly as a little girl could imagine, but for Ven, it seemed to be enough. His eyes locked onto her like magnets.

She knew then and there that Money was right, and soon their chance would pass, and they would never get away. However, she still didn't quite understand what they would do after that. She had no choice but to put her faith in her new friend and hope for the best, as she had no clue. Still, it terrified her to try to seduce such a dangerous man.

I hope Money knows what he's doing. Here goes nothing.

"Ven, can you please give me something to drink?" Annie asked in a sweet little voice. "My mouth is so dry I can hardly speak, and my teeth are sticking to my lips. Only a little something to wet my tongue. It doesn't matter what it is. I'm not fussy."

Money sat three feet from her, acting like he had fallen asleep, when in truth it had been days since he had slept much more than an hour or two. All he could think about was getting away with his new friend, Annie. He had told her she was their only way out, so she did as he said and hoped with all her might that it would work. As soon as Hawkeye returned, she knew they would be doomed. Then the trade would take place, and they would never be able to escape. They would be on jail wagons heading west along the Oregon Trail.

As Ven turned all his attention to the little girl, Money quietly bunched his three feet of chain in his fists, making sure he didn't make a sound. When Annie touched the top button of her new dress, the outlaw gasped. His eyes locked onto her as a wicked grin graced his face, and the malevolence reflected in his eyes.

Reaching into his jacket pocket, he pulled out a flask of whiskey. "I've got just the thing to unstick those pretty little lips and calm you down." He held the flask in his hand as he poured some into a tin cup.

Ven boldly walked up to her and tried to stare down her blouse. The top button was undone. The look in his eyes made Annie cringe. That was when Money used both hands and all his might to hit the twisted man on the temple with his fists full of steel. He drew back to hit him again, but to his surprise, he was out cold. Money dropped to one knee and felt his pulse. His heart was still beating.

"Is he still alive?" Annie asked.

Money nodded as he quickly grabbed the keys to the chains and unlocked them both. Annie rubbed her reddened wrists, which bore touches of black and blue. Then he removed his gun belt. It was too big to wrap around his waist, so he strapped it over his shoulder. The belt was full of bullets, so now he had something to defend themselves with.

"Pull that key from the string around his neck. Quick now, we've gotta hurry."

"We should kill him. I won't be able to sleep at night unless he's dead. Hit him again, Money, for me."

Money shook his head. "We can leave that to some-body else. We've won for now. That's enough. We've got to put as much distance between us and this cabin as we can, so we don't have time to think about anything else. I don't know how long Ven will be out, but I reckon he'll wait for Hawkeye's retrim from Fort Boise to chase us anyway. As soon as his boss gets back, they'll be lookin' for us, that's for sure. If we don't move now and fast, it will have been all for nothing."

As soon as they slipped the beam holding the heavy timber door closed, the hinges ground, and steel against steel screeched. They ran outside, and both took a deep breath of freedom, even if it might only be for now.

Annie gave Money the key with the broken red string, and he ran around to the side of the building where Indian captives were locked up. He heard voices as soon as he slipped the key into the lock and the rusty steel turned.

"Sho'daache Kahee," Money yelled in Crow Indian, which was a formal greeting. He could only hope that someone inside understood the words.

He didn't want to be attacked as soon as he opened the door. If they knew they were saving them, they should leave them alone. Although the boy knew it was a risk, after being captive twice, he couldn't walk away and not save the others who had been taken too. He would never be able to live with himself if he did.

"Sho'daache Kahee!" he heard someone reply from inside as he sighed a deep breath of relief.

When he opened the door, the stench was over-whelming. These poor people had been locked up like so many animals, left to defecate and urinate in over-flowing buckets without food and only a limited amount of water, which was already dry. These brave people were forced to live in their own filth.

Annie was in awe at how silently they all disappeared. One moment, they were standing in the doorway, each stopping for a moment to nod at Money for his kindness, then they vanished into the shadows, as if they held some strange magic that White men didn't understand. They seemed to walk with the shadows. She wondered if that was what she and Money were going to do.

Annie felt a sudden urgency to escape and turned to go without asking Money which way. She ran for the only path she knew, which was the main trail. All she could think about was escape and putting distance between herself and the scene of the crime.

"Stop! We can't go that way, Annie. We'll have to follow the rabbit paths so nobody will accidentally run across our tracks. I take Hawkeye for a first-class tracker, so I'm gonna need to use everything I've learned from Levi to save us. But don't you worry. I can do it. All you've to do is step exactly where I step, and we won't make a sound, and the tracks will be hard to see. We're gonna move between the shadows like Rusty Steel does, just like those captive Indians did. I haven't learned a lot in my short time as an apprentice, but the first thing Levi taught me was how to hide and travel unseen."

———

HAWKEYE'S BLACK, grimy fingernails followed the wavy lines over the stained wanted poster, illuminated by the light of a nearly full moon. He hadn't had an opportunity to have a bath, but he knew that time was of the essence. The time for new clothing and cleaning up would come once they conquered the Oregon Trail and reached the West Coast.

He looked at the wanted poster again and saw Farnsworth Claymore's face looking back at him. There were a lot of zeros above his head, and his full name was listed at the bottom, along with a brief physical description. There was no doubt in his mind as to who it was, even if he did look a little younger in the picture.

He quickly folded the piece of paper and shoved it into his pocket before anyone noticed. It said he was wanted for interfering with government affairs and offering money to Indian agents as bribes. It didn't say anything about being a slaver, though. Maybe in the territories, such actions didn't merit a crime? He seemed to have his fingers in several pies. There was a thousand-dollar reward on his head, alive, not dead. Whoever caught him would have to transport him back east to Washington, no less. Nobody in their right mind would take such a chance.

More useless decisions were made by the people in the capital, along with President Polk. He was responsible for the largest territorial expansion in American history and would soon sign the declaration of war against Mexico. To those in Congress and then the Senate, it all looked like excellent progress, but they had no idea at what cost, nor were they particularly interested.

But then again, Hawkeye had already known that. As usual, he had done his homework on the man he was working for. He himself had a reward on his head, too, and he wasn't worried about it this far west. Few men were prepared to take him on to retrieve it, especially if they intended to bring him back alive, but he doubted it. Unlike Farnsworth, his *Wanted* poster stated, *dead or alive.*

When he looked to the north, the sky was dismal, depressing, and dark. It looked like bad weather was approaching. Then again, on the Great Plains, you just never knew what the weather would be two or three hours away. The severe climate cursed the Plains with temperature swings, strong winds, tornadoes, and blizzards. The only constant was the wind blowing southwest in the summer and northwest in the winter, and it never seemed to stop.

All these climatic changes were due to its proximity to the Rocky Mountains and varied topography across the region. These changes were particularly pronounced when nearing spring, when it was a roller-coaster ride of weather, like the one just opened in Paris, France. It featured a singular vertical loop, which was an innovation from earlier Russian snow slides. It was just published in the newspaper, complete with a picture, and the news was on everyone's lips.

As he snuck along the path to the ramshackle cabin, he stopped every hundred feet to listen for out-of-place sounds. He had to make sure he wasn't walking into an ambush. He knew that hostile Indians didn't frequent the Fort Boise side of the Snake River, but they were known to be brave and even hostile, with the river separating them from the soldiers. The Paiute, Bannock, and the most dangerous, the Western Shoshone, claimed the western side of the river as theirs. White people called this coming together of tribes *The White Snakes*.

The night was full of sounds unlike the ones he had left behind. Night birds, owls, and coyotes filled the evening with their coos and howls. Hawkeye traveled just as carefully as he always did, looking for trouble before it could find him. Finally, he saw a thin line of smoke coming from the stovepipe and cursed. He had explicitly told Ven not to make a fire, so there was no smoke to follow while he was alone.

He suddenly became suspicious and wondered what else he had done that he told him not to. Suddenly, a bad feeling came over him. He wasn't quite sure of what it was, but he knew that something was wrong. Years of Indian wars and living in the wilderness had honed his senses like few men.

He rapped on the door three times, then waited five seconds and rapped on it twice more. He could hear Ven remove the heavy beam. When he opened the door, a wedge of light spilled onto the porch. Ven stood before his boss, holding a wet rag to his head as he staggered back to his seat at the table. He walked like a drunken sailor.

Venom looked at his boss like a little kid who had done what he was forbidden to do. Now, Hawkeye and the *Evil One* shrank away and retreated deep into his mind, and the Good One emerged to try to save the situation while the other two skulked in the dark recesses of his twisted mind.

"Where the hell are the children, fool? Did you kill them despite what I told you? Did you rape that girl, Venom? If you did, you're gonna die right now."

"I didn't kill anybody, Hawkeye. That young fella with yellow hair is the one who knocked me out. He did it when I wasn't looking. He was sneakier than we thought. Why, I never laid a hand on that little child. The boy's a snake in the grass, though."

"You mean, sneakier than *you* thought. So, if you were sittin' in the corner like I told you to do, how did that little kid get close enough to hit you—and from how it looks, knocked you out? What did he use to put a lump on your head like that? And where in the hell are your guns? Son of a bitch, I knew I couldn't trust a damned fool to watch them kids. I'd have been better off payin' those friendly Tonkawa Indians than my right-hand man. What's the world comin' to when a man can't trust someone his own color?"

"Now what are we gonna do, boss?" Ven asked. There was none of the bravado he usually had, but instead, he looked like he was ready to cry. It was clear that the meek one had taken charge.

"Here, unlock that trunk," Hawkeye said as he tossed him a key. "Inside, you'll find two extra pistols. When you're ready to leave, let me know. And don't forget your rifle. We've gotta catch those two and fast. I have a meeting to sell 'em at first light tomorrow morning, and I had planned to leave forthwith."

Ven reached over the fireplace, grabbed his long gun, and headed for the door.

"Wait a minute. Are the Indians we captured still in the shed, too, or did you let them get away, too?"

"And why would I do that, boss? I ain't that big of a fool."

Ven immediately grabbed for his neck, but his red string necklace with the extra key on it was gone. He patted his pockets but to no avail. Hawkeye stormed for the shed, as angry as hell. He felt Hawkeye might shoot him this time, and rightly so. He was ashamed of what he had done. Two wicked voices, deep in the darkest recesses of his mind, laughed and snickered, but they didn't dare come out and show themselves.

When they walked around to the side of the building where the door was, both their jaws dropped to their chests. The lock was on the floor. It was still attached to the red string that had been around Ven's neck. Hawkeye pulled his pistol and walked into the dark, foul-smelling room.

"Damn you to hell, Venom! You let 'em all get away. I bet all this had something to do with that little girl, didn't it? That scrappy little boy knocked you out and released all our captives. You couldn't have made a bigger mess, had you tried."

"I swear, boss, it was the little girl. Something came over me, and I couldn't help myself even though I tried. I've never told anyone, but it's like there are more than one of me inside my head and they're all talkin' at once, so I'm not sure which one I should listen to."

"What kind of horseshit is that you're feedin' me? Shut up and get your ass moving." Hawkeye was as mad as a hornet.

He walked up behind Ven and shoved him hard, nearly pushing him to the ground. He cringed as he waited for the bullet, but it never came. For now, his boss was going to let him live, but something told him that if they didn't find the children, his life wasn't worth squat.

A WOMAN RODE up and slid easily from the bareback horse and into the slosh in front of the town boarding house. Passersby stared at her ravishing, youthful beauty and her wild black stallion. She greeted Farnsworth Claymore in broken English. "Are we ready to go, darling? I'm getting bored in this one-horse town. There's nothing to do. I would rather be traveling than living in this squalor."

Her face suggested she was of Latin descent and possessed a certain mysterious beauty beneath her sun-darkened skin. She smiled like the rising sun, easing the frown off Claymore's gruff face. His heart pattered as she neared, and he smelled her expensive perfume. Regardless of who you were, if you wanted to go to San Francisco from back east, the only option was to go overland along the Oregon Trail.

"Why, it isn't even a town, my dear," Claymore replied. "This is no more than a settlement full of heathens and trash. Just wait until I get you to San Francisco, California. There is nothing like it in Madrid, or anywhere in Spain."

"I won't sleep another night in that bug-ridden bed. It's populated with fleas, bedbugs, mosquitoes, and cockroaches. I won't spend another night there. I'd rather enjoy the comforts of our tent."

"Don't be such a fancy-pants. We've gotta work to earn our money, but the job is almost done. For us, anyway. As soon as Hawkeye Burns brings the last load of slaves, he can send the three prison wagons on their way, but first, we'll leave. We'll wash our hands of the whole thing and disappear."

"Good, I didn't want to travel with those dirty, disgusting prisoners. Who knows what diseases they carry?"

"Don't worry, I've arranged it, so you won't have to. It's only four hundred forty miles to civilization. All our belongings will come behind us by wagon train, so we make better time on horseback with pack mules to carry our supplies and our large tent. We'll have four guards with us to ensure nobody bothers us along the way. Before you know it, we'll be in San Francisco. Every stop of my plan worked, and when we reach the West Coast, we'll be rich and have done a favor for the Californianos. Connections will be important as soon as it becomes a state."

"So, what's holding us up? Why don't we go right now? The sooner we leave, the quicker we'll get there."

"I have one more business deal to tend to first thing tomorrow morning. As soon as we've exchanged the goods and my people have them locked in the prison wagons, we can leave. The heavy steel cages will be much slower than even a wagon. Twelve more hours and we will have made a successful trip and made a good sum of money in the process."

"And what did I hear you say about two little kids. You're making children slaves these days, too?"

"That's the cream on the top of the cake. I know men in the big cities who will pay top dollar for good-looking White children. There are some twisted people in San Francisco, but I reckon it's the same in every big city like Montgomery, Alabama, or Atlanta. Where you have men with too much money, you'll find people with strange habits. Only things that the rich can afford."

THE CABIN

TO REACH A PLACE WHERE THEY COULD FORD ACROSS THE Snake River, they had to ride thirty miles west. Sure, there were ferries, but they didn't want anyone to know they had crossed to the other side. It would have been better if they had traveled unperceived until they knew where Money was. For now, they were working on rumors they had heard in McKay's Saloon back in Fort Boise and along the riverbanks. There, the gossip and tales were much more plentiful, but of course, not all that was said was true.

When the captain and Levi topped the rise, it was thick with weeping willows and cottonwood. It blocked their view until they reached the top. They came out of the trees and climbed down the riparian shrub-strewn steep hillside that led to shallower water where they could cross without losing a horse or a life. The part of the river in front of Fort Boise was treacherous and impossible to cross by horse.

They led their mounts into the slower-running water and grabbed their saddle horns while holding their rifles over their heads. They allowed their powerful horses to pull them across the river as their eyes watched for movement on the opposite bank. Finally, the horses began to get footholds in shallower water and climbed out of the river with Levi and Will on their backs. In their six years in the wilderness, they had forded countless rapid waters, and they didn't give it a second thought.

Once on the other side, they dismounted their horses and hobbled them while they grazed, and the scouts searched for signs of human tracks. They wanted to make sure they weren't on a main trail. Most people who couldn't afford a ferry or were afraid of boats rode these thirty miles to cross without mishap. Even Levi had a good luck charm for river crossings that Rusty had given him. He put the wet rabbit's foot to his lips and kissed it one more time.

The captain shook his head in disbelief. "At least you're not like old Rusty, fraternizing with mesmerists and clairvoyants with lucky potions and charms to ward off evil spirits," the captain said.

"He has some of the strangest ideas I know," Levi replied. "It must have been his time living with the Flat-head people. They don't put up so much of a fuss when a White man marries into the tribe. I believe a man makes his own luck, good or bad. Now, let's go and see if we can't find this abandoned cabin we heard about. For now, that's our only lead."

"It's supposed to be right across the river from Fort Boise, but inland some," Will said as he shook the water from his long hair.

"It's off the beaten path and is in a blind of trees and grown-over brush. That fisherman on the river said you could walk right by it and never notice it was there, so we're gonna have to keep sharp."

"I'm always sharp and at attention, Levi. You know that. Some things don't need to be said."

After riding most of the day and into the night, they were surprised when they saw smoke in the sky. It was black and thick enough to discern before a clear blue night. The moon created long shadows to the east.

As they drew nearer, they heard a noise in the dwelling—a boot scraping against the floor. Suddenly, there was a second man standing in the light of the doorway, silhouetting himself. He was a dark-bearded man, streaked with gray. It looked like it had never been trimmed. He appeared indifferent as he watched. A Colt Patterson hung from his hand by his side. His eyes were like two chunks of coal.

The man with the shotgun moved his thumb to the hammers. The range-clothing-clad man was burned brown from the sun, and his shirt and pants were soiled and sun-bleached. They both held their guns like it wasn't something new to them. However, they didn't resemble the men they were looking for. Neither had hawk-like eyes nor a flat nose.

"Who are you two to be snoopin' around where you shouldn't be?" The silhouette of a man was framed in the doorway with a sawed-off shotgun hanging from his hand.

Beaver pushed his gun belt lower on his hip as he tightened the buckle. He was ready to go to work. He stood with his Sharps in the crook of his arm.

Behind Beaver, he heard boots squeak softly, and then the captain was standing at his side. His rifle was in his fist, and his pistols in his wide leather belt.

"Last I heard it was a free country," Levi replied, smiling, but it didn't reach his eyes. "We're lookin' around for someplace to build a hunting camp."

"You're on the wrong side of the river. This is Indian Territory, mister."

"Why, you two are here, aren't you?" the captain asked. "How bad can it be for two greenhorns like you fellas?"

"Who do you think you're talkin' to, mister. I don't take kindly to sass."

As soon as the words got out, the one-armed man made his move, and the mouthy one had Will's pistol barrel in his mouth. His eyes grew wider when he drew back the hammer.

Levi kept an eye on the second one with his thumbs hooked onto his belt. "Don't make me shoot you, too, mister. You haven't caught us in the best of moods. Now come on out here nice and slow or I'll plug ya before you can wrap your fingers around your pistol grip."

"You seem awfully sure of yourself, big fella. Have you ever heard, the bigger they are, the harder they fall?"

"I'm Levi Johnson. Maybe you've heard of me and my partner, Captain Will Forrester. We've been livin' here in the wilderness for some time, now."

"I read about you two in one of them dime novels. I think it was called *Trouble in the Rockies*. Well, if you're lookin' for trouble, you've come to the right place."

"Now we're getting somewhere by creating a dialogue. That's the civilized man's way to negotiate without harming his fellow man. All it takes is a little talk and understanding, and everything can be worked

out without bloodshed. It would be a shame to ruin a
perfectly fine day."

"You won't find many civilized men around here.
Especially on this side of the river. All you'll find over
here is trouble."

"All we wanna do is ask you two a few questions and
then we'll be out of your hair," Levi replied. He raised
his hands and added, "Look, no guns."

"Look out!" the captain shouted as he pulled his
Colt Walker, and two quick shots rang out. The man just
inside the shack tumbled to the floor with a pair of
holes on either side of his chest. Then the man leaning
in the doorway was moving to level his gun, but the
captain pulled his trigger for a third time, and a single
shot blasted the stillness. Both men had crumpled to
the ground. The problem was that dead men didn't talk.
They obviously weren't there to bluff. They were there
to play for keeps.

One wore a low-slung cartridge belt. His other
revolver was still in his holster. They dropped off their
horses, and Levi pushed the man in the door over with
his moccasin. He appeared motionless until he blinked
his eyes open.

"This one's still alive. Maybe we do have somebody
to answer some questions."

He was gutshot, and although at first the shock
masked the pain, soon the waves of agony would fill his
very being. The bullet ripped through his stomach,
intestines, and nicked his liver. He was shot all to hell.

They were suddenly aware of gunpowder smoke.
The man framed on the floor in the doorway, who had
groaned as he dropped to his knees, was still alive,
although it was anybody's guess for how long.

"You were itching for us to pull on ya, weren't cha?" Beaver huffed. "And why was that? What did you have against us? Or do we have money on our heads?"

"And if so, how much is it?" the captain asked, amused.

"We thought you might be the law."

"Have you ever seen lawmen dressed like Indians? I ain't."

Levi stood over the man, who was lying halfway in and halfway out of the doorway, and watched as his eyes fluttered, fighting to stay open. He waited with his hand hanging with his Colt Walker in his fist. "Now, who are you working for? Before you reply, let me give you a warning. If you lie to me, I plan to pull the trigger until the revolver is emptied into your face. Then nobody will ever know who you are, and you won't get a proper burial. I wanna know what this place really is and who it belongs to. Were there two men here recently? One with a flat nose and another with eyes like a hawk?"

"That'll be Hawkeye Burns and Ven Grim. Some say his real name is Venom. Watch out for him. He's as crazy as a Mexican bullfighter with about as much sense as a monkey. They were the last ones here." The man looked into Beaver's eyes, pleading. "I'll tell ya what you wanna know, but in exchange, I want you to end my life and put me out of my misery. A man with a gunshot wound to the belly can take hours to die, and I don't fancy the agony. Now, what else do you want to know? If you don't mind, hurry up, I'm in a lot of pain."

"What was this place for?"

"It's a holding station to transport slaves from back east to the West Coast and back. It all depends on who they kidnap. Sometimes, like now, it's slaves, and others, it's rich folks kidnapped. That's why we were sent here to clean up the mess before somebody else finds it and the word gets out."

"I have one last question for you, mister. Do you know anything about a kidnapped boy by the name of Money Penny? He's about nine years old."

"Why, I thought there were two of 'em: a boy and a girl, and both of 'em were White. Then again, I only know what the other employees told me. I'm pretty much at the bottom of the totem pole."

"You've done fine, mister...?"

"Gordo. At least that's what my friends call me. I'm sorry about the boy. Was he kinfolk of yours?"

"He is my friend's son and my mountain man apprentice. Thank you kindly for what you've told us. It'll go a long way to finding the boy. So, how do you want it?"

"Not in the face. My folks live in the fort, and they'll find out soon enough. Everybody knows who I work for, so nobody will be surprised. But at least I'll have a proper burial."

"And what about your dead friend there?"

"I just met him, so I can't tell you much there. The slavers have hired men from here to San Francisco."

"And what mess was that you had to clean up? It looks tidy enough in there." Levi eyed the cabin, but did not notice the shackles on the floor.

"The mess is over there in the shed where Hawkeye and Ven locked up the slaves until they're bought and paid for and shipped out. The gossip said that something went wrong with the last batch, and some escaped. Ven and Hawkeye were out looking for them. Whether it's true or not, I couldn't say for sure."

"And it was full of slaves, you say? How long ago was that?"

"That was our real job. You know, cleaning up the cabin and the holding pen. The boss owns the property and just rents it out for special occasions or loans it to bad outlaws he's in cahoots with. That was yesterday, before dawn, when the trouble was supposed to have started. What happened here, I'm not quite sure, but the only blood I found was on the cabin floor, and it wasn't much. Nobody was shot or stabbed, that's for sure. I reckon one of 'em got knocked around is all."

"This Hawkeye fella has to be the gang leader, and Ven is his second," the captain said.

Gordo nodded, his eyes full of pain. He struggled to gobble air, as he was doubled over and blood pooled under his body on the wooden floor. The claret from his liver was black.

Levi slipped his pistol out of his holster and whispered as he kneeled beside the blood-draining body. "I wish we'd have met in different circumstances. We might have been friends and all. You seem like an honest man caught up with the wrong people. It happens too often these days. At times, it's hard even to get by."

Beaver put the end of his revolver to Gordo's chest right over his heart. With an expressionless face, he pulled the trigger. The round sounded dull across the flat land. The fire flash made his cotton shirt burn and smolder around the gunshot wound in his chest.

Despite the shock, Gordo managed to mouth the words, "Thank you," before he died.

"I wonder if he was thanking me for killing him and putting him out of his misery, or was he thanking me for getting him out of a life not befitting of an honest man."

"Maybe a little bit of both, Beaver. Now we have names, and all we've gotta do is find out which way they ran."

When they were ready to go, Levi said, "Make sure you tighten that lash rope on the supplies on the pack-saddle. We can't afford to lose any food because we don't know how long we're gonna have to follow these two."

"Always worried about your next meal." The captain laughed. There was a nervousness about it that made it sound strange. Now that they had two names, the tension rose even more.

When they looked back at the small cabin, they saw where the wood paneling was full of bullet holes. After the rounds went through and through the bodies, the wood paneling exploded under the blast of the heavy loads, making splinters fly like tiny projectiles. Where some of the bullets hit, they could see lamplight where the rounds from the nine-inch barrel penetrated the door and shutters, and penetrated the walls.

Crows were already crowding limbs, cawing in harmony, even though it was still dark. In minutes, coyotes were at the edge of the clearing. Soon it would be daylight, and the sky would be full of circling vultures.

HIDE HUNTERS

DESPITE THE KIDNAPPING OF LITTLE MONEY, THE mountain men, at least the elders, knew that life had to go on. Their winter supplies were nearly depleted since they had another unplanned mouth to feed, with Kit Carson spending the winter with them. Levi was bad enough, but when you added another hungry mountain man, Angus's stocks dwindled.

Now, it was time for Rusty and Joseph to ride out and hunt for some fresh meat for their next meal. When Levi and the captain returned with provisions for a few days, they would all go on a big hunt where they wouldn't return until they had enough food to last them the summer.

Virgil and the women would hold down the fort in the men's absence. Dahteste, Levi's wife, was a war chief and had a dozen battles under her belt. Betty, the captain's wife, was a Crockett, the niece of the famous Davy, who fought and died at the Alamo in Texas. She had been a frontierswoman since she was a child and should outshoot most men.

Silvia, Bar-Chee, and Pine Needle weren't warrior types, but they, too, knew how to use their guns from living deep in the wilderness. If attacked, they could defend themselves from the main cabin, which was nearly impregnable. In the earlier years, they had been repeatedly attacked, and no one had breached the cabin walls.

Rusty and Joseph sat, sipping coffee, exhausted from the tension and worry, as they stared into the fire, listening to the snap, crackle, and pop. Both their minds were on the young boy, Money Penny. Although they missed him, they knew there was nothing they could do but wait until Levi and the captain returned, hopefully *with* the boy. The wilderness was like that. Every day could bring the unexpected.

"Do you know what the Crow and Blackfeet call White men married to Indian women? Squaw Men." Rusty chuckled. "How do you like them beans, Marshal *Squaw Man* Walker?" The federal lawman frowned. He didn't think it was very funny.

"I dare anyone to call me that to my face."

"Why, if they did, they'd be talkin' in Crow or Blackfoot, and you probably wouldn't understand anyway."

The thrums on Rusty's buckskins fluttered in the wind, as did his long, gray hair, as soon as he removed his hat. As he faced the wind, his long beard lay flat against his chest.

"Did you know that the first guides and scouts called the Rocky Mountains the Shining Mountains? I reckon it's a fine name," Rusty said. "I wonder why they ever changed it. Sometimes, well enough should be left alone."

"Why, aren't you a wagonload of information today.

Or are you just trying to piss me off? You haven't stopped talkin' since you got up."

Rusty laughed. He seemed pleased that he could get under the marshal's skin. Then again, when they first met, Joseph was the angriest man he knew.

"What's that smell?" the marshal asked, sniffing the air and making a face. It kind of smells like tobacco, but both sweet and rotten. Who would smoke somethin' like that?"

"It's Kinnikinnick. It's made from tobacco leaves, leaves from other plants, and tree bark. Only Indians smoke that mix. Potak uses something like it in his pipe, but his smells a little different," Rusty whispered and took another whiff.

"No, that ain't him. It sure doesn't smell like White man's tobacco. Keep sharp, we probably ain't alone." Joseph continued to follow his nose.

Suddenly, a Blackfoot Indian stepped out from the trees and onto the path, appearing right in front of them, not thirty feet away. He held a pagamoggon in his fist. The three-pound stone was attached to the two-foot-long leather-covered handle. If you got hit on the head with that, it would crush your skull like an egg.

"He doesn't look like he's in the mood to palaver, is he?" Rusty said dryly. If the Indian was at all scared, he sure didn't show it. "To me, he looks like he's come here to raise our hair. See that scalp lock on his head. He's challenging us to take his. He's taunting us, Joseph. It looks like he's ready to kill a couple of dog faces, like us, to make his bones. He ain't old enough to be an experienced warrior."

"Why is he jumpin' up and down and yellin' like

that?" Joseph asked, with furrowed brow. "Maybe he's touched in the head."

"He's tryin' to scare us, is what it is. Or maybe he's been eatin' peyote or loco weed. Who knows, but he's certainly acting crazy. Mind ya now, if he gets close enough, he'll use that club on us. His intentions are clear enough. He wants to kill us both, even though he came poorly prepared."

"Whatcha wanna do? I know that neither of us is the psalm singer that Virgil is, but he does keep us walkin' the straight and narrow. It's your call, hoss."

The young warrior's face was painted red with yellow circles around his eyes and fangs down his lips and chin. It did make him look like a dangerous character, but Rusty knew behind all that war paint was only a boy dying to be a man. Still, he showed clear and present danger, and if they didn't stop him, he would try to kill one of them. There was no doubt about it.

Without a word, the marshal pulled his Colt Peacemaker, as quick as spit, drew back the hammer, and fired. The bullet hit the Indian dead center in the chest, making him stop his erratic dance and freeze as still as a stone as he looked down in wonder. It was like he couldn't believe there was a ragged hole where a second before there was none. Joseph held his pistol on his target until the truth set in, and he plopped down on his but. When he growled, he showed blood-stained teeth.

Joseph didn't even wait to see it out. He slammed his gun into his holster, clearly angry, dropped off his horse, and turned and walked into the bushes to have a leak without so much as a word. Rusty just shook his head at the waste of life. Sure, the marshal could have winged him, but then they would have to take him with them, which was out of the question. That, or leave him to fend off the mountain lions, bears, and wolves. The grizzlies would probably smell him first, and it was better not to be around when they got there, especially if there was more than one.

The smell of fresh blood in the air brought all the predators to the mountain. The bears could smell the wounded man twenty miles away. Their sense of smell was two thousand times that of a human and seven times better than a bloodhound's. If they were near enough to arrive before the others, the kill would still be fresh. They were usually the first to find the wounded, and once claimed, no one would dare to try to take it away from what was the true king of the wilderness.

Rusty wheeled his horse to the trail past the dead Indian on the ground. He stopped at the edge of the clearing and turned in his saddle and asked, "Are you coming or not? We sure as hell can't stay around here unless we wanna get et too."

Joseph was clearly angry as he buttoned up his britches and pulled his gun belt tight again. He pulled out his revolver and ejected the single spent shell, and pulling one from the many in his gun belt, then he slipped it into the chamber and slapped it home. The marshal slammed his pistol into his holster and forked astride his horse and silently followed Rusty, without even glancing at the Blackfoot Indian. His lungs made their last rattle as he struggled to draw air, then he was gone. Instead of making his bones, he had recklessly lost his life. Unfortunately, his bravery outweighed his skills, and the captain was forced to take yet another life.

When they rode beneath the apex of the sun, they

noticed the flies first. Initially, they didn't know what it was, but they heard something distinguishable in the air. When they got close enough to smell the pungent odor, they began to see blowflies by the hundreds and soon in the tens of thousands. It looked like every fly in the Rockies was there. Finally, the cloud of insects hanging over the unseen valley was in the millions.

As they continued to ride, they pulled their Sharps rifles from their sheaths and laid them across their laps. It was anyone's guess what lay just over the next rise or two, but what was certain was death. A lot of it, judging by the hundreds of turkey vultures that made lazy circles in the sky before them. Dozens folded their wings into dives and disappeared over the tops of the trees, only to rise again minutes later with meat in their talons and beaks.

Both men remained silent, their ears pricked to hear any out-of-place sounds. Their eyes stretched into the distance, but still they saw nothing. The closer they got, the more overwhelming the smell was. When they finally reached the next ridge, they braced themselves for the worst, but what they saw was another gully. The trail squirreled down their side and up the other and over another rise. The mountain men exchanged looks, then nudged their horses' flanks and carried on.

They stood in their stirrups as they walked their horses down the steep grade, then they began to climb, grabbing their saddle horns as they struggled up the sharp incline. Finally, they were just about to reach the second ridge. Question marks filled their heads as they exchanged looks. Now, the sound of crows cawing was deafening.

Rusty gasped when he saw what lay before them,

and the marshal growled and spat a brown stream of juice, then rolled his chew to the other side. His eyes blazed angrily. Despite the size of the flat valley, it was covered with carcasses of dead animals. Blood was everywhere since the buffalo had been skinned where they died.

It was obvious that a team of buffalo hide hunters had struck, killing all the dumb animals before dropping into the valley of death and taking their hides. By the time the local Indians located the valley of dead beasts, they would be rotten and of no use to anyone but the boners. The boners were at the bottom of the totem pole. They traded in animals and even human parts of the dead, especially bones. They could be crafted into tools like hoes, knives, awls, and scrapers. They were also used as ornaments and pieces in games.

They reluctantly made their way down. When Rusty pulled his horse up to the first big bull, he leaned over and touched the raw skin with his hand. They sat on their horses before a sea of dead bison, one and all lacking their beautiful fur, leaving ugly naked bodies in their wake.

"Why, this one's still warm. They must have left this part for last. It's obvious they had just left when we got near. Lucky for us and them, we didn't run into each other. They did a sloppy job of butchering, too, but I imagine they wanted to get their furs and get off the mountain before the Indians caught them here. They don't take kindly to White folks stealing their furs and food, but they like it even less if they leave most of the animals to rot, doing nobody any good. It's a damned shame, this."

"I reckon those hide hunters have up and moved, lock, stock, and barrel," Joseph said.

"It'll be better if the Indians don't catch 'em or their scalps will end up on some braves' buckskin shirts," Rusty snickered. "Pass me that flask of tanglefoot. I've got to get rid of this bad taste in my mouth."

Joseph reluctantly passed his personal stash of whiskey. "After seein' all those slaughtered buffs for their hides, it left a bad taste in my mouth, too."

"Those buffalo were hit by hide hunters. All those carcasses with the meat rotting are a total waste. This is what ticks the Indians off."

After finishing off half of Joseph's liquor, Rusty dug into his possibles bag for his pipe and leather pouch of tobacco. In seconds, he puffed it to life, and the bowl reflected orange in his eyes, and smoke swirled around his head.

"Maybe we should take a chance and cut some steaks and harvest us some sweetbreads. These animals haven't had the time to go ripe. It's still cold enough to keep the meat from going bad, too. There's no sense in letting such an opportunity pass us by."

Rusty didn't wait for an answer but nudged his horse and began the descent to the killing fields. By the time he got to the bottom, the flies were so thick they lit in his eyes, his ears, and even tried to crawl into his mouth. The air seemed thick and humid, and everything was tinged with a red hue.

By the time Rusty was done, he had blood up to his elbows, but he also had stacks of steaks already on salt. In one stop, they had complied with their planned hunt from the compound, and it hadn't taken over a few hours without a single shot.

"How about a cup of buffalo cider, pard?" The fluid found in the buffalo's stomach was a favorite thirst quencher among both mountain men and Indians.

"Buffalo cider don't tickle my fancy, but I have some of that bull cheese," Joseph asked as he grabbed a piece of buffalo jerky, just salted, and gnawed on it raw, like a dog.

They also had their fill of sweetbread from the bison's belly. For the Plains Indians, the thymus and pancreas glands of the buffalo were often considered a delicacy. The mountain men gobbled them up. Rusty knew how to prepare it to a delicate, creamy texture. He made these from the younger animals because the thymus glands degenerated with age.

"Come on, let's get moving," Joseph said as soon as they were full and had the pack mule loaded. "We've already been here too long for our own good. Now we can head straight home."

They rode on for the rest of the day, but now they were headed back in the direction of the compound. When the sun was eight fingers from the world's edge, they saw a silhouette walking on foot in their direction. It was a black, moving figure against a background of glowing light, accompanied by a four-legged animal.

"There's something familiar about how that fella walks, but with the sun in our eyes, I can't tell who it is," Rusty said as he removed his hat and held it high to shade his face, but to no avail.

"From here, he doesn't look like a threat, does he?" Joseph replied.

Rusty shook his head, but still he moved his hand toward his revolver in his cross-draw holster, just in case. When he finally recognized him, he dropped his hand to his side and exhaled a sigh of relief.

Potak, the Tonkawa Indian and medicine man from the Crow stronghold, carried his medicine bag slung over his shoulder. The end of his medicine pipe stuck out the top. An odd-smelling tobacco smoke swirled from his hand pipe, drooping from his thin lips. When he saw Rusty, he smiled, and his eyes reached his face, but they were emotionless when he turned them to the marshal. It wasn't that he didn't like him. He knew he would never be one of them, like his mountain man mentor. Few White men were blood brothers with an important chief. Rusty even spoke good Crow, along with a bit of several of the languages of the Yellowstone Valley Indians.

"Whatcha doin' way out here, Potak?" Rusty asked.

"The same thing you're doing. The hunter's tracks led me first, but it wasn't long before I could smell their mess. I reckon that was a field of bison they shot and killed, over that rise, didn't they? I can see the turkey vultures from here."

"What were those fools thinking about letting all that food rot? We have some bison steaks and sweetbreads if you want to follow us home. You're welcome to break bread with us. Mi casa es su casa."

"I saw some tracks from a lobo and wondered what timber wolves were doing so close to humans. I believe you have found the answer. I think they'll be after the orphaned calves, of which, judging by how many vultures are circling above, there are many. And the circle of life goes on, although faster and faster with the White men's presence."

"Their hides weren't valuable enough for the White

hunters to spend a bullet to put them out of their misery," Rusty huffed. "Now they'll be easy pickings for scavengers of all sorts, not alone the wolves."

"Every coyote on Bear Tooth Mountain will be here soon with their constant yapping," Potak said. "When a distant coyote hears one of these, he'll start howling too, and thus the chain starts, covering miles. The scavengers will be eating here for days, and then the bugs and worms will come."

PRISONER SWAP

VEN LAY IN THE CORNER NURSING HIS INJURIES. ONE EYE was so swollen he could hardly see. His nose was even flatter than it was before, and continued to bleed with no stopping in sight. Bells rang in his ears from the blows to his head. He still didn't know how that little boy hit him so hard, but the beating from Hawkeye was more brutal, and it damaged his ego, too. Between the two, he had difficulty seeing straight. Every time he stood up, he felt dizzy.

"Now do you see, you damned fool," Hawkeye said. "If you had listened to your orders and done as I said, you wouldn't have gotten these beatings. For letting those two get away, I should've shot you then and there. Now we've gotta go out and look for 'em, although I doubt I'll have much trouble with my skills. They'll be easier than a bear cub to find. They're just two stupid kids. The Indian captives are another matter. I'm sure all six of them are long gone. But don't give up hope yet. I figure the kids are the most valuable of the lot."

"What would happen if we showed up with the kids but not the Indian slaves?" asked Ven.

"That's not an option. Why don't we snatch a half dozen Indians from outside the fort and pass them off as savages from the mountains? If they think they ain't locals, nobody should care. Once they're locked up, who's gonna be the wiser? They'll mix in with the rest. But we're gonna need to move fast. We've gotta grab the kids, snatch six slaves, and get back to the rendezvous to collect our money in gold coins. As soon as we get paid, we'll be off, and we won't look back. Somebody is gonna be offended that we snatched six fort Indians, but I doubt it'll be anything they can't live without. Then again, there'll be no use in hanging around to find out. I wanna get to California so bad that if I could, I'd leave today."

"So, what do we do first, boss?" Ven asked, his lust hardly veiled. "If you want, I'll go after the little girl and boy on my own, especially as it was all my fault. I'll find 'em, all right. And when I do, I'll tan both their hides. But don't worry, I won't mark their faces and they won't get away again, but I'll give that little runt what he deserves for hittin' me like that."

"Like hell you will. It was your fault you let a little boy best you. You'd like that just fine, you and that little girl alone, wouldn't you? I've trusted you for the last time, Venom. I'll go and find the children, and you get the six Indians."

"But you're bigger and stronger than I am. Why, I figure, you're part Indian. Now, a couple of White kids must be easy enough to find, even for the likes of me."

As soon as the words came out, Ven knew he had said the wrong thing. It was the evil one who had opened his mouth again, landing him in more trouble than ever. It was as though the other two living in his mind didn't feel the pain when he was beaten to a pulp, like this time. Hawkeye had never beaten him so severely.

Before Ven knew it, Hawkeye had pulled his revolver and had the barrel pressed against the side of his head. He felt the click rattle through the barrel and knew what was going to come next. He closed his eyes. He didn't bother to pray because he knew that God didn't listen to lost souls like him.

"Are you going to start doing what I tell you to, or are you going to continue to run astray from my orders, Venom? I'm tired of all the lies and bullshit. Either you follow orders, or I'm gonna have to put ya down like a dog. On this job, you've proved how worthless you are. I've had donkeys that listened better than you."

"Where should I get 'em from, boss?" Ven asked, having no idea where to start. Now he was as nervous as he had ever been and knew he was very close to getting shot. When his eyes turned dead, like they did then, he knew he was just about to blow his top. He had only seen it happen once before, and he had murdered four men in the blink of an eye and with little apparent reason. When he was like that, it was better not to ask why.

"I don't care where you acquire more slaves, just get 'em is all. Grab 'em off the street if you've gotta. We need to have our merchandise ready for dawn tomorrow, and I ain't about to give up now that we're so close. If it weren't for you, we'd just be finishing up. For once in your life, listen to what I tell you. If you don't snatch me six healthy heathens, don't bother to come back. You'll have ruined everything, and you and I will be done."

Ven frowned when he called him by name, but he knew that now wasn't the time to complain. As it was, he was lucky he wasn't already dead. He still didn't understand how those two young kids could stand up to a man like him. His problem was that his own craziness and stupidity consumed him so much that he didn't realize how dumb he really was.

If a nine-year-old could trick him, he was as dumb as mud. Then again, Hawkeye didn't have him around for his brains. He used him because he was as ruthless as he was and didn't shy away from danger. It was almost like he had an addiction to violence, among other unsavory traits, even more vile.

Hawkeye gave his right-hand man the ultimate insult. He hacked, clearing his throat, then spat a green, gooey stream down his face. The boss never noticed how red Ven's face got. It was hard to tell under the bruises. His teeth ground as his muscles tightened. Right then, he could kill his boss, but he knew how fast he was with a knife or pistol and knew he wouldn't have a chance. He could feel his neck burning with humiliation.

Hawkeye stood there watching the spit run down his face as his fingers drummed his wooden pistol grip, like he was challenging Ven to draw. He was edging him on to finish it then and there, but they both knew that he would never try such a thing. It was true—he was stupid, but he wasn't a total moron and loco beyond repair. Or maybe he was.

———

As Money and Annie moved through the woods, she could hardly keep up. She wondered why they weren't running in an all-out sprint. But he insisted they keep moving at a brisk pace, always being careful where they stepped. She didn't have the slightest idea of where they were.

"Slow down, Money. Your legs are longer than mine. I can hardly keep up. You don't walk in a straight line. To me, you seem to stagger all over the place. Why don't we just run as fast as we can? Then we can flee like the wind."

"If you walk a straight line, it's easier to track. They've got to make sense at a glance to a scout, or they're hard to read, and that's exactly what we want."

Her remark reminded him of when he had tried to follow Levi with his long strides, but he had never stopped trying to keep up. Annie was giving it her best, but she was undoubtedly slowing them down. Money looked around and then up at the great oak tree above them.

"We need to rest, but we can't stay here on the ground. Our only option is to climb as far up into that old oak tree as we can and make a bed on the bow or joint of limbs. Up there, nobody goes but the wild cats, and I doubt they come after two humans, even if we aren't very big."

"Boy, you sure do know how to paint a pretty picture. But I think I like being in the tree better than down here on the ground."

Money jumped for a low-hanging limb and pulled himself up. Then he grabbed the thick branch and reached out, pulling Annie up by the hand as she scrambled to his limb.

"Make sure you get a good hold and don't slip, Annie. I'll meet you at the top. I'll stop as soon as I see a place to make a bed."

Money scrambled up the tree, limb by limb, almost as fast as a squirrel. When he found a place where five thick limbs branched out, he knew that was where they would sleep. Without waiting for the slow but sure-footed Annie, he began chopping thinner branches to make them a bed high in the tree's bow. He covered them with leaf-covered branches from strong limbs and them with tiny branches. Some of the leaves were larger than a grown man's hand. By the time Annie reached the top, Money was already lying in their provisional bed with a grin so wide that it showed his wisdom teeth.

Annie was so exhausted, she lay down and instantly fell asleep without saying a word. Money sat there, listening to the wind whistle, making the tree sway slightly at the top. Some of the old oaks were a hundred feet tall and ranged from one hundred to three hundred years old, although some say that other species of California oaks can live up to a thousand years. This one was fifty feet tall and had a seventy-foot spread, providing a massive amount of shade.

While Annie was sleeping, Money was jumping with energy. The adrenaline from the escape was still pumping through his veins, and even more so, being so high in a giant oak. He decided to climb to the top and see what was around them. Maybe he could find a safe place to stand guard and still doze.

When he reached the highest limb that would hold his weight, he wrapped his arms and legs around it, and he felt it move to and fro with each gust of wind. Money wasn't afraid of heights, though. He and Levi had climbed mountain peaks that were truly impressive. From where he sat, he could see the Snake River and Fort Boise on the opposite bank. He saw dozens of streams of smoke from the campfires, both from the dozen or so teepees and more than fifty covered wagons.

When he scoured the countryside outside the fort walls, he saw steel wagons with bars on their sides, and they were painted black. Money gasped when he saw that two of them already looked like they were full of humans. He pulled out the miniature spyglass Levi had given him and took a closer look. He saw that all the prisoners were from the Indian tribes that lived on and around the Yellowstone Valley. To the Fort Indians, they were considered hostile, and more so to the Whites.

The captives consisted of seventy percent men, and the rest were women. A shudder went through Money's body when he realized that the empty wagon was where he and Annie were supposed to ride along with the other captive Indians, whom they had freed. He wondered if the wagon owner knew what had happened yet. It was still dark, maybe two or three in the morning. He wondered when they were supposed to meet to turn them over. Whatever he had to do, he was going to make sure they didn't end up in that jail wagon, no matter what he had to do. It looked like the prisoners already in them were in a living hell.

As he looked to the other side, he wondered where Hawkeye and Ven were. He knew too well that they would be out there somewhere looking for them. All he had to do was avoid them until Levi showed up, and he knew that he and the captain would undoubtedly show up. That, or they had to make it to the fort without being discovered. While they were out in the wilderness alone, they had to consider the dangers posed by wild animals as well. They were just small enough to be an appetizing treat for a grizzly bear.

If his mentor and the captain were around, the fort was where he suspected Levi would be, and where Beaver went, the captain accompanied him. With this, he knew he had a skilled and deadly force of scouts looking for him. Knowing his mentor, they would probably come alone because anyone else would just slow them down. He briefly wondered if they were still there in the settlement. If he could only get inside those fifteen-foot walls, he might find his mentor, and he knew he and Annie would be safe.

He briefly wondered what would happen to his new friend, Annie. Then, it suddenly came to him that one of the kind souls that populated the Fort Boise settlement would probably step up. He had heard Rusty say that Chief Wanata had a fuss when he was informed of Money's presence in the compound on Bear Tooth Mountains and didn't dare make promises he wouldn't be able to keep. Levi said that despite the riffraff that sometimes traveled through, the long-term residents were solid citizens with good hearts.

As he stared at the reflection of the moon on the river between him and freedom, he wondered where it would be safe to cross and not get discovered. It was apparent that the currents were strong, and he had noted that no wagons or horses waited to cross near the fort docks. Everyone moved by ferry from one bank to another or even up and down the river to deliver supplies to distant neighbors who, too, had cut out their little world among the often-hostile Indians.

It took a particular kind of man to live in a place like

this. It was even more susceptible to violence than where they lived on Bear Tooth Mountain. There, they had a massive Crow stronghold, only a few hours' ride. Despite the tension between his mother's brother and his uncle, Chief Wanata, he knew that he would never let harm come to them. They were much safer back in the compound than they would be, even living inside the walls of the fort.

He continued to watch for another half hour, but by then his eyes became heavy and he was afraid of nodding off and falling out of the tree. He carefully climbed back down, taking twice as long as it had taken to climb up. He carefully lay beside Annie, but she was dead to the world and never stirred. Money yawned deeply, and his eyes drooped until they closed, and he began to snore. In minutes, he was sleeping like he was at the bottom of a deep well where there was no sound, sight, or danger.

———

EVEN THOUGH HAWKEYE hadn't spoken a word since they left the shack, Ven knew all the signs telling him his boss was beyond himself with anger. Every time he shot a hate-filled glance over his shoulder, it sent a chill up his right-hand man's spine. He knew with every step he was walking closer to his own death.

When they got to the river, the two Tonkawa Indians appeared from the shadows. With them came an odd smell. They had rifles in their hands and braces of pistols in their belts. Their deadpan eyes seemed to look right through them.

"These two will paddle you across the river. You can

get the slaves wherever you want, but I don't want to get involved. It was your mistake, so if you're caught, you'll be the one who pays for it. Like I said before, if you don't come through, you had best not show your face again, because if I see you, you're gonna get shot. And don't go and ask these two Indians to do your dirty work. They weren't paid for that. They've honored their agreement, and I plan to honor mine. That's more than I can say for you."

After climbing into the bull boat and grabbing the rudder, the Tonkawa pushed it off the riverbank and into deeper water. They climbed aboard with sea legs and quickly rowed the boat across the river to the Fort Boise side. As soon as they hit shallow water and ran aground, Ven jumped out. Despite what Hawkeye had said, he looked back with pleading eyes, but by then the Indians had vanished again. He looked around but didn't see them anywhere, still her knew that they were there.

"You two stay right here. I won't take long. I'll take that bag of shackles and irons. I figure we've got a couple of hours before the first crack of dawn. When we get back to the other side, Hawkeye will probably have the youngins, and we'll come back one last time and finish this."

Ven realized that even if he was successful, but Hawkeye wasn't, upon his return, he would be walking straight into a trap. As promised, he knew that his boss would shoot him on sight, and neither the Tonkawa nor the slaves were going to try to stop him. They already knew what he did. The looks in their eyes told the whole story.

Ven left his heavy rifle on the buffalo boat. He knew

a pair of short-range pistols was always best in close quarters. They were lightweight and easy to handle and even to hide. Now to find some healthy candidates for the prison wagons. He needed six, and not even one less would do. There appeared to be many more Indians on the outside of the fort than on the inside, so Ven started to sneak around the dozen teepees surrounding Fort Boise. Almost everyone he saw was still asleep or only beginning to stir as the first hint of light reached the end of the world.

Many of the Indians slept around the campfire to keep warm, and others occupied their teepees. There were many more people living around the settlement than he had imagined. Now, how to figure out when to take a few Indians with him. Until then, he hadn't seen any groups as small as a half dozen. They were all in bunches of a dozen or more, with some topping out at twenty bodies sleeping around the fires. That was when he saw six women, drearily walking to the river with dirty clothing and wash pans under their arms. It was apparent these were starting early to tend to their daily chores.

Go ahead, and grab the woman, the evil one popped into his head and said.

No, that's not what Hawkeye said to do. We had seventy percent men before. Ven argued with himself. *We can't come back with all women. Then he'll shoot us, for sure. Stop it! I can't think straight as it is.*

Still, no matter what his mind said, he headed for the six women who were just squatting on the water's edge. It was far too easy to resist.

Ven counted, "One, two, three, four, five, six...seven? But I only want six."

It was easy sneaking up on the women as they gossiped and splashed their clothing in the water, rubbing it against rocks and using river sand as soap. An evil smile suddenly crossed Ven's face as he realized what he was going to do. Four gunshots rang out as the other women snapped their heads at the man with a gun in his hand in terror.

Ven put his finger to his mouth as he drew back the hammers to let them know he meant business and would shoot them, too. He tossed the irons to the Indian women and mimicked putting them around their wrists. As soon as they were on, he locked them tight and turned and jogged for the buffalo boat. He didn't know what tribe they were from and really didn't care. To them, they were like a side of beef, priced per pound.

When he arrived, he huffed, gulping air. "Keep an eye on these three while I get us three more. This is easier than I expected." He turned and was off again.

MONEY & ANNIE

WHEN MONEY FINALLY WOKE UP, HE FELT SPARKLING RAYS of sun peppering his face as the leaves fluttered above him. He sat up and realized it was long after first light. The sun was already four fingers from the horizon. He used the heels of his hands to rub the sleep from his tired eyes. He looked down at Annie, and she was dead to the world as her chest calmly rose and fell. Finally, she was calm, but he knew when she awoke, she would remember everything that had happened. That terrified face would return and change from her now peaceful expression. Asleep, it was as though she didn't have a care in the world.

He sat for a moment while he got his bearings and debated whether to wake Annie up or not. For now, they appeared safe up there in the tree. Maybe it would be best if they stayed there all day until it was dark again and they could continue to travel unperceived. If Hawkeye or Ven discovered their tracks, it would only be a matter of time until they cornered and captured them. He was sure that Hawkeye would know the area well, since he didn't seem to be a man who ran off unprepared, and his clothing said he was a mountain man.

Without a concrete decision on what to do, Money waited there until she awoke on her own, whenever that might be. As seconds became minutes and minutes turned into an hour, she never seemed to awaken. When she finally did, he watched her face go from calm to bewildered, and in seconds, to fear again. His brain raced for something positive to say, but he came up with nothing. The only good news was that, for now, they were free.

Money suddenly blurted out, "I have an idea. Do you know how to swim?"

"Swim?" Annie asked, barely awake. "Yes, I can swim, sort of. I can dog paddle, if that's what you mean. Everyone who travels west has to cross a creek, river, or pond at some time or other, if not many. We crossed so many, I lost count."

"If I can find a log to help us float, do you think you can help me kick our way across the river somewhere the current isn't so strong? I figure the only safe place for us is in Fort Boise. If my friends ain't there at least, we can go to the sheriff. Tom Hand is a friend of my mentor, and I figure he'll help us as he's the law. Maybe he'll let us sleep in his jail cell bunks. I can't think of anything safer nearby, unless you want to stay here in this old oak tree until my friends find us. Then again, I'll have to go down to rummage for food. I'm not a very good shot with a pistol either, but the long rifle was too big to carry."

"Won't we be too hard to find up here in this oak? Maybe a mountain lion will find us before your mentor does. I know you said they would be afraid of two humans, but I'm not so convinced that they'd be wary of a couple of kids. We'll look like baby calves to them. A big wild cat might eat us both. I think our best chance is to reach the law, even if we have to cross that dangerous-looking river. If it comes to swim or sink, I reckon I'm gonna have to do it or suffer the consequences."

"I figure our chances are best downriver from what I've heard the mountain men say, but I have no idea of how far we'll have to go. If we try to cross here, we'll drown before we get halfway. Everybody in the settlement will see us, too, which we might not want until we find out more about what's going on. I saw prisoner jail wagons from the top of this oak we slept in."

"Well, we can't stay here forever, so we might as well go now, shouldn't we. I feel like we have to do something or I'm gonna go crazy."

"I was gonna wait for dark, but that is when the panthers and packs of wolves are on the prowl, lookin' for somethin' to eat. Maybe it is time to go. To tell the truth, I was plannin' for us to head out at first light, but I slept in, which was my mistake. That better be my last bad move, or we might find ourselves caught out again."

"At least we know that somebody is out there looking for us. Just knowing your mentor and an army captain are looking for us makes me feel a little better. We still have a chance of getting out of this."

"The problem is there's more than one group looking for us, and half of 'em are up to no good. Come on, I'll help you climb down. It's always harder getting down from a tree than climbing up."

When they got back down to the limb they swung up on, Money held out his hand, stopping Annie as he had a careful look and listened closely. When they didn't see or hear anything, they dropped to the ground and ran for the first shadow they saw. From there, the mountain man apprentice led them from shadow to shadow and the hard places to see, behind growths of brush, trees, and boulders. It made the going much slower, but that way, Money was pretty sure that nobody would see them. The youngsters slowly picked their way through briars and brambles as she carefully followed on his heels.

After a full day of carefully picking their way along rabbit and raccoon trails, they could finally hear the water lapping at the river's edge. The vegetation was so thick that they had to fight their way through. When they pushed the last of the drooping willows aside, they discovered several logs washed up on the bank. They bobbed up and down in the slow-moving water.

"We can use the biggest log of the lot and float it across the river. See that wood drifting downstream. It's not moving as violently as near Fort Boise. You must be tired. We can rest for a bit before we carry on, if you don't think you can make it yet. We need some food to give us energy, but it's just too risky. We can't take the chance when we're so close. Are you ready, or would you like to take another nap? I don't think anyone will discover us here in all these weeds and overgrown trees."

Annie was afraid to answer, so she just nodded her head. Money forced a smile as he waded into the water, pushing the log. He held onto one end and Annie the other as they kicked their feet while trying to steer, but sideways it was impossible.

"This isn't gonna work. Instead of pushing the log sideways, we need to push it lengthwise, like a boat, or there will be too much resistance. We'll have to hold on with one arm and paddle, stroking with the other while kicking our feet. Are you ready?"

Again, Annie only nodded, but now she had a determined look on her face. "Let's do this."

Money guided the front of the log while Annie did her best with the back. Sometimes all she could do was hold on for dear life and let him do the work while she caught her breath. Then, after a few seconds of rest, she would give it her all again. Back home near the compound, they had rivers, creeks, ponds, and even lakes, and he spent much of last summer frolicking in the streams, so he was like an otter in the water. In a few minutes of intense work, they arrived, clinging to the log on the Fort Boise side of the river. They were nearly to safety. At least that was what they hoped. Living this deep in the wilderness was sometimes hard to say.

Again, Annie became frustrated because Money insisted that they continue to sneak around the trail without ever stepping on it. For her, he seemed to do everything the hard way, but the truth was, he was doing a better job than she could ever do. Up until then, nobody had seen them, not to mention trying to apprehend them again.

———

WHEN THEY WALKED past the fort's wall torches, their shadows danced boldly on their faces, but they were small enough that the guards didn't give them a second glance. As far as they knew, they were just two more children from one of the continuous wagon trains that constantly frequented the town. The large courtyard stood in the middle of shops and buildings all along the sides. Money's eyes were drawn to a glass window with a large silver star painted on it. Above the star, it said, *SHERIFF*.

When Money knocked on the door, it sounded like a hammer. He looked around, nearly panicking, as he wondered if he had made too much noise. A key rattled in the lock, then came the sound of squeaking hinges. The sheriff stood in the doorway, yawning. They had awoken him from his siesta. Since he had to do the graveyard shift rounds late, he had a nap at midday or whenever he found a moment to rest.

The marshal stared at him with his thumbs hooked on his gun belt and his eyebrows raised. "Well, well, what do we have here? Are you two in trouble or somethin'?"

"We come from across the river where some slavers were holding us, but we escaped their grasp and made our way here, to the old fort."

"How in the world did you two youngins make it all the way to town from across the river without being seen or drowned?" Momentarily, he was stern, then he relaxed into a grin. "You must be one clever little fella."

"Levi Johnson is my mentor. I'm Money Penny, his apprentice. I figured the safest place for us to be right now is in one of your jail cells until Beaver comes and fetches us."

Sheriff Hand leaned back in the chair, showing a

gold chain that disappeared into a vest pocket. His shiny tin star was pinned on his chest. "Sit down, you two, and tell me everything you know about your abductors. I need to know every detail that you can remember."

"Abduc...what, Sheriff?" Money asked.

"The folks who stole you, young man."

"A buckskin-clad man by the name of Hawkeye Burns and his man Venom Grim. He's dressed more like a normal person, but they both have smooth hands, so they aren't farmers or ranchers. There were two more, but as soon as we arrived at a cabin on the other side of the river, the gang leader paid them off, and they left. When the boss came here to Fort Boise to arrange for the sale of us eight slaves, I got the drop on Ven, that's what they call him, and knocked him out."

"You mean to tell me that you knocked out one of your abductors? With as little as you are, but then again, you did say you were Levi Johnson's apprentice. I reckon he's teachin' ya quicker than he thought. How is it they didn't catch you before you could cross the river? You did say one was buckskin-clad, didn't ya? That usually means they're mountain men."

The sheriff spread his hands on the desk and leaned forward so there were no misunderstandings. "Don't you two worry a minute more. You're gonna be safe and sound here in my jailhouse with me. I usually live here anyway, of late. I'm too busy to go home, but don't you worry. I'm not going anywhere until Levi or the captain comes here and fetches you. And what have you got to say, young girl? What's your story?"

A mist of uncertainty clouded Annie's face. She didn't realize it when her voice got louder as her raw-boned jaw tightened. "My parents were killed by the

Indians who captured me and kept me as their own. The truth is, even though they murdered my folks, my Indian mother treated me like a true daughter. She claimed she never had a child of her own. After that, another Indian stole me again and sold me to the slavers. But I reckon I can't go back to her, now, can I? I don't have anybody else like Money does. What's gonna happen to me, Sheriff?"

"Did you hear that, young man. Do you know how lucky you are to have such a family to take you in?"

Money nodded so profusely, his head looked like it was on a spring. He thought it strange that a person didn't know how good they really had it until they lost it all, like him and his new friend.

"Don't you worry, little girl, we'll work something out." The sheriff's voice said he was honest and unhurried. "There are a few good husbands and wives here in Fort Boise who can't have children, and I bet one of them will take you in. We can have a word with Reverend Raymond Smith. He'll locate a good family for you here in town, so you won't have to worry anymore."

As the sheriff listened, he pushed his hat back from his forehead, easing the hot grip of the headband. It showed a white band of skin under a sun-darkened face.

They heard the faint, faraway rumble of wagons. The creaking and churning of wheels and jingling harnesses came racing by in an explosion of wood, leather, and horseflesh. The streets outside were busy with people, and they all seemed in a hurry to get somewhere. Most of the carts and carriages were to deliver supplies to the businesses. With so many overlanders, there was never a moment of peace. It suddenly dawned on Money that maybe Ven might come to town to look for them.

"I forgot to mention Mr. Farnsworth Claymore. He was the fella who was supposed to buy us. At first, we hid high in an old oak tree so nobody could find us, and we didn't leave any tracks for someone to follow. When I climbed to the top, I saw three jail wagons a way down the trail, westbound. Two of 'em were full of slaves already. I reckon Annie and I were destined for the empty one, along with the other six slaves we set free. They were all from the Yellowstone Valley tribes."

"This is sounding more serious all the time. You say you set six more slaves free? Were these White, Red, or Black folks?"

"They were from different Yellowstone Valley tribes: four Indian men and two women, plus us two White kids."

The sheriff carried a brace of revolving pistols at his sides. A Bowie knife handle stuck out from the top of his boot. Not a year ago, he had been a poor excuse for a sheriff, but during this time, he had stepped up to the challenge and proven that he deserved the badge, and the townsfolk appreciated him. He had gone from a political pawn to an experienced lawman with a set of cojones.

He officially worked for the British fur trading company, like most of those in the fort. At least that was who paid their checks to keep their business going, and they arranged for the soldiers to keep the fort from being overrun. They were sent there unofficially as Washington continued to force its agenda on the local Indians. He was voted in as the town law when he had little experience, but he had surprised one and all, and now he excelled at the job and never shied away from danger. At times, Fort Boise was a perilous place.

Dust danced in the light falling through the window, making yellow squares on the floor. More rays slanted through the open door. The sun said it was two o'clock, crowding the sky with its bright, white light.

Money sat beside Annie and could hear her hard breathing close and loud. Despite having made it to the only law within three hundred miles, she still wasn't convinced they were out of danger and on the road to a safe and ordinary life.

Money let breath pass his lips in a long sigh when he saw that Annie was still half scared to death. He didn't know what more he could do to calm her. Even now that he had led them to safety, she still had paranoia sitting perched on her shoulder.

When they walked onto the sheriff's porch and sat down, their heads swiveled from one side to the other, taking in everything they saw. The sheriff looked over everyone with an eye-squinting sternness.

Tom chewed on the end of a dead cheroot as he looked up and down the street at every person he didn't know. He pulled out a self-striking, friction match, invented by John Hucks Stevens in 1839. Smoke billowed from the phosphorus as the smell of sulfur filled the air. He ran it across the wooden plank floor and put it to the end of his cheroot. In the second, smoke swirled around his head, but he didn't take his eyes off the pedestrians on the boardwalk and on the street. He took another puff and watched with the palm of his hand shading his eyes.

WHEN ANNIE suddenly saw Ven Grim out of the corner of her eyes, she worked her mouth into a scream, but all that came out was a moan. He was the last person in the world she expected to see right there in the middle of the settlement.

"What's the matter?" the sheriff asked.

But Annie couldn't find the words. She did all she could and pointed with her finger. That was precisely when Ven locked his eyes with hers. He was almost as surprised as she was. An evil grin unconsciously crept onto his ruddy face as his fantasies bubbled to the surface. Money followed her finger and jumped up and shouted, "That's him! That's Venom Grim!"

Suddenly, Annie found herself alone on the porch when both the sheriff and Money took off running after the slaver. She wondered what in the world he was doing in town. The fact that she was sitting there alone hit her in the face like the hot kiss at the end of a wet fist. It nearly knocked her out. As chaos prevailed, she became unmindful of time.

Sheriff Hand was so drenched in the excitement of the contact as it washed through him that it took all the nervous tension along with his reason for life or death. As soon as he saw his chance, he aimed and fired a shot. The bullet was off and hit Ven in the shoulder, spinning him around like a top.

"Quick, help me grab him before he gets away," Sheriff Hand shouted. Money's actions were so adult-like that he spoke to him as an equal, forgetting he was only a little kid. He certainly hadn't hesitated when he told the sheriff to help chase an outlaw. He even pulled one of the guns he had stolen from the shed on the other side of the river.

As he held the heavy revolver on the slaver, it trembled in his hand, and his tongue slid over his cracked, dry lips.

His skin tingled as a restless urge to vomit came over him, and he had to fight it back, so he didn't embarrass himself. He had acted like a man up until now and didn't want the sheriff to think less of him.

A hint of a smile softened the straight lips of Tom's mouth. Now he understood why Levi Johnson took this young man as his apprentice. He had all the signs of an excellent choice.

"Come on, you, you're comin' with us," the sheriff said. He pushed the barrel of his gun into Ven's back and steered him toward the jail.

They saw his fear in Annie's wide-open eyes. After they shackled Ven's hands and feet and locked him up in a cell, they went out to the porch to have a cup of coffee and gave themselves some time to settle down. Annie hadn't moved from where she was sitting before. All that had happened since they arrived in town had overwhelmed her, and she was distant and alone again, lost in her own world of terror. The man who was after her to abuse her was sitting in a jail cell, not thirty feet away. Although the men thought it all fine and safe now, she lost all hope.

"You surprised me, Money. I never expected you to have so much spunk and grit when needed." Sheriff Hand smiled. "For a minute there, I forgot you were no more than a kid. Now I see why Beaver chose you, or was it you that chose him?"

Money pondered as he took a sip of coffee before he

spoke. He was proud of what he had done, even if it was more from instinct than anything else. He didn't ruin it all by saying something stupid or trying to show off.

"I did the best I could, sir. You can thank my mentor for that. I reckon he's taught me better than I thought."

THE AFTERMATH

"YOU *DO* KNOW THAT WHEN SOMETHING LIKE THIS happens, the animals go wild," Potak said. "First comes the scavengers, then the other predators that'll feed off them. It's the chain of life. Some animals even eat the turkey vultures if they can catch them off guard and grab ahold of one of their seven-foot wings. The animals won't be the only ones upset about all that mess you just saw, either," Potak said as he stared into Rusty's eyes.

When he spoke, everyone gave him their full attention. He was said to be one of the wisest men in the Rocky Mountains, and the local tribes swore he is the best medicine man within hundreds of miles. Rusty and the marshal listened with undivided attention.

"The Indians who consider this to be their hunting grounds will be angry with the buffalo hunters, too. There were sixty million buffalo here ten years ago, but now the numbers are dwindling faster every day with the endless number of White hunters coming west for the slaughter. Some say there is nearly half that now. If we're not careful, they'll follow the path of the beaver and become extinct, just like these men, who only take their hides to make blankets back east. The Indians also call them hide hunters and have a deep hate for such men. Once the word gets out, the news will go up in smoke signals, and every Indian warrior and hunter within a hundred miles will know what happened. The White men won't know it, though. They won't be able to read smoke like you and the captain. There are a few Easterners who know such secrets of the Indian Nations."

"I reckon we can add some angry warriors to the list of dangers on the way home, then," Rusty said. "If we just hunt for what we eat, the local Indians usually leave us be, but when something like this happens, every Native American that sets eyes on such a slaughter is gonna be angry with any White men they encounter, including us. What was going to be a quiet stroll home might turn into a running battle. Situations like this are heard increasingly often, and nobody living in the mountains likes it one bit. I agree that one day the bison will be gone, too. There's no end to modern man's greed. Sometimes I can't understand how they think, and I'm one of them. It almost makes me feel foreign to my own people."

"You are no longer White man or Indian, Rusty Steel. You have lived in the mountains for so long and had a Flathead wife, you are part Indian too, and from several nations. This gives you the good fortune to learn from both Red people and White. You are more like us than you realize. I can see it in your eyes."

"Maybe we'll get lucky, and they'll find the hunters that did it with the hides before they find us," Joseph said. "Then they won't be able to deny what they did. The Indians might do everyone a favor and scalp the lot. Then again, if they ventured all the way up here to hunt, it means that they'll be ready to fight, too. There's no room for daisies in these mountains. As soon as they shoot a warrior brave or two, all hell is gonna break loose, and the only safe place for us will be back in the compound, still a full day's ride away."

"Well, we're waistin' time standing here talkin'. If you wanna ride off on your own, we'll understand, Potak. No Indian tribes around here are gonna mess with a medicine man as famous as you. There's no reason for you to take such a risk. We'll take our chances on our own. Plus, we've got some meat from those bison cows. It'll be hard to deny with blood running down the flanks and rumps of our horses from the buff steaks on their backs."

"But then who is going to take care of you two?" asked Potak. Curls touched the edges of his lips. "With me, you might just make it back home in one piece. Without me, you may have to fight part of the way, if not the whole distance. There will be a lot of angry people around here soon, and they'll be looking for somebody to take their anger out on. Plus, you two only speak Crow and English. That little bit of Blackfoot and Shoshone Rusty knows will be enough if you want to be polite, but not good enough to talk your way out of a mess. Tryin' to speak a language you don't dominate usually gets you into trouble. Indian languages are complicated, and the slightest error changes a compliment into a threat or challenge."

"So, what does all this mean?" Joseph asked. "To me, you seem to talk around the answer. I know I ain't

Indian, but I can usually understand English and Bar-Chee is slowly teachin' me Crow. Are, are you comin' with us or not?"

Potak frowned when he looked at the marshal. "You're always so brash and in a hurry, Joseph. You could learn from Rusty and Beaver if you only listened. However, you *do* have a good reason. Levi, you and your family have helped me in the past, and I'm in your debt, so I will set things straight and make us even. Yes, I'll go with you, and I appreciate the invitation to the meal. Angus knows how to make the best deer steaks on the mountain. I try to never miss one of his feasts when the chance arises. If the truth be known, I'd have probably gone with you two just for Angus's cooking." He arched his back and laughed.

"I wonder how Levi is doin' findin' Money," Joseph said, trying to hide his concern.

Although it was only natural to worry and be preoccupied, the marshal was the kind of man who didn't show his feelings easily, if at all, but lately, he had been struggling, and tiny cracks in his façade began to show. New wrinkles showed on the sides of his mouth, and bags drooped under his eyes from sleeping poorly. The truth was revealed in his tired face, and for those who knew him, like Rusty, in his eyes.

"Don't fret, Joseph. I've taught him everything I know and then some," Rusty replied. "If anyone can find the boy, Levi and the captain can. It's a good thing Captain Forrester is along, too. Beaver has a kind heart and might be moved by a good story, but the captain will cut the man's throat who harmed Money, whether Beaver likes it or not. These men are not going to live after what they have done."

"Daylight's burning, gentlemen." Joseph climbed astride his horse and turned for the trail.

"I thought I was leading this party," Potak called out, again put out with Joseph.

When the marshal pulled up and turned, he saw both the Tonkawa Indian and Rusty were looking at him with perturbed expressions on their faces. Only then did he realize he had gone too far. He was in such a hurry to save Money that he had forgotten his manners and what had just been said.

"Sorry, Potak. I do appreciate you leading us. It could be a labyrinth of angry Indians, and you'll know which path to take better than me. Which way do you wanna go? Of course, you'll lead the way. Sometimes I charge off like a Spanish bull without thinking. Rusty can tell ya that. I'll try to do better next time."

Rusty was so surprised to see Joseph apologize to anyone that he burst out laughing. Potak was already tickled, so all he needed was a nudge. They ended up rolling around on the ground, holding their bellies, and all the time, Joseph with a questioning face. At times, he felt he would never understand Indian ways, and he was married to a Crow woman.

———

RUSTY PUSHED his fists into the small of his back, arching away the stiffness, and swung back into his saddle. He pulled his coat tight across his shoulders as the sun hid behind the clouds, and a chill began to set in.

"We won't travel at night because we know the warriors looking for the buffalo hunters will, and we don't want to run into them in the dark," Potak said. "It would be better to travel in daylight so they can see who I am if we encounter trouble. We don't want to hide either. We will ride the main trail. We don't want to do anything that appears suspicious."

"What about the fresh buff steaks?" Rusty asked.

"Men have to eat. We'll leave it at that. I don't want to throw them away. Remember, you invited me to dinner. Maybe even more than one if I do a good job. It is seldom that I get to eat food as good as Angus makes. He has truly adjusted to the mountain ways. Now he hardly leaves. Maybe he's discovered he likes the Indians' ways and living free, and no longer feels he has to search for peace when he already found it here.

"You sure are the philosopher today." Rusty snickered.

"But that is my job. Shamans philosophize—it's what we do."

"Lately, trouble is my middle name," Joseph huffed. "And here I thought my old life was over when I married Bar-Chee, only to have to run down wicked men to kill for what they've done to us both."

"I know it sounds easier than it is, but focus on the target, Joseph," Rusty said. "First, let's get back to the compound in one piece. Maybe by then, Beaver and the captain will have returned with Money, and you'll have been fretting for nothing. Stop runnin' around with a half-empty glass. It's better to have one that's half-full."

"What do you think about how the Indians will react, Potak?" Joseph asked as they rode right down the middle of the main and well-traveled trail back to the compound. It was a path used by them and three Indian tribes. The chances that they ran into trouble were about as high as they got.

"I would do as any Indian would do, because these men are not of my tribe. I would take revenge and instruct my people to do the same. I assure you, if we run into any Indians, they will be hostile. And if we run into the White hunters, it would be best if we shot them and took their scalps as proof. You know they're going to try to convince you and Joseph that they will have more strength in numbers, but he who sides with them will be all the tribes' enemies, and there are many more of them than there are of us. Hopefully, some Blackfeet or Shoshone will find them first and solve the problem, and it won't fall to us."

"I don't know if I can just shoot these men on the spot. I usually need to be challenged first. It sounds too much like murder to me. There's little doubt we can take 'em if we want to, but killin' 'em in cold blood. I don't know about that. Whatcha say, Marshal? This is a decision I can't make on my own."

When the marshal thought about the men who kidnapped Money, he felt the anger rise hot on his face, but he forced himself to calm down. Now wasn't the time to make rash decisions. It was time to stop charging like a bull in a china shop. He talked softer, but there was still an edge to his voice. "If we run into the buffalo hunters, I'll take care of 'em. If Rusty has a problem with that, then I'll do it myself. Just help me get the right opportunity. I can't scalp 'em, though. It's not that I mind, because they put our lives in jeopardy. I don't know how and would make a debauchery of it."

"I can do that much. Once they're dead, takin' their hair is just like skinnin' an animal, and if it means the difference in us living or dying, I don't have a problem with it at all. It's just, I never shot anyone that wasn't trying to kill me, and don't know if I can."

"My old job as marshal out of Leavenworth gave me the right to shoot any man who killed another, among other various lesser crimes. It was my job and the best way to stay alive. If every encounter were a gunfight, I'd be dead by now."

"As an Indian medicine man, I can kill none of those who follow my beliefs. I even have an acceptable relationship with Blackfeet. If we do run into anyone, other than the White hunters, whatever you do, don't go for your guns or make any threats. If you can, smile like you're strolling in the park. This will put them off guard and might make them think us innocent. Confide in me. I will talk our way out of it. We have truly done nothing wrong."

When Potak abruptly stopped, he shaded his eyes with the flat of his hand and stared into the distance, and both men automatically went for their guns. The medicine man shot them an angry look, even though he knew they did it out of habit.

"That looks like a good gully to lie up in for the night. In the deepest part, we can make a fire that can't be seen from above unless they are standing right over us. We can risk a coffee, but we should eat hardtack and stale biscuits, so we don't make too much of a smell. Remember, Indian's noses are as good as their eyes.

"I still have some sweetbread made up," Rusty said, and his stomach grumbled as if on cue.

Half an hour later, they were chewing on salted meat and gobbling down steaming hot coffee. They knew they were so tired it wouldn't keep them up. When it hit their bellies, they instantly warmed up.

Rusty sat up the remainder of the night listening to his thoughts as they flashed through his mind at a million miles per hour. Now he had two dilemmas on his mind. Money was still missing, and now they had to run the gauntlet because of a bunch of reckless buffalo hunters. He cursed himself to stay focused. If he lost his scalp, he would never see the boy again, anyway.

———

THE FOLLOWING DAY, under the blazing sun, they saw tracks of shod horses and a string of mules with deep tracks like they were heavily loaded. It was undoubtedly the hunters.

Rusty dropped and kneeled on one knee as he touched the track with his fingertips, like they had some deep, dark secret that only a few men could read. Potak kneeled beside him, scooped up a handful of dirt, and sniffed. He let it fall to the ground, filtering through his long, bony fingers.

"Everything stinks of dead buffalo carcasses. I expect that soon we'll see and hear the flies." Potak held his hand to his eyes and looked up. "The turkey vultures are already here." He stood and looked all around the sky until he saw puffs of white smoke. "And there are the smoke signals. As Levi says, the cat's out of the bag."

"They probably followed the buffalo hunters, eating what was left behind as they traveled," Rusty said. "You would think that all these critters would be over feasting on that valley full of dead bison."

"It looks like we ran into those responsible for the

slaughter before the Indians did," Joseph said. "What do you wanna do now, Potak? I don't have any ideas, but I'll shoot 'em if you want."

Potak snickered. "Well, they're in our path, and I hate to make scum like them make me stray off my planned route. Maybe we should keep going, and if they aren't camped off the trail, we might as well see what they have to say for themselves. If they're camped a distance away, we can sneak around them without them ever knowing we were there. I'm all out of ideas, too, so we'll let destiny decide for us."

Joseph shook his head and swore under his breath, but managed to hold his tongue. He was trying hard to be a better friend, but he hated people hacking on him, even if they had good reason.

In a few minutes, they had the White hunters in sight. They didn't appear to be making any effort to avoid being seen. They had a roaring fire, and they sat around the flames as they sawed in the wind, sending sparks scampering down the mountain. The smell of cooking meat was overpowering, as was the body odor of the hunters who still had bloodstains up to their shoulders. Aparejos filled with bound hides were stacked high, ready to reload on the mules first thing tomorrow.

Marshal Walker walked right up on the camp like he owned the place. He smelled of lawman, and there was an underlying authority that no one could miss.

"Afternoon, gents," Joseph greeted in a friendly tone. "And what might you fellas be up to way the hell up here? I was wonderin', are you boys the kind of fellas that walk under a flock of birds and don't expect to get shit on your faces?"

"What kind of question is that?" the hunter asked, standing and looking puzzled. "And here I was going to ask you to step down and part bread with us. I don't know about you, but I'm a Christian, and we're taught manners and treat other White men the same as we would have them treat us."

"Up here on Bear Tooth Mountain, it is only a rude man who leaves hundreds of skint buffalo to rot in the sun," Potak hissed like a viper. "Only a greedy man would take more than he needed."

"And who the hell are you? What's this heathen taking about? Why is he even talkin' at all? He looks as wild as an ape I saw back in the Chicago Zoo."

"You came all the way across the country to shoot our buffalo?" Potak spat. "Are you too stupid to make a living where you live?"

All five White hunters looked on in shock. They had never heard an Indian speak like that to a White man. The anger in their eyes was visibly apparent, but none of them moved their hands toward their weapons. The mountain men watched their every move. Even the twitch of a muscle. If they drew on them, they would have no choice but to put them down or at least try. Five against three wasn't a deadfall.

"Your buffalo? And who said that all of God's creatures belong to you?" the White hunter retorted. He growled then spat in the dirt. The friendliness in the hunter's voice disappeared as it turned coldly polite. "By my count, there are five of us and only two of you, plus that old rude Indian. He ain't a Christian. But I bet you boys are, ain't cha? Then again, maybe you ain't since you're hanging around with heathens." He scowled.

The leader of the hunters was past forty with a thin,

wizened face. When he removed his bowler hat, they saw a receding hairline. His forehead looked pale and was as white as snow. From the bright red color of his face, he wasn't used to so much sun like he found high in the mountains. Especially when it reflected off the snow. With his hat off, his head almost glowed under the sunlight, making a perfect target.

———

THE BULLET ROARED out of the barrel and closed the distance between the gun and the target as the chunk of lead shattered bone and ripped into his head, turning his brain to mush. They didn't see from where it came, but when the bullet hit the hunter's leader, his head snapped back, and his body followed. His heels dragged in the dirt and toppled him over, spread-eagled on the ground. He was dead as soon as the bullet hit him.

His four friends stood there with their mouths open and shock on their faces. Rusty and Joseph forced themselves not to touch their guns and managed to muster the most unnatural smiles imaginable. They were so surprised their feet were frozen on the spot, and luckily, none of them had the mind to go for a gun. They were totally unprepared for what was to come.

Potak turned and looked at the warriors like they were dead trees: completely free of emotion. He looked at the Blackfeet warriors like they were trespassing on his land.

"This is what you get when you come to Bear Tooth Mountain and don't respect our customs," the medicine man spat. "We don't kill animals and leave them to waste. Our people make homes and blankets from those bison, and they also supply us with ample food. You have come here to destroy this? Come on, Rusty, Joseph. This is not the place we want to be. These dogs have no respect for us humans."

Rusty and Joseph watched their faces carefully, but not one warrior gave away their feelings. The only thing they allowed the White men to see was their contempt, and this reflected in all their eyes. The marshal chanced a lightning-quick look at Rusty, but he had a shit-eating smile on his face that was almost convincing. The harder the marshal tried, the more twisted his forced grin looked. It appeared more like a grimace.

"We won't stop you and your White friends because of your fame for helping all tribes, including mine, medicine man. Potak, the Tonkawa peacemaker. That is what the Blackfeet People call you. Today, your friends are lucky. If we caught them alone, we would have killed them. We were watching when you arrived at the hunter's camp, but you didn't seem to be hiding."

"Why would I hide when I have done nothing wrong?" Potak chuckled. "Sure, we took some steaks when we found the valley of slaughtered and skinned bison, but I am sure that many other Indians did the same. It is important to try not to let it all go to waste. These men have committed a serious crime against both the Indian Nations of Yellowstone Valley and Mother Earth. They must be punished for what they have done."

As he spoke, more warriors came out of the bushes and made a tight circle around the remaining four hunters. The mountain men realized that they would have been hopelessly outnumbered hadn't they taken Potak up on his offer. He had clearly saved their lives.

Rusty's mouth was so dry his tongue stuck to the roof of his mouth, and Joseph's heart roared in his chest and hammered between his ears. Sweaty palms clutched their guns, but they refrained from pulling like Potak had warned. Rivulets of sweat ran down their backs despite the cold.

A knot tightened Rusty's mouth. Still, the smile remained, but now it didn't reach his eyes and lost its meaning. Despite his anger at what these men had done, he resisted and left his gun in its holster. He looked at Joseph, giving him a warning, and shook his head. There was no way they were going to take on so many braves and have even a minute chance of surviving.

The Shoshone had streaks of green and brown paint crisscrossing their faces, as did their ponies, which resembled sticks and flowers that blended in with the surrounding foliage. The Indians had drapes of ghostly black hair that hung around their painted faces. In the night, they were nearly invisible. That was why they hadn't seen them: that and the distraction of the discovery of the five White hunters.

One already lay dead on the ground. All the warriors were armed and had their guns and lances pointed at the hunters, but strangely enough, none at the mountain men. Maybe the Shoshone were more afraid of Potak than Rusty thought. In normal circumstances, they would also have their guns on them.

Ever since Chief Hachta died and Wanata took over, Potak assumed the role of spiritual leader for the Crow tribe, and he also kept the new chief on a tight rein. Everybody in the tribe knew that the Tonkawa shaman was more potent than the actual chief. This was something that Chief Wanata suspected, but his narcissistic ways wouldn't let him acknowledge it.

"I wonder what those Blackfoot warriors are gonna do with the other four hunters," Rusty whispered. "I doubt it's gonna be a pretty sight."

"That trash wasn't people: they're no more than prairie maggots carryin' a cross, claimin' to be better than everybody else," Rusty spat. "Back east, if they did the same thing, they'd be run out of the state as fakes. Too many folks come here and do what they can't do back home, and that ain't right. It seems like as soon as they reach the Great Plains, they forget all their laws and manners. I can tell the difference between a real Christian and a false one. All you've gotta do is compare them to Virgil, who's the real deal, and we're lucky to have him. Some folks twist their own interpretation of the Good Book to meet their own agendas, like this bunch, God save their souls."

"After they scalp them, with no hair, they will roam the spirit world, lost forever," Potak said, as a matter of fact. His false smile turned into a real one, and it reached his eyes. "This doesn't mean that we're out of the woods yet. Just because we convinced one group that we are innocent, it doesn't mean that everyone will fall for the same story. Maybe I can fix that, though."

Without explaining himself, Potak made a fire with a mix of dry green wood, as well as rotted, damp leaves, to create the dense, visible smoke needed to send signals that were visible from long distances. As he pulled out his blanket, he nodded to Rusty to help. The Blackfoot Indians watched them as everyone went still and nobody said a word. Their faces were full of curiosity. The White hunter's eyes were nearly popping out of their heads.

As they watched the Tonkawa and frontiersman busy at work, they saw the message rise high into the sky as they covered the fire with a blanket, removing it to send up individual, thick puffs. They would be seen for many miles and then relayed by more tribes to cover a vast part of the area. With one small move, Potak had secured their remaining journey home. He always seemed to know what to do, especially in dire situations.

As quickly as the rest of the war party appeared, they grabbed their prisoners, trussed them up, gagged them, and ran off with them on poles like pigs on spits. Nobody said another word as they shuffled into the night. One of the hunters managed to cry out, but a stout bash of a tomahawk to his head stifled the sound. No one knew exactly what they had planned for them, but they were sure it would be very creative. The four men alive would suffer a long and painful death.

Squinting, they studied the riders on the ponies as they rode off. Joseph took a moment to look away, but when he looked back, they had nearly vanished. He had to squint to see the last black dot disappear over a fold in the land. Thunder rumbled overhead, and a minute later, it began to rain. At first, it came down in big drops exploding on the ground, but it quickly wore itself out and turned into a warm drizzle. They removed their hats and turned their faces to the heavens as the rain washed away the dirt and sweat.

It hissed when it hit the flames and threatened to douse the fire. They had a moon, so they all stayed gathered within the circle of glowing cinders of the now crackling flames as they leaped up, sending cinders into the sky, only to disappear a few yards over their heads. Beads of water accumulated on the grizzly bear blankets as comets raced across the sky high above the rain clouds.

———

THE FOLLOWING DAY, they rode into the compound. The rain had washed away the blood down the flanks and rumps of the horses and the hands and faces of the men. Joseph's eyes were full of worry and expectation. As soon as they walked their horses into the corral, he said, "Take care of my horse for me, will ya, Rusty? I've gotta know if they found Money or not."

"I'll do it for you," Potak said, smiling. It was the first time he had looked at the marshal that way. "Go ahead now and ask about your child, but if he's not here yet, keep your faith in Levi and the captain. As long as I've known them, they never fail when it's important."

Of course, there had been no sign of Levi or the captain. The mood among the compound's members was somber. Only Angus was as cheerful as always, especially with such an important guest who had come to eat his food. He couldn't think of a better compliment. He didn't worry about Money because he knew that the man who lived with a heart full of worry was a weak man. What would come, would come, and there was nothing anyone could do about it.

He and Potak dined alone that evening. They didn't let the absence of the others bother them, though. They were too old and wise.

FOLLOW THE LEADER

LEVI'S FACE SAGGED, AND HE SAID, "IT'S TIME TO GET TO work. We're never gonna catch up with him sittin' here."

Levi's jaw had a mouthful of canteen as his eyes opened as wide as his mouth. His sunburned face showed through his scraggly beard. They had their hats pushed back on their heads and were dirty and tired.

The captain's face was beard-stubbled. He rubbed his face, brushed his blond mustache with his knuckles, and frowned.

"Don't tell me, you wanna shave." Suddenly, the amusement from Levi's eyes was gone, and his mouth tightened. He tried to make light of things, but it was hard with what they were looking at. Levi had managed to follow the tracks of the outlaw mountain man. His accomplice had run, making them pick one, the leader of the gang. When they got back to Fort Boise, they would probably find Ven, in a brothel or drunk in some bar.

The captain knew the type. When facing the crossing of the Oregon Trail, a few shots of whiskey were easy to make him put off the laborious journey another day. He had probably been paid, and the money was burning a hole in his pocket.

"I figure that Hawkeye is the biggest threat," Levi said. "If Ven gets away, it won't be long before someone shoots him if he's not traveling with his boss. We need to focus on the man who runs the show so we can stamp it out once and for all."

They rode all day long until Levi dropped to the ground and looked up and said, "These tracks are so fresh I can smell his buckskins. He's no dummy. He's runnin' all right. We should be seeing him in the distance at any time now."

When they caught their first glimpse of the sun reflecting off metal, they knew their target was just ahead of them, but still out of rifle range. Levi looked at the captain and nodded, and they broke into a gallop.

"He knows somebody is gonna be comin', but I don't think he knows how close we are, or he'd be pushing his horse harder. If we can sneak up on him from behind and get close enough for a shot, we might be able to end this before he reaches the Boise Foothills and then the Boise and Rocky Mountains, and we will never find him."

They had to catch up and finish this now, or they might lose their last chance at getting restitution. They still didn't know if Money was alive or not. They knew after so much time that he could easily already be dead.

When they saw they were advancing on the outlaw, they dug in their spurs. It was a race to get close enough to shoot before he disappeared into the deeper woods and mountains. He was a good tracker, and anyone less than Levi never would have found his sign. That's what they were counting on. If he was so good, he wouldn't think that anyone could pick up his scent.

After an hour pushing their horses to their limits, they pulled up to a sliding stop. They watched the black speck that gradually grew as they got nearer. Finally, the black dot turned into a horse and rider. Right then, Levi knew who it was. He kicked his leg over Trigger's neck and slid to the ground, covering his moccasins in mud. He pulled his rifle from its sheath, and he leaned against a rock where he lay his bedroll to rest the fore-stock as he peered down the telescope. He was riding away from them, and he was almost out of range, even for Levi.

"It was strange that he didn't turn around and look to see if we were following."

"With the snow wet, there was no dust cloud. Maybe he looked, and we didn't see him. For a long time, he's been in and out of sight."

"Should I take a chance and try to catch him or take a shot from here?" Levi asked.

"You'd save a lot of riding if you shot him now, but you'd best get to it or he'll be more than a thousand yards out," the captain said. "That is your record, isn't it?"

"Once I hit a buff from a thousand two hundred yards, give or take ten yards. He's not movin' around or anything, so I should be able to hit him, but not if I wait too long."

The sky burst into a pink, rose, and crimson prism as the sun began to sink. It stretched to the western horizon. Levi knew that it was right now, or never. If he didn't make the shot, Hawkeye Burns might just get away. Then who would be left alive to tell them where little Money was?

Beaver opened the fifty-two-caliber, inserted a round, and levered it into the chamber, then rested his finger on the safety trigger as he scoured the country before him and the single silhouette in the distance. Levi pulled a tuft of grass and dropped it, checking the direction and strength of the wind. As he inhaled a deep breath, he pulled the safety trigger. The click was hardly audible. Then he slipped his finger back into the trigger guard and rested it on the firing trigger.

He clearly outlined the silhouette and centered his sights, adjusting for the wind and the terrain. He was slightly higher than where they squatted. The captain sat on his boot heels as he waited for the bang.

Levi's eyes glowed orange like branding irons in a fire. "This should tell the story." Levi emptied his lungs and pulled the trigger.

The BOOM echoed across the countryside. They waited, looking through their spyglasses, to see if the bullet hit its mark.

"One thousand, one. One thousand, two, one thousand, three," Levi counted under his breath.

The pony's front knees buckled, and it tumbled its rider head over heels.

"Damn," Levi growled as he slipped a three-inch bullet and slammed it home, returning the rifle to its resting place to take the second shot.

They couldn't believe their eyes when Hawkeye jumped up and started dancing like a chicken, with his thumbs in his armpits, flapping his wings. It was clear that he believed it to be a lucky shot to hit the horse.

"Now let's see who the smart ass is. I reckon I'm gonna have to toot him back," Levi said.

The rifle BOOMED again, making birds break from cover not a hundred feet away, and they all flapped in a frenzy to escape what they took as predators. But Levi and the captain were only there for one man. The person who was personally responsible for taking his apprentice against his own will, and who knew what else they did to him.

Levi laid his rifle down and grabbed his collapsible spyglass, watching the black dot acting a fool a thousand yards away. When the 50-90 Sharps round hit him, it knocked him backward fifteen feet. The heavily charged bullet exploded in his chest. He was dead before he flew through the air like a magician.

They sat and waited for twenty minutes, their eyes glued to their telescopes, but they didn't see a muscle twitch on Hawkeye Burns's body. Finally, they stood, walked back to their horses, and forked astride, turning them for their target. They still had to confirm it was him and that he was indeed dead.

When they slowly walked their horses to where the dead man lay, it struck Levi as strange. Lying there, face down, it almost looked like him, but this man had taken another path in life and had ultimately paid the price.

"It's too bad you shot his horse," Will replied. "We will have to make a travois. I don't want that stinky body on the back of my horse.

"We won't get too far tonight. The moon won't be up for a while yet," Levi said.

"We might as well call it a night and get a full night's sleep. We haven't slept for eight hours in weeks."

MARSHAL JOSEPH
WALKER

IT WAS LATE AT NIGHT, AND THE COMPOUND WAS
uncannily quiet. Not even the owls cooed to their mates
in the dark. Old Dog, Rusty's canine companion, didn't
even snore. As quietly as he could, Joseph slipped out
from under the covers and rolled off his bedroll. He
glanced at Bar-Chee. She had her back turned and
breathed slowly in and out, in a deep slumber. It was
unusual not to hear the mice scampering around the
house at night. His ears were so focused that he could
hear a pin drop.

Silver light from the moon's rays spilled through the
window, providing enough light for the marshal to
make his way through the cabin without bumping into
anything. Virgil was sound asleep in his bunk in the
back corner, by the cast-iron cookstove. He was hardly
visible under the thick grizzly bear blanket.

When the planks groaned under the marshal's feet,
he froze like his blood turned to ice. He held his breath
and looked over his shoulder. He was startled when he
saw Virgil snort twice, then began to toss and turn, until

he finally settled in again and began to breathe deeply and long. Joseph took another step, as the wood planks gave, but nobody woke up, despite the noise.

Often, Bar-Chee and Joseph slept in their teepee in the compound yard. As a couple, they needed their privacy, but since Money was taken, Joseph wanted to make sure that one of the men was always close by. He not only worried about her safety but was also afraid she might strike out on her own to save her newfound child. Of course, logic would tell her that it was an impossible task, but to a grieving mother, this mattered little. There was no logic in the equation. He knew she was ready to give her life for her boy, even though he wasn't hers by blood.

When Joseph got to the window beside the entrance, he had a glance outside. Everything was bathed in silver light. The full moon was so bright it almost looked like dawn. Far above the white orb were millions of twinkling stars. They looked like tiny fireflies in the heavens.

When he lifted the door latch, it clicked, making the marshal freeze again, turning his head. He shrugged off his paranoia and opened the door just enough for him to slip through, and closed it again before the cold night breeze ruffled someone's feathers, and they woke up. It looked like he had made it without a hitch, just like he had planned.

Boot heels softly clopped across the wooden porch. It seemed that everywhere he stepped, he made noise. Then he dropped off the porch into the thinning cover of snow. Slosh stuck to his boots as he headed for the stables through the corral. As soon as he opened the barn door, the horses began to nicker and blow as their attention turned toward the noisy intrusion. Their ears rotated independently, a hundred eighty degrees. They could hear both lower and higher frequencies than humans. While not possessing as fine a dog's sense of smell, their hearing was far superior to a man's.

Marshal Walker carried his sawed-off double-barreled shotgun in his fist, and a brace of Colt Patter-sons hung from holsters at his waist. A Sharps rifle was in his other hand. The moon shone against his face, and it only took a glance to see he was ready for war. There was a dark, determined glare that wasn't there before.

He had made the decision the previous evening as he watched his wife burst out in tears, yet again. At this point, he wondered if she would take her life if Beaver and the captain didn't return with her adopted son. The attachment was as if she had given birth herself. She was all consumed by the loss, even though before the boy, she had accepted that she would never have children. She and Joseph had never spoken of the possibility until Money arrived for their adoption.

Sure, the marshal was attached too, but he knew he could never feel what a mother felt. That much he understood from his own mom and family. Way back before he was a territorial marshal out of Cantonment, Leavenworth, he felt the pain deep in his soul, but his heart wasn't broken like Bar-Chee's was. Joseph felt that if the boy were truly lost, he would also lose his wife. Then, he, too, might suffer from a broken heart. She was the mate he always wanted but never had the time for. For her hand in marriage, he had fought for his life against her brother to win the right. He was the Crow stronghold's chief.

All this was why he decided to risk his life and make

a desperate attempt on his own to find his son and bring him back to his wife and mother. Only then would things return to how they were before Money was taken. Deep down, he knew that what he was about to do had little logic and was doomed to failure, but he felt he must do it nonetheless. For one time in his life, he wasn't going to act like a lawman and instead would act like a grieving father: dangerous and out of control. All those rules he had taught and abided by for all those years were just about to go out the window. He just realized that love was a thicker bond than any human law.

When he rode his sixteen-hand quarter horse out of the barn, he had to duck to keep from hitting his head as he tightened the reins. In his other hand, he held the lead of his backup horse. He knew if he didn't have two, he could ride one horse to death. As it was, neither one might be able to continue the journey once they hit Fort Boise.

He had no idea how far he would have to ride, but it didn't matter. Joseph would ride south to the end of the world if he had to. There was no distance too far or mountain too high. He didn't plan to ease up even if both animals died on the way, and he was forced to go it on foot. Once he was in the corral, he wheeled toward the gate, removing the hemp rope loops and swinging it open just enough to get by, then he closed it behind him.

He didn't bother hiding his tracks. As soon as his friends awoke, they would know what had happened and where he had gone. Fort Boise was the only reference he had, so he would begin his search there. The marshal knew that he couldn't think farther ahead than that and had to take one step at a time. If he let the enormity of the challenge sink in, he wouldn't be able to organize his thoughts, and what he needed now was to be precise and fast, without allowing anything to distract or hinder him. Anyone who stepped in his way would die.

Lucky for him, the only one in the compound with the skills to track him was Rusty. Angus had the knowledge, but he was too old to run down a man at his age. Rusty would stay behind because he knew that if someone attacked the compound, he would be needed to lead the defense. Plus, he and Angus were probably the only ones to understand and knew they had no say in the matter. Every man had to make his own decisions in life, especially in a situation so dire.

As soon as he rode out of the south gate, he began his bumpy descent down the steep trail as he stood in his stirrups. Soon, he was snaking down the worn path a hundred feet below the edge of the compound and the south gate. Soon, he would be home free without being discovered, or so he thought.

In the shadows near the south entrance, someone moved. Even though the marshal had thought he was alone, that wasn't the case. After he was far enough away, Bar-Chee walked out of the shadows and looked down at her husband as he picked his way through the squiggly brush crowding the trail far below.

Somehow, she knew what he was going to do, perhaps even before he knew. The previous evening, before dinner, she had noticed the change in his demeanor. He hardly spoke, and when he did, he was gruff, as though he was angry, perhaps with himself. She waved goodbye even though she knew he couldn't see her and blew him an invisible kiss. She sniffled, but she didn't cry anymore. Now, they were totally invested.

For some reason, she felt that her husband would make the difference, even though he wasn't half the tracker and mountain man that the captain and Levi were. Still, she knew something else. The marshal was the only killer, like a White warrior, and she believed he had a better chance than the others, because if needed, he would become ruthless. She not only wanted her son, Money back, she also wanted those responsible, dead, and Joseph was the only one hard enough to do it, even if he caught them alive. His Crow wife knew that once he found them, they would walk this earth no more.

Joseph rode the rest of that night and continued after the sun rose. He only stopped when he had to change horses, water, feed the animals, and give them a short rest. When he felt it was safe, he dozed off and on in the saddle, refusing to give in to exhaustion, and carried on. He had always chased outlaws with unmatched vigor, but this time it was personal, and the law mattered little to him any longer. He planned to rescue Money, kill the men who were responsible for stealing him, and take him home to his mother, alive. Before he could bring him back in a shrouded wrap, he would die himself. If Money was already dead when he arrived or sold to an untraceable source, he would kill every last man who aided in his capture, resulting in his death. Then, everyone who ever laid eyes on him would die.

Joseph removed his hat and looked up at the heavens and said, "I swear to this, with the last breath I take. Every man, or even woman, who had a hand in this will die. If I find my little Money, dead, their families go with them. I'll teach them how it feels to be cheated out of your loved ones, and I don't care how many there are." He knew right then and there that if he lost Money, he would never be happy again, because he would surely lose Bar-Chee too.

On the sixth day, the spare horse suddenly dropped to the ground, spilling the marshal off in a puff of sludgy snow. He crawled out from under the animal and stroked its neck, whispering calming words into its ear. The horse blew and squealed one last time and gave up his ghost, and his eyes rolled back into his head. He had breathed his previous agonal breath. Joseph had run him to death, but he knew the risks when he started. No matter what happened on the way, he wouldn't stray off his target.

Marshal Walker stood over the animal and recited a short prayer he had learned from Virgil Lovejoy. It appeared that some of his religious ways were rubbing off on the most unlikely member of the compound. Then again, maybe losing Money had changed him in little ways. Now he knew about a thing called hope, and that was pretty much all he had. That and a burning anger for revenge, unlike he had ever felt. He knew that with such acts, he would no longer be a religious man, but he couldn't change who he was any more than he could change the color of the sky.

Joseph knew he didn't want to lose his second horse. He had been riding his American Quarter Horse for years and wasn't ready to part ways, so he slowed his pace from a gallop to a trot and gave him more downtime to rest. If the truth were known, the marshal's age was rearing its ugly head, and he, too, was tiring more than he had expected. He suddenly realized that maybe he was too tired to walk so far and was even more careful. If he didn't arrive at his destination, failure was inevitable, so he knew he couldn't let his anger take over and had to use his head.

For the last two days, he had been running on pure adrenaline and nothing more. Something that would not have happened a decade before. He was getting on in years, but was yet to be an old man, but still, he knew that, like the spare horse, they all had their limits, and if he pushed himself too hard and died on the way, he wouldn't save anyone, and he would die a disgrace.

After all he had done and been through. Would this be the straw that broke the camel's back? He quickly pushed the thought out of his mind and scolded himself. He had never been one to tolerate negative thoughts, and now wasn't the time for him to start.

———

WHEN ANGUS WENT OUT, headed for the outhouse for his morning leak, he noticed Bar-Chee sitting on her porch staring through the trees. He wondered if she had spent the night there crying like she had for days on end. But upon closer inspection, he saw that her eyes were dry, although baggy. There were wrinkles on her face that weren't there a month ago. But now there seemed to be a different air about her. She seemed to have a positive note on her face today. Yesterday, she was full of dread and negativity.

He turned right and used the well-worn path between the cabins. When he was just about to arrive, Virgil walked out the door while slipping his suspenders over his shoulders with his thumbs. He looked at Bar-Chee, then turned his head to Angus. He knew he was always up early to prepare breakfast. At his age, cooking for the compound was his only job, but as their numbers grew, he was busy all the time.

It had been a couple of years since he had ventured down to Fort Boise and back, and he doubted he would do so again before he died. He risked the rare buffalo hunt if the herds were nearby, but beyond that, he was happier in the compound with his family. This was his peaceful place and was where he would stay until the end, when he too would be put to rest with his brothers, under a white cross in the small cemetery in the corner of the compound. The numerous grave markers indicated that he would have plenty of company from old friends.

"Whatcha doin' up so early, Bar-Chee?" Angus asked in a soothing voice. "Why, it ain't even daylight yet. You should be in bed asleep with your husband to keep you warm."

"That was what I was just about to ask," Virgil added. "And where's the marshal? He ain't in bed. I checked."

When Bar-Chee first answered, they couldn't make out what she said. She spoke in a light whisper, as though if she spoke up, she would break some spell.

"What did you say, darlin'?" Angus asked. "You'll have to speak up a little. I can't hear as well as I used to."

"I said that Joseph went to get Money." This time, she said it so loud that she startled herself. Bar-Chee hadn't meant to shout, but it just came out with all the emotions she was feeling right then.

"What in tarnation has that fool gone and done

now? I told Rusty that was going to happen, but he told me every man had the right to deal with his problems as he saw fit. What kind of an answer is that for a friend to say?"

"The right one," Bar-Chee replied. "You've never had children, Angus, so you don't know what it's like. The rules change when it's your young boy who has gone missing. That's something that you'll never understand. Joseph did the only thing we could have done. I'd be with him myself if I didn't slow him down. I want revenge for what was done to us, and my husband will assure us that restitution will be ours. I know that Joseph is an angry man. Now it is time to turn that anger toward something deserving."

By then, everybody had heard Bar-Chee yell, and they all jumped out of bed and headed for the noise. Rusty came out with a brace of heavy Colt Walkers in his hands, thumbing back the hammers, ready to fight. They hung by his sides in anticipation as he stood frozen with a puzzled look on his face.

"Put those guns away, Rusty," Angus growled. "Just like we said he would do, the marshal's run off."

"It's about time he got off his lazy ass and did something," Rusty growled. "I know I would have. Whatcha think, Bar-Chee? Did he do the right thing or not?"

She was surprised that Rusty was taking her side instead of Angus's, so she just nodded her head, but her eyes were full of gratitude.

Finally, she muttered, "Thank you, Rusty. Yes, he did do the right thing. He did the only thing he could. If I were him, I would have done the same. But I am a woman and not even a warrior like Dahteste, so he did what was best."

"So, you have talked about this, have you?" Dahteste asked.

"No. We never exchanged a word. I think I knew he would do it before he did, though. He snuck off this morning thinking I was still asleep, but I was pretending. Is that the right word?"

"It is," Virgil replied. "He did right, ma'am. Joseph wouldn't have been able to live with himself had he not gone. For a man like him, he had no choice. Beware, the men who cross his path. Deep down inside, the marshal is still that lawman he was, and he won't retreat until his business is completely done. I guess between Levi and the captain and now the marshal, the kidnappers' chances are getting slimmer all the time."

Angus huffed and puffed, but there was nothing left to say. Joseph had taken off on a wild-goose chase, and there was no getting him back, though nobody could blame him. But he wasn't like Beaver or even Captain Forrester. They knew how to live off the land. They had been Rusty's apprentices and learned every lesson he had to give, and Levi, even some that he didn't teach him.

Beaver was a natural when the captain had to struggle with himself to learn everything his best friend did, but he was so determined that he always kept up, even though he was missing an arm. That gave him all that much more credit for his accomplishments. He acted like his lost appendage didn't hamper him in the least and had apparently even convinced himself that it didn't matter. He did his job as well as ever, so nobody could complain.

"Well, now that we're all awake, I might as well put a kettle of coffee on." Angus stepped off the porch and scurried out of Virgil's cabin to his own and disappeared behind the open door. He slammed it with a bang to accentuate his anger. Still, he knew as well as anyone, in the wilderness, a man did what he felt he had to do, even if it didn't make any sense. He couldn't remember the countless times he had done foolish things himself. Back then, they didn't have a mentor and had to learn everything on their own.

THE HUNT

MARSHAL WALKER TOOK NINE DAYS TO MAKE IT TO FORT Boise, and he nearly killed both himself and his horse in the process. When he was younger, near Fort Leavenworth, he could ride for nine days in one direction and turn around, doing it again without stopping for a whole night and getting a good rest. Now, as he passed the fifty-year mark, he noticed in the small things that he was beginning to slow down. He wasn't as spry and chipper as he had been five years prior.

He knew he would have to stop in Fort Boise, even if he obtained information on Money the moment he arrived, neither his body nor his horse could do what they both did half a decade prior. He needed to brush his mount down, hang a feed sack around his neck, and let him rest in the town's stables, where it was warm at night.

Joseph would put up for the night in the fort's boarding house. He needed the downtime almost as badly as his horse. It wasn't a luxury hotel, but it was better than the bunkhouse with the poor overlanders and the odd cowboy heading for California to work as a buckaroo on the West Coast ranches. The promises and stories the newspapers wrote about the Oregon Trail drew people like magnets, luring them with an impossible dream. The wagons continued to roll along in the hundreds for the end of the trail and whatever reality awaited them beyond. That is, if they made it.

Joseph had planned to go straight to his room and to sleep for a full eight straight hours, but his mouth was so dry from riding for days that he was dying for a whiskey to cut through the trail dust. It was caked in his mouth like hardening mud. When he spat, his saliva was a brownish color.

Joseph left his saddlebags with the receptionist at the boarding house and walked across the fort yard to McKay's Saloon. Perhaps Charlie could offer some insight into Levi and the captain's whereabouts. Buckboard wagons raced up and down the front of the business, delivering more merchandise to be sold to the overlanders. Wagon after wagon unloaded as they brought goods from large warehouses. They could hardly keep up with the demand. The owners and wholesalers were making money hand over fist.

People of all ages, colors, races, and genders filled the compound yard. There was a constant flow of humans passing in and out of the main gates. It was the only way in and out, and covered wagons traveling the Oregon Trail jockeyed for positions closest to the entrance as they loaded up their wagons and pack mules with supplies.

When he walked into the settlement's largest establishment, McKay's Trading Post, Saloon, and Restaurant, he saw Charlie, the bartender, straight away. He had a line of overland customers a mile long and was working as fast as he could. From exhaustion, Joseph plopped down on the nearest chair to wait.

Finally, Charlie looked over and said, "Grab a bottle, Marshal. Mark the label for me and help yourself."

Without a moment's hesitation, Joseph stepped up to the bar, reached over, and grabbed a whole bottle. "You'll know how much I owe you by how much I drink." He popped the cork and helped himself to a glass.

He turned the bottle up, as his Adam's apple bobbed up and down, and the sour taste of spirits filled his nose and mouth. Before he set it down, he had drunk two fingers of store bought whiskey. Suddenly, he could breathe again. The harsh liquor cleaned his clogged pipes and opened his eyes as it burned down his throat. He grabbed a glass and dropped back into the same chair. Now, he calmly poured another glass and sipped on the bitter spirits. He knew he should be back in the boarding house, asleep, but now the refreshment woke him up again.

When the line of people waiting for drinks dwindled, Charlie finally had a chance to welcome his friend.

"Whatcha doin' here all alone, Marshal Walker? Levi and the captain left a few days ago. They hung out in town for quite a while, trying to gather information. I hope you weren't hopin' to catch up with 'em. They told me what happened. It's a damned shame, is what it is. Why would someone steal your boy? Your misses must be frightened to death. If there's anything I can do, just let me know."

"Do you know if Beaver and Will found out

anything about the kidnappers or suspicious characters in the settlement? Somebody must know when there's slavers in town."

"Hell, I didn't even know there were any White slavers in these parts. I thought all the child theft was between the tribes as they try to repopulate their camps from warriors killed in action. This ain't the case this time, though. I wonder what kind of man would want to steal a young boy, and for what. That's what I can't figure out."

"When I was working back in Leavenworth, there were such men. Some had spent too long in prison, and when they got out, they did terrible things to adults and children. Maybe it's something like that. All I know is that we've got to find Money before he completely disappears from these parts, then we'll never find him."

"I wouldn't worry so much if Beaver is on their trail. Not even Rusty Steel, his mentor, can track like him. With the captain along, they'll take on just about anybody who might go against them. I didn't know you were a tracker too, Marshal."

"I *ain't* a tracker like them, but I've chased down enough outlaws to know where to start. I was hopin' I'd run into Levi and Will here in Fort Boise, but it looks like I'm too late, don't it? They didn't mention where they were going, did they?"

"Why, they didn't even say they *were* goin'. One minute they were here and the next they were gone. I don't think that they told anyone where they were headed, or I'd have heard. This is the center for territorial gossip, ya know. If I were you, I'd go down to the waterfront and ask around," Charlie leaned in and whispered. "The fishermen who live on the riverbanks know about everybody who comes and goes by ferry. At least that gives you a place to start."

"Well, it's too late now. I've been ridin' hard for nine days and I've gotta get some shuteye or I won't be able to think straight tomorrow. When a man goes asking questions, it's best to keep an eye on who you're talking to. At least I'll be able to find out if anyone suspicious has been snoopin' around of late. If you don't know anything here, maybe they will."

———

IT FELT like Joseph had just fallen asleep when he heard a rooster crow and sunlight from the open window warm his face. When he opened his eyes, the room was cold enough that the marshal could see his breath, but he slept best in a cool night breeze. He never noticed the chill buried deep under a thick grizzly bear blanket. He took a deep breath of fresh air and sighed as he suddenly remembered where he was and why he was there.

The marshal looked down and saw that he still had his boots on. He swung his feet to the floor and rubbed his eyes with balled-up fists. He suddenly realized that time was ticking by, and he still didn't have any information about where Money was or even where Levi and Will had gone three days prior.

That was yesterday. Today makes four days, he thought.

Joseph stood to his feet, unhooked his gun belt from a coat rack, and strapped it around his waist. Then he checked both guns to ensure they were loaded and ready to fire. He had the feeling that soon he was going to need his six-shooters. He was prepared to fight and didn't plan to take no for an answer when questioning the people who lived along the convergence of the Boise and Snake Rivers. He knew he had to take the gloves off if he wanted to find Money in time to save his life. There would be no more Mr. Good Fellow.

Before he headed for the short walk to the river, he stopped in to see Charlie again for a morning coffee. No matter when he went to the McKay's Saloon, he seemed to always be behind the bar. If he didn't know about any gossip regarding Money, nobody within the fort walls would know anything unless they were involved in the crime. It didn't hurt to ask him one more time before he started to check the town, house by house, business by business. Maybe he had seen or heard something last night.

His silver US Marshal's star had tarnished, but that morning, before he went out, for the first time in months—if not years—he polished it to a gleaming shine. It flashed in the sunlight on his vest. He knew kidnapping a White child was a crime no matter where you lived, so he was going to use his marshal's badge to do what he had to do, no matter how the cards fell.

Marshal Walker had the sort of face that needed the brim's shadows to soften his hard, strong features and hard lines. If you didn't know him, you would think he was the kind of lawman who liked doing his job, and those who objected paid the price dearly.

As soon as Marshal Walker leaned his arm on the edge of the bar, Charlie rushed over.

"I heard tell that the slaver is here in town—or at least he was. That means he must know you're here, too, by now. I have no idea where he is, but they say he was fillin' three jail wagons full of prisoners. They claimed they were Indians who ran off their reservations and were being sent to a new plot of land out west. That's why there was a mix of men and women. They didn't mention anything about a child, but someone I spoke to did. A fellow by the name of Ven came in here to have a drink after all this happened, saying there was a White boy with blond hair and blue eyes. That sounds like Money. There was a White girl too, a little younger than your son."

"Did this fella say anything else, Charlie?" Joseph asked. He could feel his heart hammer in his chest.

"I think he realized he had already said too much, 'cause he was drunk, and paid his bill and ran off. I never saw him again. I reckon he must have had something to do with all this. Who else would know such a thing?"

"Let me go and have a walk around town to see if I notice any faces I've seen on wanted posters in the past. I've still got to go down to the dock to ask around, too. Now I have some food for thought."

When Joseph reached the double doors, the marshal's eyes continued to scan the distance from inside the saloon. As the country yawned wide, his eyes inched over the expanse. He carefully pinpointed the positions of two riders. On the outer rim of the fort campsites, he saw two men with badges. From the look of their horses, they had been riding long and hard.

Both lawmen looked hard-shelled and mean and carried more guns than was usual. Bullet belts crisscrossed their chests like they were headed for war, as was sometimes seen on Mexican banditos or rebels against the state, south of the border.

When the riders came into shouting distance, Marshal Walker took a step forward into the mud. Little white snow remained as brown slosh covered his boots.

"You two might think you have everybody else buffaloed, but not me, not by a long shot." The marshal gave them an alarming smile. "You don't remember me, do you, Sam? And you, Earl? Why do I remember both of you?"

"Oh God," Charlie said, cursing, but his words sounded more like a prayer.

Both strangers were tight-jawed and solemn. They made no effort to answer, knowing it was now or never. They had confidence that at least one of them would live, if not both. With two against one, they felt the odds were in their favor.

Marshal Walker hoped he was right as he squinted down the barrels and his fingers took in the slack on the triggers. The pistols bucked in his hands, and the riders were knocked off their horses like they were hit in the chest with a sledgehammer. Both shots hit their marks simultaneously, dead center in their hearts.

"Why in the world did you do that, Marshal Walker?" asked Charlie.

"Because they weren't marshals, for one. They were just pretending. What better way for wanted outlaws to ride across the country than acting like they're the law? I recognized them both from my marshaling days, and they both have money on their heads. I'm pretty damned sure they were sent here to get me out of the way, since I've been askin' questions about my stolen boy. Whoever sent them is our man, and he's movin' quick."

"But if they're both dead, how are we gonna find out?"

"Come with me, Charlie, quick. Maybe if the man who hired them doesn't know they're both dead, he might just show himself. Where the hell is Sheriff Hand when you need him?"

The citizens looked dumbfounded as the marshal pushed his hat back from his forehead. Sun glinted off the shiny badges of the dead men: the *supposed* marshals.

"Somebody call Dr. Jason Betz. We've got a wounded man here," Marshal Walker shouted. "Keep back, folks, this ain't a circus. Now go on with your business and let me take care of mine. They weren't marshals after all. They're both wanted men. I'm pretty sure I can get the one left alive to talk."

Marshal gave Charlie a conspiring look and winked. He had to admit, when it was important, he caught on quickly.

Unfortunately, the man they saw running toward the dead men wasn't the doctor. He was tall with a stern face, fiery gray eyes, bushy eyebrows, and short hair under a wide-brimmed hat. It was Pastor Raymond Smith, just the man they didn't want there at that moment.

"Stand back, Pastor Smith. We're carryin' on an investigation here. There's no need to interfere. Your time will come, soon enough." Joseph still had his revolvers in his hands, and the smell of cordite was strong.

"But you called for the doctor. Maybe the dying man will want to confess before he passes."

"Nobody else is gonna die," Joseph said.

"But they're wearing badges, and neither one of them looks to be alive to me. Are you sure they're not dead?"

"Come with us for a moment, Raymond," Marshal Walker said, leading him by the shoulder. "We know they're both dead, but we can't let anyone else know. These men were sent to kill me for trying to find the men who stole my son. That much we can see as clear as day. As soon as they rode into town, they came right for me. I recognized their faces from wanted posters. We're not the bad men, here, pastor. We're on the good side. Sometimes a lawman's gotta tell a little fib, to save a life, and this is one of those times. To make it worse, it's my son they stole."

"You might not like this, but there's a life at stake, and this little trick might save two children," Charlie whispered. "The only way we're gonna trick the kidnappers to scare them enough to come out of hiding is for them to think one of the men they sent to kill the marshal might talk. If I'm not mistaken, it'll be like walking into a dark room with a light. Cockroaches will be crawling out of the woodwork."

"Once we're done, you can say a few words over their graves up on Boot Hill," the marshal said. "But mark my words, Reverend, these are evil men who have done despicable things. There was no room for mercy for them."

SHERIFF TOM HAND

WHEN MARSHAL WALKER HEARD A GUNSHOT, HE RAN FOR the saloon exit. He hit the batwing doors so hard that one flew off its hinges and clattered across the floor. He pulled his pistols as he scoured the street. When he saw people running in panic, he turned to look for the source of the shot. His eyes locked with those of the Fort Boise sheriff.

"It's him, Ven Grim!" Sheriff Hand shouted as gun smoke rolled from his barrel and pointed with his finger. "Quick, Marshal, grab him before he gets away!"

As soon as Joseph heard the shout, he turned and spotted the man with a bloody shoulder. He instantly knew that this was one of the two that nabbed his son. The gunshot man had his back to the marshal as he tried to hide in the crowd and limp away, but he came upon him hard from behind, like a steamroller.

After quickly slipping his guns into his holsters, Joseph waded into Ven Grim, clubbing his back and then his face with his hammer-like fists. He backed him into a corner and hit him with a roundhouse haymaker and then an uppercut that jarred his teeth and lifted him off his feet. His eyes rolled back in his head, and he slumped to the ground.

The marshal grabbed him by his hair and jabbed him three times more, flattening his nose. When he nudged him with his toe to see if he was still alive, he moaned. For good measure, he kicked him in the gut. Just as he raised his foot to stomp him on the head, he heard a familiar voice yell in a panic.

"Marshal, stop, you're gonna kill him!"

If the sheriff hadn't been there, he would have beaten him to death. Just one look in Joseph's eyes told the story. They were glazed and full of violence. He looked like a bull standing there, huffing as his chest rose up and down. In the cool air, puffs of steam came from his nose.

The marshal thought about what the sheriff said, but it just made him angrier. He pulled his guns while drawing back the hammers, ready to fire. He wanted to see life go out of this Venom's eyes. He was so furious he hardly remembered who he was.

"Don't make me pull on ya, Joseph! We're friends and we have no cause to fight. Now simmer down, and we can take this person to the doctor and then to jail. If you kill him, right in front of me, you'll go to prison. You know that I can't lie in a court of law. You know the rules better than I do. When they lock you up and throw away the key, who's gonna take care of Money?"

"Money?" Joseph whispered as he tried to blink away the fury. "Have you heard something about my son?"

Just as quickly as the marshal's anger rose, now it seemed to evaporate as he turned his thoughts to someone whom he hadn't really believed he would find alive. He had been a US Marshal for too long and knew how some men were this far west. He would never admit it, but he had given up hope days ago. He was running down those responsible with the intention of bringing everyone involved to justice.

The girl was stolen, just like him, but from some Indian tribe. Don't worry, I've got the only keys, and those jail cells are unbreakable. The locks are as thick as two-by-fours."

Joseph froze for an instant, like he was trying to understand what Sheriff Hand had just said. Thoughts collided in his brain, and reason and logic clashed. He had to shake his head to clear the cobwebs from the violence and try to think with a level mind. His focus abruptly turned from revenge to a possibility of hope after all.

Joseph turned his head toward Tom and asked, "Is it really true?" His voice was hallowed, strange, and void of confidence—nothing like the Joseph Walker the sheriff had always known.

"Do you think I would say it if it weren't true? Now keep those guns on this rascal while I slip some handcuffs on him. Then we can lock him up and get you together with Money. Boy-oh-boy, is he gonna be one happy fella."

"Here, I'll do that for ya."

"Ouch, don't ya see I'm shot in the shoulder? You can't put those on me. Dogs get better treatment than this," Ven complained, as the marshal jerked his arms and easily slipped the cuffs on his wrists. He had done it a thousand times over the years as a lawman.

Joseph pushed Tom aside and stared hard into the

eyes of the man who stole his boy. "We're gonna walk you to the doc's and then to jail. Do you understand? We can do this the easy way, or we can do it the hard way. What's it gonna be? For me, I'd prefer the hard way, so I can keep on beating you until you die."

From then on, they didn't hear a peep from Ven Grim. He knew he shouldn't have stayed behind on the chance to see the little girl again and maybe steal or buy her for himself. He recognized that these feelings were an obsession, and he could no more control them than stop the passage of time. Now he was in a mess that he didn't see any way out of. He only had himself to blame for letting his urges control what he knew was wrong.

He knew if a vigilante mob didn't beat the law to the task, the judge would see that he swung by the neck until dead after a rigged court. There was no prison anywhere reachable around Fort Boise, so there was only one possible punishment unless he was tarred and feathered and hung from a tree before the law got to him. Either way, he was going to die, and it wouldn't be long before it happened. It looked like no one had any interest in stopping it either.

"Come on, Sheriff, and I'll help ya get him to the doctor in one piece," Marshal Walker said in a gravelly voice. "I owe you, Tom, and I won't forget. By the way, how *did* you save my boy?"

"You don't owe me. Money and this little girl, Annie, came to my office all on their own. He said he knocked this Ven out with his fists full of chains, and they hid high up in an oak tree before they forded the river thirty miles downstream and made their way here alone. It looks like the only hero in all this is your son, Money. He said he saved the lives of six Indian slaves, too. He's gonna make one hell of a man." The sheriff spoke with such solemnity that Joseph didn't doubt a word. He hesitated, knocked off balance, not quite sure of what he had just heard.

Ven felt the war drums beating in his chest. He wondered what it was going to feel like with a noose around his neck. As soon as the doctor was done, they led him toward the jailhouse. He felt like he was wrapped in a blanket of doom. Grim knew that he was damned and that even God could not save him. He doubted the Lord knew he was on the planet. The devil would know all about him, though. His guts turned to slush, and he went rigid like an icicle.

The Indians outside the tall walls huddled in groups, staring at the White people as they came and went from the fort. Some of their eyes were like feral dogs, and their clothing was ragged and filthy. Others were neat and clean, looking like honest men and women doing their best to survive. The overlanders were another matter. Most of them were people with no experience or wilderness skills, and some of them didn't even know how to shoot a gun. Many of them didn't speak English, so most of the time the shop owners didn't even know where they were from.

"Most of those overlanders are as useless as a bunch of two-legged donkeys," the sheriff said. "By the time they make it to the Willamette Valley, they'll be experienced enough to make a go at settling, though. That is, if they survive the Oregon Trail. Tens of thousands of travelers have already perished, and tens of thousands more will die in the future. Until they lay those shiny tracks from east to west, people will continue to perish on the only trail across this part of the country. It's said that one in ten doesn't complete the trek alive. It's tough on the women and children. They're the ones who die first."

"How about you stop yappin' and take me to my son, and we can get rid of this smelly bum." Joseph grinned now that he knew Money was safe. "I doubt he's had a bath in a year. That or he lives with polecats. Maybe both. Ain't that right, Mr. *long gone and soon to be dead*."

As soon as Sheriff Hand unlocked the door and opened the heavy timber door, Money ran across the jail cell floor and office, his feet pattering as fast as a raccoon, and jumped into Joseph's arms. The little boy wrapped his arms around him like he would never let go. Joseph sat him down for a second, and held him back, at arm's length, and looked him up and down to make sure he wasn't hurt. Then he embraced him again. He had thought he would never see his son again. A tear ran down the rugged old lawman's face, but the smile in his eyes was priceless.

Until he saw his father, Money had shuddered like a feather in a windstorm. Even though he was in Fort Boise, he was still afraid that the slavers would find him again and take him away forever. That, or something would happen to Levi and the captain. But embraced in his father's arms, he never felt safer in his life.

The sheriff began rearranging papers on the polished surface of his desk and clearing his throat. It was clear he was nervous. When he glanced up, Joseph was looking at him strangely. Both he and the boy in his arms were grinning from ear to ear.

"What's the matter, Tom?"

"I was wondering if you could stay here tonight and keep an eye on this Venom, rascal. You and Money can have my cell. It has the best mattresses of the bunch. That way, I can sleep in my bed for a change. I ain't been home for a full night for nigh on three weeks. I'm married, ya know."

A girl's tiny voice came from inside the cell block. It was young and soft and called Tom's name.

"Who's that?" Joseph asked.

"It's that little girl that your son saved from the slavers. I thought I'd take her home tonight and let the missus feed her and clean her up. I think she needs a woman right now, and I don't want her anywhere near that Venom Grim. I saw the way he looked at her when he walked into the cell block. He's as evil a man as I've ever seen."

"Maybe you should have let me kill him and turn a blind eye," Joseph said. "I'll do the job if you want, and it won't bother my conscience at all."

"I guarantee you that if we weren't here in the middle of the settlement, I'd have killed him myself. At least we know he's gonna hang." The sheriff turned his head and shouted, "Did you hear that, Venom Grim? You're gonna swing before the whole town. I can guarantee you that."

The marshal's knuckles were dark with blood from the last go he had at Ven.

"You sure don't scare easily, do you, Money?"

"I reckon I never had the time to think about it, Pa. Everything was happening so fast that I had to give it all my focus just to keep up. I reckon Annie was afraid for both of us. I just did like Levi taught me. A man always needs to plan carefully and act decisively. There's no time for wishy-washy second thoughts. Plus, I reckon I'm hard to catch and kill," Money grinned. "At least after the first time. Now, I'll always keep one eye on my surroundings."

"A lot of cemeteries are full of men who said the same thing." Tom smiled.

Joseph sat for a moment, chewing on what Money said. He slapped the tabletop and laughed until his stomach hurt. "I reckon that Levi is gonna be as happy to see you as I am. We've got to get you back to your ma, though. She'll be the happiest of us all.

"And why is that, Pa? Why would she be happier than you or even Levi?"

"That's a question that I doubt even Virgil could answer. We men will never know exactly what goes on in a woman's mind. I reckon she'll be just about as happy as she's ever been in her life, but in a different way than we are. Men and women are as different as night and day. To be honest, they're a mystery to me."

ANNIE OAKS

WHEN TOM WALKED ANNIE TO HIS HOUSE, SHE GRABBED his hand and looked into his eyes. Hers were sparkling with gratitude. Inside, he was more nervous than when facing a hardened criminal. He wanted his wife to be happy, and they had been married for a long enough time, but she had never become pregnant. He didn't know whether it was due to him or her, but that mattered little.

In a desperate attempt to save his marriage, Tom considered bringing Annie home and possibly letting her stay there, if only for a while. Maybe it was fate that brought her to his door, even if it was the jail. He thought maybe she might do the trick. She was lost and needed a home, and he believed his wife needed something to look forward to every day when he was away. His job paid well but demanded most of his time, leaving his wife lonely with little to do. Fort Boise wasn't a place where she could get a job. Most businesses were small and family-run. There were always the saloon girls in every bar west of Saint Luis. But Pearl was a refined woman who found herself in a dangerous, rough, man's world, trying to survive. Not a threat to her life, but her sanity from living such an uneventful life confined to the fort and the camps outside. It was too dangerous for a woman like her to stray farther, even if her husband was the sheriff.

Of course, she could help him in jail to tidy things up, but with the violent events he had seen, he preferred her to be anywhere but there. Now, perhaps he had the solution to all their problems—someone to give all their love mutually.

Lately, his job had been taking up all his waking hours, and he left his wife at home alone for days if there was trouble in town. Since it appeared that they would remain childless if they didn't adopt, perhaps this would enable her to fulfill her dreams, and he might make a greater effort to spend more time at home.

If he had a deputy, there wouldn't be any trouble, and he would have much more time, but the fur trading company would only pay so much. He felt it better to keep his salary for himself if he had to pay extra officers from his wages.

Initially, when he was voted in as the town sheriff, it went straight to his head. He had meetings with the mayor and the business owners in the settlement, and thought he was something he wasn't. He even dressed in a clean suit and an ironed white shirt every day. Not until Levi Johnson and his friends transformed him into the man he was now. He had been humbled by his peers and had learned a hard lesson, but it had made him a better man.

"What's your last name, Annie?"

"I don't know," she replied with puzzled eyes. "I can't

remember. I think I forgot some things when I got really scared. I can remember what my real mother looks like, but I can't remember the face of my father or brothers. I remember my Indian ma too, but that was only a few days ago. I also remember that vile man you brought into the cell block. He saw me, too. When he looks at me, my skin crawls. He's the one who stole us, along with Hawkeye, his boss. I'll never forget their faces, either of them, even though I want to forget."

Annie sat silent for a moment, then she said, almost afraid, "Oaks. I remember now, that's it. My last name is Oaks."

"Don't you worry, these band men can't get you in my house. Everybody knows I'm the town law. I'm gonna stay here tonight, too, so that you can sleep tight and feel safe."

"What's your wife's name, Tom?"

"Pearl, Pearl Hand. I have a sneakin' suspicion that you're gonna like her just fine."

"Where am I gonna sleep?"

"Why, anywhere you want to. We'll let you decide as soon as I introduce you to my wife."

Tom knew that would be when this made or broke things with his spouse. He believed that if something didn't change, she might leave him and go back east within the following year. Hopefully, this small opportunity they had to give to someone needy would make all the difference they needed.

Sheriff Hand lit a cheroot, inhaling deeply as he observed the situation and tried to figure out what the right thing to do was, or was he making a grave mistake. He knew he didn't have the heart to go around asking who would take Annie in anyway. It would break his heart to have to do something like that. Or was that just an excuse, too?

Tom exhaled a blast of cigarette smoke as he wiped the sweat from his brow. His eyes were full of fear as he clamped his jaws and gritted his teeth. He still didn't know what he was going to say to Peral. He tried to formulate something in his mind, but it went completely blank.

When Annie had first arrived in his office with Money, she looked like a frightened animal cowering at the end of a boxed-in canyon with nowhere to run.

They walked along the boardwalk until they arrived at a small house painted green with a brown door. Sheriff Hand stepped up onto the small, quaint porch of his home, slipped the key into the lock, and knocked, then turned the knob. "Darlin', I'm home. I've got a surprise."

When Pearl came rushing to the door to see if Tom had brought her a gift, she found the unexpected. He was standing in the doorway with a cute little girl. She noticed that the little lady was holding her husband's hand. The sheriff swiveled his gaze to his wife and then back to the person who might be their new daughter.

"Who is this little girl, Tommy? What's this all about? I don't understand."

First, dread crept in like a ton of bricks. What if she rejected Annie, and all his plans were terrible and for nothing? Then he would lose his wife for sure. And what would he do with the little girl? His mind began to spin into a panic. Tom cleared his throat and managed to speak.

"This is Annie, Annie Oaks. She was saved from a bunch of slavers along with Marshal Walker's little boy,

Money. We got 'em back, safe and sound. She doesn't have anywhere to stay, darlin'. I thought we might let her visit for a spell. Whatcha say, girl? Or have I done the wrong thing?"

Women's minds were a mystery to Sheriff Hand, too, and he had no idea what was going through his wife's head right then. He said a little prayer, under his breath, and hoped for the best.

Annie's eyes swelled at the extravagant notion of staying there with Pearl and Tom. She shocked them both when she whooped with joy and ran, grabbing them both and burying her teary eyes in her new mother's dress, catching Pearl completely by surprise.

Pearl smiled excitedly and said, "All right, Tommy." She was the only one he let call him that, like when he was a kid. Then she mouthed, "Thank you for this."

The sheriff's wife stared at him, glistening with emotion. Until then, he hadn't realized how much she truly loved him. Now he saw she would never leave his side, nor that of Annie's.

He sighed in relief. He had made the best choice possible, after all. He had found a safe home for the abducted girl and made his wife happy, which made all the difference in the world for Tom. He felt like he was on top of the world.

THE FRONTIERSMEN

THE SUN CAME FROM OVER THE HORIZON LIKE A BIG RED rubber ball. A glaring orange light spread across the sky as the stars vanished. Long black shadows lay to the west of everything in sight. Soon they all started to move, and the city's first breath of a new day began.

Two men, two horses, and a sled with a salted, wrapped body bounced in the water as they forded the gap. Men rowed as others pulled ropes swiftly, taking them to the other side of the choppy Snake River. They forked astride their horses, slipping their feet into the stirrups and nudging them up the steep riverbank. At first, their hooves slipped, but then they got traction as they took their riders to the top with a jerk.

The sled with the dead body was pulled by a one-armed man with a saber at his side, riding a stallion. It clopped its hooves nervously. It was clear it didn't like pulling the travois, but his rider lost by the flip of a coin.

They snaked through the Indian village and the wagons of every size, shape, and color parked every which way. It seemed like chaos was the order of the day. People crossed their paths without even looking. They had to tread carefully not to knock someone off their feet.

Inside, Levi was torn to pieces. Sure, they had Hawkeye and his sidekick, but still, there was no sign of Money, and it made his heart feel like a lead weight. The captain was affected too, but he wasn't the father type. Sure, Money was only Beaver's apprentice, but he felt like he was his son, too. He believed that probably everyone in the compound felt the same.

"We can drop Hawkeye off so they can confirm his death. If he has a bounty on him, all the better," Captain Forrester said. "Then I'm going to go straight to the barber and get a shave."

"Some things never change, do they?" Levi chuckled. "To be honest, I wouldn't have you change a thing about yourself, amigo mio. You stay just like you are, and we'll continue our lifelong friendship."

Will looked at his friend in puzzlement. Sometimes he didn't understand precisely what Levi meant to say, but he usually got the drift. Then again, he had been stranger than usual since Money was abducted.

Roosters crowed behind the towering fort walls, and people just waking up hacked and coughed. Men lined up in the alleys to take a leak. Suddenly, the settlement was bustling with people, horses, mules, carriages, and wagons. The odd drunk lay on a saloon porch, passed out. Music still blared from the small Mexican cantina in the corner of the courtyard.

As they walked their horses down the street, everybody stopped, pointed, and stared. It was common enough to see a dead man in Fort Boise, but unusual when Levi Johnson and Captain Forrester brought it in.

Everybody in town, except the overlanders, knew who they were. They had both been in the newspapers back east, and a few copies had made their way this far west, making them something special for the locals.

When they pulled up to the sheriff's office, the shutters were closed and the heavy door locked tight. There wasn't any sign of life.

"Maybe the sheriff had a late night and is sleeping in. That, or had a slow night and went home. I'd like to get rid of this smelly Hawkeye. It'll take a week to get this stink off my clothing." Levi stepped down. Planks gave as he walked across the floor. He wrapped his fingers into a fist and knocked like a man on a mission, but still, no one answered. He put his ear to the wood and listened, but didn't hear a sound. Then he pounded his fist like a hammer, but still, there was no answer.

"Are you in there, Sheriff Hand? It's Captain Forrester and me, Levi Johnson. We found that critter, Hawkeye, and expect his partner Ven is here in town." He knocked on the door one last time, but still no answer. He turned to Will and said, "Maybe he is at home. The problem is, I don't know where he lives."

Just then, church bells began to ring from the tall white steeple within the fort's walls. The crisp sound traveled through the air like shockwaves, making everyone turn their heads and gawk.

"Is it Sunday?" Levi asked the captain. "Or maybe it's a funeral. That sounds more likely. That or someone's getting married. That would be the best. Then there'll be a wedding cake. If we know 'em, they might invite us to a piece, or maybe three."

"It beats the hell out of me what day it is. At this point, I'm not even sure what month it is. Drop that sled and let's tie our horses here at the watering trough, and we can walk over to have a look. Maybe the sheriff is over there. I hope they ain't burying someone. I hate funerals. Is Sheriff Hand a religious man?"

"I don't rightly know, but I bet his wife is."

As they walked toward the crowd, their curiosity was stimulated, and now, they couldn't turn away if they wanted to. The people massed around the church was bigger than they expected, and they saw many familiar faces. Levi and the captain had been coming to Fort Boise for six years, sometimes more than once or twice a summer. Of course, in the winter, the trip was too dangerous, if not impossible. Still, they were well known in town, especially as they first arrived with Rusty Steeel.

"Nobody's wearin' black, so it must not be a funeral." Levi sighed a breath of relief. He didn't want to see anybody buried today other than Hawkeye Burns. He might even get a little kick out of that. But now his stomach was guiding his mind as he sniffed the air for the smell of food—especially cake or pie.

When they rode by the gallows, they didn't even look up. They stopped tearing it down just to build another when they were often needed to punish a crime. Out of the corner of his eyes, Levi saw two pairs of feet swinging and kicking back and forth. From down there, they couldn't make out who it was, but they had the best seat in town for whatever was going on.

———

"HEY, BEAVER, UP HERE!" a small voice yelled.

Levi froze dead in his tracks. They both recognized

the voice, and it both, surprised and startled them. They turned toward the small voice.

"It's about time you two came back." Joseph smiled. "Did you find Hawkeye? Ven is already in jail. The stupid son of a bitch walked right into town like he wasn't wanted or anything. Maybe he is crazy like he keeps claimin'. But I doubt that's gonna change his future much."

"Is that really you, Money?" Levi forgot himself and raced up the thirteen gallows' steps to the top and whisked his apprentice off his feet. "How'd you find him, Marshal? I knew you would follow along. I wouldn't have been able to wait back at the compound either."

"I didn't save him. It turns out he saved himself along with a half dozen more Indian slaves and a little White girl. And all by himself. He said he just did what you taught him to. I reckon I'm gonna have to give you more of his time, ain't I? But this time I won't mind, 'cause I know it's for his own good."

Beaver ruffled Money's hair as he grinned like an opossum. He had to resist kissing the little fella, but he knew it would just embarrass them both. They were mountain men above all, even little Money. He was on his way to becoming a real frontiersman.

"I'm mighty proud of you, boy." Levi grinned. "Well, it looks like we've killed or locked everybody up, don't it?"

"What about Mr. Claymore?" the little voice asked. "Ain't ya gonna save the other wagons full of slaves? There must be another fifteen or sixteen in all, and they're all headed for California in steel-barred wagons."

Joseph and Levi exchanged glances, then they looked down at Money with their faces full of surprise.

"Who is this Claymore fella you're talkin' about?" Levi asked. "What did he have to do in all this? And where are all these slaves?"

"Why, he was the man who was gonna buy Annie and me, along with the six Indian slaves. They were to make the exchange the next morning on the banks of the river, but we escaped, so I reckon we blew their plans up in their faces."

"Prison wagons, you say?" Will asked as his blood began to boil again. It didn't take much to set him off.

"Yep, steel cages painted black. They're about ten miles downstream on this side of the river. We saw them when we arrived in town, but I was careful, and nobody saw us. The guards didn't even notice two little kids with all the ruckus going on."

"Where's Sheriff Hand when he's needed?" Will asked.

"Why, he's right there at the church with his wife Pearl, accepting their new adopted girl into their home," Joseph said. "Tom's wife goes to church every Sunday. I reckon she prays for her husband, so he'll come home every night."

"That's what all the ruckus is about. Pa and I are waitin' for the food that comes after."

"Well, it looks like we're not done yet, Will. We don't want to take the marshal from his son again so soon after all this happened. This one falls on us. I guess we'll give Sheriff Tom a break since he has a new family and all. Is this the same girl who was with you when you walked into the sheriff's office, Money?"

"It sure is, Levi. I reckon she got about as lucky as I

did when you all found me. It's not like you always say, Pa. You know, the only luck you have is bad. Sometimes you've gotta forget the bad to be able to see the good things."

As soon as the crowd by the church began to break up, the mountain men headed for the spread of free food. They knew everybody there and felt right at home.

"I saw you and the captain sitting over there on the scaffolding with Marshall Walker and little Money. Why didn't you come over and join our family? You and the captain knew you were always welcome in our place of worship."

"Well, Reverend Smith, we had as fine a place to watch the ceremony as there was in town. I must say it was an impressive do and for two deserving parents." Levi winked at the pastor. "You know me by now, Raymond. I ain't sittin' in confined groups of people when I'd rather watch from afar. I ain't much for crowds. We all have our own way of worshipping, Reverend. Mine is more private, and I keep it to myself. You have yours and I have mine."

"You and the marshal might think about young Money. You have a big responsibility, Joseph. You, too, as his mentor, Levi."

"As his mother is a Crow Indian, we'll have to let Money grow up and decide such things on his own. He's growin' up so fast that I think he's already smarter than me, so who am I to tell him what to do."

"A wild bull is smarter than you are, Joseph." The captain chuckled.

Once they had eaten all they could and then some, they congratulated Tom and Pearl and let them take their little girl, Annie Oaks, home. Now she would be Annie Hand like her ma and pa.

"What about Hawkeye?" Will asked as the sheriff walked off. "We can't leave a dead body in the street like that."

"Why, I plumb forgot. The smell of food always does that to me. We might as well drag him over to the undertaker. We can look through Tom's wanted posters later and see if we're owed any money."

"Joseph said that the sheriff gave him the keys," the captain said. "With Tom out of the way, I can question the prisoner and find out where this Claymore is. It's time to put an end to this once and for all. If we're lucky, we can hang both Ven and him at the same time."

"Come on, I don't want to be at this all night. Let's find this Claymore fella if he's still in town, and if he ain't, we're gonna have to chase him, too."

Once they left Hawkeye at the undertaker's, Levi and Will helped carry him inside to be measured for a pine box, and then headed for the jail with a plan. The captain knew that there were some things that Levi didn't find acceptable, but the captain was an officer in the United States Cavalry and knew how dangerous it was to leave an enemy alive. Leaving loose strings could come back at you at a later time.

Captain Forrester would question the man in the privacy of a cell, while Joseph and Money took a walk around town. This wasn't the kind of thing that they wanted Money to see.

———

"HERE'S THE KEY, WILL," Joseph said. "Whatever you do, don't kill him. He's already a doomed man, so don't walk away with his blood on your hands. Just do what you've gotta do to get him to talk. Once we have the location of the fella running this operation, we'll run him to ground and that'll be the end of it."

"There's an awful lot of things that we don't know about yet. We don't even know how many of them there are. Now that we have Money back, before we go chasin' ghosts, we might wanna cut our losses and leave it alone. If they've already left town, they could be a good way along the Oregon Trail by now. Don't worry, I won't kill him, unless his heart gives out."

Then Levi and Joseph turned and began to walk down the street with Money in the middle. By how Levi walked, Will could tell he was as tense as a high wire at a circus. His eyes constantly shot all around, while the marshal seemed totally distracted by his son. One was paying far too much attention, while the other wasn't paying any attention at all.

Will slipped the large key into the industrial lock. It clacked when it turned the tumbler, and the bolt drew back. Hinges squeaked as he pushed the door in.

"Who's out there?" Ven asked in a whiny voice with a stopped-up nose. "Is that you, Sheriff? Come on, speak up." But nobody answered. Still, he could hear the floor groan under the weight of a full-grown man.

Are the vigilantes here to get me? Ven thought.

He held his breath and waited to see who it was. He was sure he was there for all the wrong reasons. Otherwise, he would have answered when he called out.

When he saw the man with long, blond hair and baby-blue eyes, he felt like he was looking at the devil.

There was something about him that oozed danger. The man with the missing arm had a short saber in his only hand. He lay it on the table, unbuckled his gun belt, and hung it on the wall. Then he slowly removed his hat and coat. It was like a surgeon preparing for an operation. When he turned back to Ven and picked up his shiny blade, Ven gasped as his heart hammered in his throat and sweat rolled freely down his face.

It came so fast he hardly saw anything except the flash of steel in the lamplight. Ven didn't feel anything until something warm ran down the side of his head and across his neck. The captain flicked an object from the floor with the tip of his saber. It flew through the air, landing in Ven's lap. It was red and bloody.

When he saw his ear lying on his lap, Ven screamed so loud, they had to have heard him in the street, but the town's folk weren't about to interfere in the law's business. They knew that some wrongs had to be righted, no matter how they were done. Everyone in town was aware of what had happened to Money and the Hand's new daughter and approved of getting the facts, no matter what it took, and the captain was the perfect man for the job.

"You cut my damned ear off!" Ven screamed.

"Can you hear me better now, or do you still have shit in your ears?"

Ven slapped his hand to the side of his head to confirm it wasn't there. He groped around but couldn't find his appendage. His palm came away sticky with blood.

Another flash of light, and Ven screamed again and slapped his hand to his left ear. He laughed like a madman when he felt it was still there.

"Tell me, sir, what should I take off next? What don't you need, Ven? That other ear or your nose? It's awfully flat, but I think I can slice what's left off. Wouldn't that be an ugly sight? I bet you could look right into your skull then. That would get the ladies' attention."

"Aren't you gonna ask me any questions? I'll tell ya whatever you want if you stop cuttin' me up."

"Who's this Farnsworth Claymore I heard about. And the three prisoner wagons, with two full of slaves. You said I could ask a question. Don't make it your last."

Ven went silent for a while. The blood had soaked into his wool shirt. He gasped like a fish because he couldn't breathe through his broken nose.

"He's the one who hired Hawkeye and me, along with two hired guns, to steal six people for slaves to take to California for the revolution. Two other gangs filled the other two wagons."

"A revolution?" Will asked. "What revolution is that?"

"That's what he said. I don't know all the details because Hawkeye wouldn't let me go along. But he had three groups of men, all hired to fill prison wagons. Four of us were one of those groups. If I'm not mistaken, they left the day before yesterday, but they'll be moving mighty slow with all that weight. If you leave now, you could catch them in a day."

"And this is where I'll find this Claymore fellow?" the captain asked as he traced the tip of his saber down Ven's shirt, slicing the buttons off one by one.

"No, he won't be anywhere near the wagons, sir. He's a politician, or so he says, so he's shifty clever. He'll be with his new Sanish wife, who he brought from back east. He said he was with Californianos, whatever that is, and they're about to have a war with Mexico and claim an independent state."

"Why, you sure are full of information, Ven. Sorry about the ear, but you don't look like the type of fella that listens much anyway. You sure won't need it where you're going. Too bad you weren't a harder man to break. With a man like you, I would have spent a while, and it wouldn't have bothered me at all."

PLAINS MASSACRE

WITHOUT A WORD, LEVI AND THE CAPTAIN TURNED FOR
the corrals and rented two good horses. Theirs were too
tired to push any longer without a good rest and plenty
of feed. They didn't want to kill their animals, but they
wanted to catch up with the prison wagons as quickly as
possible. Every season, large numbers of people died on
the Oregon Trail. Since the slaves would be out in the
weather and probably only fed bread and water, some
of them would succumb before they arrived in
Willamette Valley, and beyond. It was said that Claymore's destination was San Francisco.

There was no need to watch for tracks. There was
only one trail, although in places it was wide, but so
many people had passed through that there were hoof
prints and boot prints everywhere they looked. They
had one thing to their advantage. A heavy wagon would
be limited to the main trail that would hold its weight
and wasn't impassable or prone to busting axles or
wagon wheels.

All they had to do was travel as fast as they could

without crossing paths with hostile Indians. Tribes often lay in wait for the White people to come to them, then they ambushed and murdered them all, and after they would strip them of all their valuables to take back as trophies or presents for their wives.

They rode all day and late into the night by the twilight of the stars. Still, the path was so worn that they continued at a gallop. In the wee hours of the morning, they stopped for a break, each taking a two-hour watch while the other slept. Four hours later, they were riding again.

It wasn't long before they saw wagon ruts different than the covered buckboards and makeshift wagons seen every day as they headed west. Only the heavy Conestoga wagons pulled by oxen left a deeper track, but they weren't used on the Oregon Trail. They were too large and cumbersome for the long, arduous journey west. Most of what they saw were prairie schooners and small cargo wagons, although some families walked the long trek, sleeping in their tents at night. Many of these risked losing their lives on the deadly cross.

It was eight fingers from the sun's horizon when they finally saw two black wagons drearily pulled along by six stout mules each. Around the wagons rode four armed guards. When Levi pulled out his telescope and peered into the distance, he saw the men were nodding off and on as they traveled forward at a snail's pace.

"See that brush down there at the bottom of that next hill? I'm gonna ambush them from there. There's no doubt about a man's guilt when the stolen goods are still in his possession. I'll use my bow and arrow, so the other two won't have time to react before you rush them and finish this once and for all. Make sure we don't hurt any of the animals, so these people have a way to make it home. They won't be too fast, but they'll get them there."

Will pulled to the side of the trail and tried to keep the boulders and scraggly trees hiding him from the men around the wagons. If he timed it right, he should be able to get close enough to get off a couple of shots. Levi would take care of the other two, so he focused solely on his job. He trusted his friend with his life.

The Indian slaves inside the wagons didn't say a word. There was somber silence all around. The wagons' wheels spun, churning up a cloud of dust that followed the two, making them even more visible. Will counted the time in his head and knew how many seconds he would need before it would be too late, and the guards would have time to get off a shot. All it took was one well-placed bullet to end his life.

Captain Forrester shrugged off the danger and continued counting. *Five, four, three, two, one.* He set his spurs into his stallion's flanks as its nostrils flared, and it burst into a run. Its acceleration was such that someone who didn't know the horse would be thrown off from the start. As it was, Will held on for his life as he hugged his horse's neck and urged him on.

Will saw when the other two guards fell off and hit the dirt with arrows piercing their necks. The other two turned for Levi before they heard the heavily pounding of the stallion's hooves behind them.

They turned just in time to see a wild man on a black stallion bearing down on them with his reins in his teeth and his revolver in his hand. The pistol jerked in the captain's hand as a flame shot out of the barrel, and the first guard went down. In a split second, before he could shoot the second man, the outlaw threw down his guns and raised his hands high in the air.

"I give up. Don't shoot me, mister. I'm just tryin' to feed my family. I don't approve of all this, but what choice did I have? Please don't kill me like you did to the other three."

"Go ahead and shoot him, Will. He doesn't deserve to live. He's just as much a part of stealing Money as anyone in this gang was. They all knew the risks, and I imagine they got paid in gold eagles in return. Bein' poor don't make it right. It's still as wrong as sin."

Will dropped the barrel, resting the butt of his grip on his leg, but he never moved his aim. All he had to do was pull the trigger, and the fourth guard would join the others in the afterlife.

"Who we really want is Farnsworth Claymore," Levi said. "You wouldn't know where he's at, would you? If you help us find him, maybe we could work something out. He's the true villain in all this."

"We aren't making deals with rats like this," the captain growled.

"Let me handle this, Will. Well, whatcha got to say about Claymore? I know you know who I'm talkin' about."

"Why, he's dead. One of the guards who survived rode back this way, not two days ago. He had to inform someone at the bank in Fort Boise of his passing. The fella was scared to death, he was. He had a festering wound where an arrow had hit him in the arm. I told him we could cut it off here, but he wouldn't have it and rode on, hoping to make it to a doctor."

"And how did this come about?" the captain asked. "Claymore's death, I mean."

"A war party of Blackfeet ambushed them as they passed some tall buffalo grass. The fellow who came by with the message said that one minute they didn't see a thing, and the next, Shoshone Indians were popping up all over the place, slinging arrows as fast as you could spit. He said they were after all the guns and valuables they had on their pack mules. They didn't travel with us because of the risk, so they got fast horses, spares, and mules loaded with supplies with four gunhands."

"Go on, what else did he say?" Levi asked.

"This fella said that they killed three of the guards straight off with arrows, just like you did to us. He said it was spooky because the only sound was the dying. He got lucky. After he got hit by the arrow, he tried to escape and hit his head on a low limb, and fell into a ditch, and they didn't discover him. When he woke up, it was dark, early in the morning, with little moon. But he said he could hear Claymore scream for hours. He said it sounded like they planned to torture him the whole night or for days if they could keep him alive. I've heard such stories on the Great Plains.

"And you expect us to believe such a story?" Captain Forrester sneered.

"I'm betting my life on it. Oh, and there was his young Spanish wife. I only saw the woman from afar, but she might be the most beautiful woman I've ever seen, and with that old man. He must have a lot of money. Anyway, she was captured by the Shoshone warriors. He said it looked like they took her as a slave. Ain't that ironic. They were slave traders only to end up slaves themselves. Sometimes life whips around and bites ya right on the ass. It's sort of like sweet justice."

"You have the keys. Let these people out and give them the mules. Whatcha waitin' on, mister? We don't have all day." Levi turned his head and spat a brown stream off the side of his horse.

Levi was not as good as Rusty, but was fair at Indian sign language. At least he knew enough to tell these poor, starving people to take whatever the guards had, including the one alive, and take the mules and ride home as fast as they could.

"Go ahead," Will said. "Give them all your valuables. That means your guns and all the horses, too."

"But how do you expect me to survive out here without a gun or a horse?"

"I really don't care if you survive or not. You'd better think about how lucky you are that you're still alive and we're gonna let you walk away from all this," Levi replied. "If my partner there had his way, you'd already be dead."

HOME SWEET HOME

EVERYBODY WAS SO FULL THEY COULDN'T EAT ANOTHER bite, except for Levi, of course, but to everyone's surprise, Potak had kept right up with him, plate for plate—bite for bite. Now they were working on their second dessert. Of course, Levi was six-foot-seven and two-hundred-twenty pounds of muscle, so he needed a lot of food to keep his body energized. The medicine man, too, was tall, at six feet, but he was thin, and his face appeared almost gaunt, with sunken eyes.

Still, he never seemed to fill up and constantly complimented Angus on his cooking skills, which brought even more food. There was nothing the old mountain man liked more than adulation on his talents as a mountain man chef.

Bar-Chee kicked off another round of questions, but Joseph and Money didn't mind. It provoked a round of cuddling, and they both knew the secret that men often fail to understand women. They exchanged conspiratorial looks and smiled as the little boy was dwarfed between his parents. Dahteste watched her husband eat in amazement.

Of course, medicine men always did strange things, so she wasn't surprised if he ate twice as much as her husband. For the Crow people, Potak wasn't quite like them. He wasn't what they considered an Earthly human being. He was closer to some sort of walking spirit they could see. Potak neither denied nor encouraged either story. He knew that no matter what he said, gossip would always dictate what was believed, even if it was an exaggeration or an out-and-out lie.

"I reckon God's blessed us," Virgil said with his Good Book in his hand. "I prayed for you the whole time you were gone."

Potak stopped eating, looked at his Black friend, and replied, "No, I saved us. The gods had no say-so in this one. Had they, Money would have never been taken, and none of this would ever have happened. God is all-powerful, but no one can control his people, no matter what color they are."

The old black dust-covered dog barked dispiritedly and lazily crawled under the porch. He had been lying on the feet of Rusty and his wife Silvia, sound asleep until the debate started. They didn't know if the shaman was baiting old Virgil, but they knew they were about to hear a lot about the Bible and what the Indians' spirits thought about it all. The two would provide the evening's entertainment, and nobody else would have to say a word.

Pine Needle had returned from the Crow stronghold, where she and Angus had a teepee, but every season it was harder to get him to trek the half-day ride up the mountain. Still, she was younger than her husband and still had her family in the stronghold, and spent half her time there and the other half in their log cabin in the compound.

Captain Will Forrester stank of duty and honor. The marshal gave him a dubious look. In the end, it was his saber that severed the lion's head, which prompted Ven Grim to talk. The courts would kill him rather than allow Joseph, and everything would stay legal. But things just didn't work out that way. With Money back home and his wife, Bar-Chee, happy, he didn't even mind as long as due process was finally done and they were all buried in the ground. He found he was no longer in a hurry to rush justice. Maybe he would learn to become a patient man and stop raging around like a bull.

"Who was the fella that saved the day?" Joseph asked, beaming at his son. "Was it you, Money?"

"Yes, sir," Money replied. His father tried not to smile from pride, but it was impossible. Bar-Chee cried, as usual, but this time from joy.

Nobody but Dahteste, Levi's wife, noticed the look on her husband's face. Worry lines traced his brow that weren't there before. Sure, he was as happy as any of them, but now he realized the enormity of being such a young man's mentor. So far, it had worked out for the better, but good luck also accompanied the boy.

He was going to focus on the things most needed and change his plans for his apprentice's future. He wouldn't be anything like when Rusty taught him as his apprentice. First, he was going to teach him everything he knew about survival. Once he really learned to sustain the wilderness, the rest would come naturally.

Beaver sat cross-legged, with his fingers tented

before his mouth as though he was deep in thought, but he didn't miss a thing. The weight of the responsibility left him more serious, though. He wondered briefly if Rusty had felt the same in the beginning with him and Will.

For a moment, Angus just stared at them all, baggy-eyed and confused. He had nodded off and had fallen asleep in his chair. He jerked his head when he startled and woke up, yet to get his bearings anew. He shook his white-haired head and blinked his eyes until he locked his on Money's.

He cackled like an old hen and ran over and hugged him. Over the years, he had shrunk, and now he wasn't much bigger than the boy, but his eyes were full of love.

"It's been a long time since we were all at the table together and with a famous guest, no less." Angus grinned, now fully awake.

"Can I have that last piece of peach pie?" Potak and Levi asked simultaneously.

Everybody at the table had a hearty laugh.

A Look At: Tornado Express
Levi Johnson Mountain Man Scout
Book 32

Shipments vanish. Forts are pushed to the brink. The Oregon Trail is one spark from exploding.

When cargo trains from the Tornado Express disappear without a trace, Levi Johnson, Captain Will Forrester, and U.S. Marshal Joseph Walker are called in to investigate. With Fort Boise and Fort Hall running dangerously low on stores, thousands of overlanders face starvation before they can reach Oregon and California.

The stakes climb higher as the trio rides west to guard the next shipment out of Laramie. Outlaw Garrot Sneed and his ruthless gang are waiting, eager to strike again. But they're not the only threat. A Shoshone war party eyes the stolen cache of weapons, preparing to turn the firepower against the settlers flooding their ancestral lands.

Panic builds inside the forts. Migrants are desperate. Tempers flare. And if Levi and his friends can't stop the raids, the entire western migration could grind to a bloody halt.

The Tornado Express must get through—*no matter the cost.*

AVAILABLE FEBRUARY 2026

ABOUT THE AUTHOR

 Ash Lingam was born and raised in Southern Ohio, not far from the mighty Ohio River. He had somewhat of an isolated upbringing on a family farm with his sisters. His best friends were his horse, Sugar, and his grandfather.

Born in 1886, the family patriarch grew crops, raised cattle, and doted on the young boy. At his grandfather's side, Ash learned about livestock and firearms at an early age. His grandad carried an old Colt with him at all times. It helped spawn a young boy's dreams of yesteryear.

Ash was only eight years old when his grandad taught him how to trap muskrats to prevent them from draining the farm's ponds. He gave him a double-barreled shotgun at twelve and taught him how to hunt to put food on the table.

It wasn't long before Ash was breaking horses. His spirited Tennessee Walker never allowed any other rider on her back. Together, they searched through the plowed fields in the spring, looking for Miami Indian arrowheads to add to his grandfather's ample collection.

Ash's family was among the early settlers in pre-

Revolutionary America. He has traced his lineage back to around 1746 when his ancestors immigrated from Europe to the aspiring American Colonies.

A retired marketing executive, Ash devotes his spare time to training police dogs and writing novels. He has found his niche in the Western, historical fiction, and adventure genres. With his vast vault of experience, he never runs out of sources for new stories. He has lived in eleven different countries and worked in a total of forty-six to date, Ash has written approximately 130 novels, short stories, and poems. More than one hundred of his eclectic titles help the American frontier come alive for his readers.

https://www.ashlingam.com/
Join the Lawless Waters Western Readers & Writers
Facebook Group